RED DIRT HEART 3

N.R. WALKER

COPYRIGHT

Cover Artist: N.R. Walker
Editor: Erika Orrick
Red Dirt Heart 3 © 2014 N.R. Walker
Fourth Edition: 2024

All Rights Reserved:

Warning

Intended for an 18+ audience only. This book is intended for an adult audience. It contains graphic language, explicit content, and adult situations.

Trademarks:

DEDICATION

For those who took a chance on me years ago, and for those
who are with me still,
thank you.

INFORMATION PRIOR TO READING AND GLOSSARY

Size matters - Sutton Station, while fictional, is based on a working property in the middle of Australia and is three hours drive to the nearest town. Sutton Station is 2.58 million acres (10,441 square kilometres). In comparison, the largest ranch in the USA is King Ranch at 825,000 acres (3,340 square kilometres). Sutton Station, while fictional, is the third biggest station in the Northern Territory and is classed as desert. Sutton Station is approximately the same size as a small country.

The Northern Territory is a federal territory in between Queensland and Western Australia. It's like a state, just don't call it that to someone who lives there.

Australian Terminology Glossary:

- Station: Farm, ranch.
- Paddock: Large fenced area for cattle; a pasture.
- Holding yard: Corral.
- Swag: A canvas bedroll.

- Ute: Utility pickup truck.
- Motorbike: Motorcycle, dirtbike.
- Akubra: Australian cowboy hat.
- Scone: American sweet biscuit, usually eaten with cream and jam.
- Pub: Bar/drinking venue, usually serves meals.
- Trolley: Shopping cart.
- Car park: Parking lot
- Driza-bone: Oiled coat farmers wear to protect from rain and wind.
- Stockman: Australian Cowboy
- In the roof: In the roof cavity/attic.
- Crook: Feeling unwell.
- To powder: "He powdered." To be of no use. Usually a derogative term.

N.R. WALKER

Red DIRT HEART 3

CHAPTER ONE

WHERE TRAVIS CHANGED SEATS AND CHANGED SUTTON STATION.

WE BOARDED the plane at Darwin, fully expecting the flight back to Alice Springs to be a non-event. People were still boarding when Travis decided he wanted to sit by the window, and then he didn't, then he did, then he didn't. And then he did.

"Too bad," I said, refusing to move seats again. "I pity the person you sat next to for twenty-something hours when you flew to Australia."

"You really wouldn't," he said. He leaned in real close. "We ended up joining the mile-high club."

My eyes shot to his, and I glared. Instantly jealousy, anger and hurt flared in my belly.

Travis threw back his head and laughed, making a few of the other people still boarding the plane look at us. "Just kidding. I totally didn't."

"I hate you."

He snorted. "I like making you jealous. You're too easy," he said, smiling. He could tell I was still a bit peeved by his comment. "Honestly, it was some woman with two kids who, if they weren't yellin', they were crying."

"Serves you right."

He laughed again. "You know, you were so much more relaxed at Kakadu," he said. He leaned in and spoke quietly, "And I just happen to know how to really relax you, so if you want to head to the bathroom first, I'll follow."

I coughed as some poor bastard took his seat next to Travis. I wasn't particularly hiding my sexuality anymore, but I wasn't up for lewd comments in front of the unsuspecting public either. I gave him a behave-yourself glare, and as Travis struck up conversation with the guy next to him, I bid that man a silent good luck, put my earphones on and closed my eyes.

I'd barely shut my eyes for ten minutes before Travis tapped my leg.

I blinked, realising we were now up in the air. I pulled off the headphones. "What?"

"Swap seats," he urged, standing up.

I looked at the guy who was sitting on the other side, and without time to wonder what had happened, I slid over —with some degree of difficulty given the tight space and Travis standing in front of me. Travis didn't look pissed off or even worried, so I figured the guy now next to me was harmless. I gave the man a nod and indicated Travis. "Did he say something inappropriate?"

He was mid-thirties with short brown hair that was kinda greyed at his temples. He had a thick-set build, and the stereotype that he played rugby was typified by his been-broken nose. He laughed. "No. Not at all."

"Good," I answered flatly. "I wasn't gonna apologise, I just could have sympathised with you, that's all."

Travis whacked my arm with the back of his hand. He leaned forward so he could include all three of us in conversation. "Charlie, I wanted to introduce you," Trav said with a would-you-shut-up look in his eye. "Blake Burgess, this is Charlie Sutton."

The name meant nothing to me, but Blake's eyebrow flicked. "Charlie Sutton? As in *Sutton Station*?"

"The one and only," I said, wondering who the hell this guy was and how he'd heard of me. I gave a quick glance to Travis to get him to explain.

"Blake here was just telling me what he does for a living," Travis said. "Thought you two might like to chat."

I was confused, and when I turned back to Blake, he was smiling at me. "I'm a buyer for Woolworth's. More specifically, I source out beef suppliers for supermarkets across the country."

I blinked. Slowly. Twice. Like an idiot. Travis laughed quietly beside me and mumbled something that sounded like "thank you Travis" before putting on headphones and before I composed myself to actually speak to this guy.

But speak we did. For the next hour and a half—the remainder of our flight—we talked beef: prices, stock rates, ratios, buying, selling, exporting, breeding. For a suit-wearing guy, he knew his stuff. He probably thought that for an outback dirt junkie, I did okay too.

As we were landing, Blake said, "Your friend was telling me you've just been to Kakadu."

I nodded. "Yep."

"How was that?"

"Wet," I answered. "And green."

Travis, who I had thought was asleep, chuckled. "Charlie thinks anything that's not red desert sand is abnormal." Trav sat up straight, took the earphones off and straightened out his long legs.

I shrugged. It was kind of true. We'd been gone a week.

A whole week! And as incredible as the holiday with Travis was, I was keen to get home.

"I'd love to see it," Blake said.

"Kakadu?" I asked. "It's beautiful," I agreed. "If wet and green is your thing."

Blake laughed. "No, I meant your farm."

The plane had taxied in and people started to move, collecting bags from overhead lockers, and our conversation kind of ended with that. We disembarked and headed toward the luggage conveyor belt.

"Thanks for the company," I told Blake as I shook his hand. "It was good to talk to someone who appreciates what we do."

He collected his bag, but seemed to hesitate before leaving, like he was making a decision in his head. He turned back to me. "Look, Charlie, I was serious when I said I wanted to see your place," he said. "In an official capacity. I'd like to oversee what you do out there. I've spoken to enough farmers in my time to know who's legit or not, and I've seen enough stock rate figures to know your name when I hear it."

"Oh." Shit. Shit. Shit. This was kind of a very big deal. His offer threw me for a six. "Oh, um..."

He smiled. "If you're interested, that is. I'll need to check my schedule, and I'll let you know when I can fit you in. I hadn't planned on meeting you, and I'm only here for two days, so it's real short notice. But I'll need to see some sales-to-weight reports and I'll require your vet to be onsite. Can you arrange that?"

"Sure." I swallowed down my excitement and gave him a nod. "Sounds good."

We swapped phone numbers and shook hands, and

when he walked away, Travis and I stood there for a long while in complete silence.

"Holy shit," I whispered.

Travis laughed. "Thought you might like to talk to him."

That made me laugh. "I can't believe you did that." I looked at him, still not quite believing what just happened. "Travis, this could be kinda important for us."

"I know," he said like I was stupid. "That's why I swapped seats."

"I owe you something big."

"Big as in eight inches?" he asked. "Or big as in a pizza oven or a week in Kakadu?"

Laughing, I pushed him to the luggage conveyor belt. Ours were the only two bags left. When I looked over to the reception area, George was there watching us, smiling and shaking his head.

Man, it felt good to be home.

***

I DIDN'T WANT to be getting too excited about this meeting with Blake, but I couldn't help it. I told George all about it in the ute on the way home, then ran through it again with Ma once we were finally sitting down at her kitchen table.

She, of course, just wanted to know about our holiday. *What was it like? Was the weather okay? Did Travis see any wildlife, like crocodiles and buffalo? What was the accommodation like?*

She looked tired, and it weighed on me that we'd left her for a whole week. I could just imagine it would have stressed her out. She'd have worried and naturally felt it her place to keep everyone in line while we were gone.

She pushed her untouched tea away. "So, what was five-star luxury like?"

"It was good—Ow!" I had Nugget, the baby wombat, burrowing under my shirt. It was his favourite place apparently. While the sentiment was nice, his sharp nails on my skin weren't particularly pleasant. But all the ouching and squirming didn't deter him. He was only happy if he had his nose was burrowed into my side or in the crook of my arm.

Ma smiled at me. "He's missed you terribly," she said, nodding to the movement under my shirt.

"Has he been keeping you awake?" I asked. "You look tired."

Ma sighed and patted my hand before she stood up. She took her cup and put in the sink. She'd gone from glaring at me when I asked if she was well to now not answering at all. She was either sick of me askin' or sick of lyin' about it.

So, again, I changed my approach to her taking it easy. "You should go," I said. "You and George. A week at the place we stayed at will do you the world of good."

"They have room service," Travis added. "And king-sized beds, spa baths, showers for two..." He smiled a little as he obviously got stuck on memories of us in the shower. There were a lot of mental images to go through. He blushed a little, which was rare from him, and he cleared his throat. "That's probably much more information than you needed."

"You think?" I asked, still trying to stop Nugget from performing an appendectomy on me with his claws. I ignored Ma's sly smile. "Anyway, as I was saying," I redirected the conversation, "I met this guy on the plane—"

Travis interrupted to correct me. "I met him first."

"Well, yeah, Trav met him first."

"I swapped seats with Charlie so they could talk business."

"And as it turns out, he's interested in Sutton Station," I said. "He called my mobile when we were driving home. Said he checked his schedule but he was a bit stuck for time."

Travis interrupted me again. "So Charlie said he'd pick him up in the chopper," he said, still excited. "It'll save time."

I took a deep breath and tried to continue. "So yes, I told him I can pick him up from his last appointment and drop him back at Alice airport before he has to fly back to Sydney."

Trav snorted out a laugh. "His last appointment is at Jack Melville's place. I'd love to see his face when Charlie flies in."

I looked at Travis. "Who's telling this story?"

"You are."

"Then stop interrupting."

"I'm not interrupting," he said. "I'm contributing."

"Well, go *contribute* with George. He said the roofing iron you ordered was delivered."

"Oh, cool," he said, easily distracted. Travis hugged Ma. "It's good to be home," he told her, then stuck his tongue out at me as he walked out of the kitchen.

Ma laughed quietly and had that you-two-are-so-in-love look in her eyes. "Keep talking," she said.

"Right. Well, you remember how I told you about Jack Melville? The old guy on the board of the Beef Farmers Association who I basically told I was gay and he could shove it?"

Ma nodded and smiled. "Yeah."

"Well, him. I get to fly onto his property, give him a

royal salute"—I practiced with my middle finger extended—"and bring this Blake guy back here. He seemed keen enough."

"What does that mean?" she asked. "He buys for supermarkets?"

I nodded. "I haven't spoken specifics, but he'd secure us a deal of some sort, a contract of some time frame, for a guaranteed income."

Ma's eyes widened, as did her smile. "Wow."

I shrugged, trying to play down my excitement. I figured it was easier to be excited once it was done rather than let on how disappointed I'd be if it didn't work out. "It's not done yet, but at least we're on his radar now, so who knows, if not this year, maybe next year."

"Do you need me to do anything?" Ma asked.

"I need you to take it easy," I said. "I know you don't like talking about it, and you shush me every time I do, but, Ma, you look like you haven't slept in a week."

She frowned. "It's just a cold or something."

"You said that before," I reminded her. "Weeks ago."

"And I thought I was getting better," she said. "Seems winter's having one last stab at me before she goes this year."

I frowned this time. "How's Nara been going?" I asked. "She can help out more if you need."

Ma smiled, and her pallid cheeks chased some colour. "Nara's doing well. I think I might have actually convinced her to pick up a schoolbook."

I couldn't help but smile. "You need to worry about you too, Ma. You're so busy worrying about everyone else, you forget about you."

"I'm fine, Charlie," she said. "Really, I am. Though I will sleep better knowing you and Travis are back." Then she added, "And that little Nugget isn't scratching around looking for you."

I pulled the neck of my shirt out, and all I could see was a baby wombat's butt and two back legs. The rest of him was buried under my arm. "I'm sorry he's been a pain."

"He's the cutest thing," Ma countered.

"He is cute," I agreed. "But how I ended up lookin' after him, I'll never know. Travis was the one who found him."

Ma smiled her ever-knowing-motherly smile and patted my hand. "Well, it's good to have you home. And Travis. It's not the same here without you. Without either of you."

"Thanks, Ma," I said warmly. "That means a lot."

"Now get out of my kitchen. I have dinner to make or there'll be a mutiny."

Yep. It was real good to be home.

I CALLED DOUG RUSSELL. He'd been our vet since before I was born, and while he was keen to help out, the short notice and distance to travel made it impossible. "I'll see if Scott can make it," he'd said. Five minutes later, he called back to say his son was happy to help. Scott Russell, his son, had wanted nothing more than to be a vet just like his dad and was now proudly following in his father's footsteps.

I smiled to myself when I thought back to me bein' an annoying tag-along kid, whenever Mr Russell and Scott came out to do a vet check. Growin' up, I didn't get to see many other kids, so to have another guy—he was only six years older than me—at the farm for a full day was like Christmas day for me.

To him, I'm sure I was nothing more than an annoyance, really. As I got older, I started to appreciate his visits for other reasons. He was wank fodder to my day-dreamin' teenaged mind. He was straight as an arrow and, in hindsight, pimply faced with braces and all gangly-awkward with a body he hadn't quite grown into yet. But I'd crushed on him hard.

What can I say? I had limited selection out here.

It made me smile thinkin' back, and I thanked the stars above I'd never been foolish enough to act upon my hormone-fuelled impulses.

I called Scott directly then and explained I'd be back on Sutton soil with the buyer by eleven. "I'll be there. See you then," he said.

I sent Blake a text message saying it was all good to go. He replied later that night, saying he was looking forward to it and reminding me of the trade reports he'd need at some point.

I put down my phone, opened my email and, ignoring my flooded inbox of a week's worth of unread mail, I sent him the files right then and there.

Travis parked his arse against my desk and smiled. He handed me a fussing bundled-up Nugget and a full bottle, which I took with a roll of my eyes. The baby wombat started to drink his bottle straight away, and his little eyes closed as he fed. I sighed, and when I looked up at Trav, he was smiling his just-for-me smile.

"Get everything organised?" he asked.

"Yep. All done."

"Ready for bed?"

"Very," I answered. I looked down at a still feeding baby wombat. "As soon as this guy's done."

Travis smiled. I'm pretty sure it was a God-I-love-you kind of smile. He poked at the pile of actual mail on the desk, envelopes and magazines. "Anything interesting in there?" he asked.

"Bills mostly. Nothing exciting," I answered. "The trade magazine's in there."

"What's that?" he asked.

"An association magazine for the Beef Farmers," I told him. "It only comes out every quarter, so there's probably a write up about my rant at Melville in there. Or how I punched the crap out of Fisher." I shrugged. "To be honest, I'd rather not know."

Travis ripped open the plastic cover and discarded the front address sheet of paper. He didn't even have to open the magazine to find out whether I got mentioned or not, because my face was on the cover.

CHAPTER TWO

ONE STEP FORWARD. TWO STEPS BACK

SITTING at my desk the next day, I was still staring at the magazine. There I was on the cover, with Greg and Allan, under the heading "Farming in the Future". I guessed it was better than "Farming for Fairies".

I remember some photographs being taken that night, but after I'd come out to a room full of fellow farmers, called old Jack Melville a few choice words and then proceeded to knock an ex-employee's two front teeth out, I never gave the photos another thought.

Last night, as he was leaning against my desk while I fed Nugget, Travis had read the article before me, I guess to soften the blow if me coming out as gay was mentioned. But it wasn't.

The article was pretty decent and very clearly Greg's doing. He'd obviously got in the ear of the interviewer and told them of his plans to change the face of farming the outback. He told them the days of the past were finished, that the younger generation, naming me and Allan specifically, were ready to take on the Australian beef industry and the twenty-first century.

There was no more than one whole paragraph of me in detail. All it said was that it was a welcome sight to see the new face of Sutton Station after the death of my father over two years ago.

Still, I stared at the magazine on my desk. It had been a restless night. It was good to be back in our own bed after almost a week away, and Travis had done his best to distract me. But I had to get up twice to feed a hungry wombat and spent a whole lotta shoulda-been-sleepin' time wide awake and staring at the ceiling.

The reception to me 'coming out' as gay within the small-town farming community hadn't been too bad. I'll admit, I expected it to be a lot worse. But I still didn't care; I would do it again in a heartbeat. I'd met brief resistance from Brian at the co-op, but shut him up pretty quick when I'd threatened to take my business elsewhere. He knew my father well enough to know that when a Sutton made a promise, it was made for life. If he didn't want to take my 'gay' money, I'd thoroughly enjoy making sure no one else spent their money with him either. Spiteful, maybe. Stubborn, yes. I was a Sutton. And as many times I'd wished it otherwise, the apple didn't fall far from the tree.

Despite the lingering issues I had with my dead father and what he might think of the stand I'd made, I'd never felt freer or more myself, than I could ever remember.

But in the last few months, since Travis's visa got sorted and I'd agreed to nominate myself to be elected on the Board of Directors of the Beef Farmers Association, life had been a bit of a blur.

I'd been doing a bit of groundwork with Greg and Allan on getting a public profile, creating a slow but steady push in the farming movement. By the time elections rolled around, we were hoping to create enough momentum to vote the redundant, afraid-of-change old timers out.

I'd been studying—and quite possibly poutin' and stompin' about doing it too, but my brattish gripin' didn't bother Travis none. He'd just smile, more stubborn than me, and tell me to shut up about it and get it done already.

And funnily enough, I was getting through it. I'd done three subjects so far and only had two to go, and the university degree I'd started years ago would be done. It was an accomplishment, another one I could thank Travis for.

I was starting to see how all his push-push-pushin' to get shit done just made me a better me.

And not just me. His influence was all over the farm, not just out in the paddocks, but in the homestead as well. His warmth to Nara, the once-frightened kid, had helped her find her feet. He had convinced Bacon and Trudy they should be honest with me about their relationship, which truthfully probably saved me from losing one or two of the best workers I'd ever known. He'd also saved the lives of two little critters I'd probably have left to die. First it was Matilda the kangaroo and now Nugget the wombat. Right or wrong, I'd have kept on my ignorant and selfish way and left them to fend for themselves, whereas he stopped and saved them.

He saved me.

Right now he was outside sorting out roofing iron with George and Bacon, and I was inside, supposed to be going through the mail and emails. I had been out there after breakfast, sayin' hello to Shelby. A week away in horse-counting-days was too long apparently, because she nipped at me and nudged me into the fence. I rubbed her neck and whispered sweet nothings, just soothing like, and promised her a ride soon enough.

When Bacon had pushed Travis's shoulder and asked him if I talked to him like that, I told them both to fuck the fuck off, left them laughing even louder, and went inside.

Where I would spend the entire day doing paperwork.

I guessed bein' away for a week let it build up, but it was frustrating that more time was spent doin' bookwork than bein' outside doing what I really loved.

But I wanted to be a farmer that Travis would be proud of, and if that meant I needed to make my way through invoices, receipts, accounts, statements and emails, then that's what I'd do.

Plus, it helped keep my mind off this meeting with the supermarket buyer tomorrow.

By the next morning, I was itching to take the chopper up and go collect Blake. I wasn't nervous, I just wanted to get it over with. I didn't doubt this station's capabilities or my own to give this buyer what he needed.

I just needed to get him here. He could see the rest for himself.

George and I went over the chopper, fully fuelled and serviced. I checked the weather station for wind direction and speed, slotted in Melville's coordinates into my GPS, and off I went.

I'd asked the boys not to make a start on re-roofing the house today. I didn't know what Blake was going to ask of us —whether he'd need one or two of the guys to be in a holding yard with him—and I didn't particularly want to bring him here, trying to make an impression on him, only for him to find the homestead roof bein' pulled apart. There wasn't anything strictly wrong with the roof; it had just seen a decade of desert seasons too many.

Right on time, I landed the chopper a safe distance from the cluster of homes, sheds and livestock on Melville's property. The man was an arse, but I respected the farming life and would never give the man reason to hate me any more than he probably already did. Not without good reason, anyway.

There were several guys standing around some four-wheelers, so I naturally walked toward them. My presence was greeted with silence and cold stares. I, on the other hand, smiled widely and spoke cheerfully. "Someone call a cab?"

Blake laughed. "I'm just finishing up and I'll be with you."

"No problem," I said. Then I looked at Jack Melville and gave him a nod. "Mr Melville."

His greeting was more of a grunt than a hello. "Sutton."

I tipped my hat to the other men, his station hands, and bid them good day. When I was walking back to the chopper, I heard Melville say he'd have his accountant forward sales reports to Blake as soon as he could. I smiled, knowing Blake had mine already. A simple email was all it took, and I wondered idly if old Melville even knew what email was.

I had no clue whether Blake had told them it was me coming to collect him, but they sure as hell knew now that he was considering putting Sutton Station on his sellers list. If Melville didn't dislike me before, he certainly did now.

I smiled all the way back to the chopper.

Blake was no more than five minutes behind me, and it wasn't until we were all buckled in and in the air that I sparked up conversation. I figured a bit of a scenic tour would be nice.

I pointed out through the windshield, over the expanse of red, red dirt, telling which stations were in which direction. His eyes were as big as his smile, and I figured he probably didn't do this too often.

"So, what's your territory?" I asked. "Which regions do you look after?"

"Australia."

I laughed. "All of it?"

Blake nodded. "I have a team, but yeah, I go all over."

"What's your favourite part?"

Blake smiled and looked out the windshield. The desert looked endless. "Different areas for different reasons," he said. "Whether it's green pastures and high rainfall, or this"—he waved his hand at the windshield—"all the farmers I talk to think theirs is the best."

That made me laugh. "Yeah, but they're not as right as me."

Blake chuckled and nodded, like he'd heard it all before. "I take it you know Jack Melville?"

I bit back a sigh, wondering what the old bastard had said. "Kind of."

"Well, he was saying times are pretty tough out here these days," Blake started. "But lookin' out across the desert, I don't know how you guys tell the good times from the bad, to be honest. I mean, the desert's pretty to look at, but I don't envy you trying to get money out of red dirt."

My laugh seemed to surprise him. "I used to think you'd have to have red dirt in your veins to do this, but I'm not sure anymore," I said, thinking of how Travis had settled in so well. "I think you just have to understand it, appreciate it and respect it."

Blake nodded. "True."

"And old Jack Melville thinks any days that wasn't the eighties are tough." Then realising I'd probably sounded spiteful, I lightened the conversation and added, "I remember my old man saying once the eighties had been good for the industry, but I wouldn't know. I'm what he'd call new-age, and I can only go by what I know."

Blake smiled and looked at me. "I see it all the time. The old farmers are still doing things the way they've always done them. And they do okay. But they're getting left behind. People are more educated these days, they use knowledge and research and adapt to suit."

"Exactly!" I agreed. And so the conversation about technology, science, man-hours and even the use of the very kind of helicopter we were sitting in continued until the homestead came into view. I told him all about the solar-powered collars Travis had implemented on some cattle on our station, and he was interested to see how they worked.

I brought the chopper down, and we were met by George, Travis, Billy and the vet, Scott. He'd only beaten us there by five minutes, apparently. I made introductions, and we didn't waste any time.

We had herded some yearlings and pregnant cows into the round yard, and Blake got down to business. He fired a dozen questions at Scott as they inspected the cattle. Then he asked to see grain storage areas, feeding bays and a transcript of all vet call-outs, vaccinations and drenches.

Scott put a call through to the office in Alice Springs, and fifteen minutes later, he had the files in his inbox. As a final step, Blake asked if he could take a look at some cattle in the paddocks. I guess he didn't want us to herd in the best-looking animals when they may not have been a true indicator to our typical quality.

I didn't hesitate. I had nothing to hide. "Sure thing," I said to both Blake and Scott. "Come inside and I'll show you how the tracking collars work first."

I led them into my office and showed them the program on my laptop. It was a property boundary outline of Sutton

Station, and inside were ten little red flashing lights. I pointed to the screen. "Ten collars. They're solar powered and monitor feeding, location, migration of those select beasts. We have the ten collars integrated throughout the mob to give us a broad indication."

I clicked on one random collar and it bought up a short, concise history of that animal, including GPS coordinates.

Scott was intrigued. Blake, on the other hand, was just smiling.

I handed Scott the information brochure we got with the collars, and he was absolutely fascinated. "You didn't have these last time I was here?" he asked.

"Nope. They're new. We've only had them for about four weeks," I told him. "I can sit here in my office and have a pretty good indication what my cattle are doing. It's a darn lot easier considering my top northern paddock is almost four-hundred kilometres away."

"So you can monitor where a select mob is at any time?" Blake asked, now seemingly impressed.

"Yep. And we can track migration, how far they've travelled over what time. We only have ten tagged, five cows and five steers," I said.

I pulled out my smartphone. "I have an app here too. You can take this into the paddock to inspect some cattle. It will take you to one of these beacons"—I pointed to the screen—"to within a few feet."

Blake smiled. "I'd like that."

"I can't take credit for it," I said straight up. "It wasn't my idea. It was Travis Craig's idea. The tall American guy. I have to admit, I thought it was pretty crazy at first, but it's a bloody good concept. You can buy the collars from the Queensland Department of Agriculture. Anyone can do it."

When I'd showed them the app on my phone and they

saw how, from anywhere we had mobile phone reception, we could track each of the tagged animals, where they were and where they'd been. It was similar to the version on my laptop, but this I carried with me in my pocket. Blake and Scott were duly impressed. "I've heard of this set-up before, but never seen it action," Blake said. "It's really rather remarkable."

I took them back outside. "You could go by horseback without my phone for a GPS, but you might be riding for a time 'til you find any cattle. This paddock right here"—I nodded to the closest fence—"is about fifty miles long."

Blake's response was one I expected. "Oh."

"The ute'll be faster," I said with a smile, handing him my phone. "Travis can take you."

Travis covered his surprise well. "Yep. Sure can," he said. He narrowed his eyes at me for a brief what-the-hell moment before leading Blake to the old Land Rover.

I chuckled as Travis got in to the driver's side, knowin' full well he hated driving in Australian cars. He could refuse with me, but I knew he wouldn't with a guy we were trying to impress.

I wanted Travis to talk to him. First, because Travis was the smartest guy here, he'd researched the collars before convincing me to buy them, and I wanted Blake to see we were a young, well-educated team. And second, because if anyone could charm Blake into securing us a guaranteed income, it was Travis.

Of that I had no doubt.

"Scott," I said, addressing the vet. "Thank you so much for coming out on such short notice."

"No worries," he said. He looked around, seeming a tad uncomfortable now that it was just me and him.

I wondered what the problem was, and then the penny

dropped. He'd heard about me being gay. It was true that not much grew in the desert, but the grapevine fucking thrived.

So I took a deep breath and raised my chin. "Let me guess, Scott. You heard rumours about me?"

I watched him swallow, and he shrugged. "Maybe."

"Can I ask you something?"

He didn't answer me, but he looked at me like he was waiting for me to continue, so I did.

"How's the cattle look?"

My question confused him. "Um, good. They look real good."

"We're expecting a two-to-one calving season soon," I told him. "Pretty good figures for around here, yes?"

He nodded, obviously still not sure where I was going with these questions. "Yeah, better than most."

"And my team here," I said, looking back to the homestead, "any one of them could run this place if I needed 'em to. And they have. I trust them, and they trust me."

He blinked. "And?"

"Just proving a point," I said simply, "that whether those rumours are true or not, it don't make a fucking difference to how I run this station."

The corner of his lip twitched, as though he fought a smile. He was quiet for a moment. "Do you remember that time I came here with my dad? I was about sixteen. You were, I dunno, probably ten."

There were a dozen times around that age. "Yeah?"

"Your dad was telling my dad that some farmer he knew was losing water out of his bore, and you said it didn't make sense. You said it was more than likely his water was too salty and his cattle were just probably drinkin' more."

I laughed. I'd forgotten I'd said that. "Yeah."

"I'll never forget it," he said. "When we left here, we were driving down the road and my dad said, 'That young Charlie isn't stupid. He'll be one of the best farmers out here if he's given the chance.'"

"He said that?"

Scott nodded. "Yep. As true as I stand here. And you know what?"

"What?"

"You were right. Dad called that guy and asked him to check his ph levels."

I snorted out a laugh. "I usually am right, about farming, that is." Then I said, "Well, I wasn't blowing my own trumpet before. I just wanted you to see that whether those rumours are true or not, nothing is different. That's all."

Scott looked out over the paddock, as though not looking at me made it easier. "So, the rumours are true?"

"About me being gay?" I asked. "Or me telling old Jack Melville to shove his old-fashioned view on farming where the sun don't shine? Or that I punched Jason Fisher in the mouth, several times?" I shrugged. "Actually, there ain't no point guessing. They're all true."

This time Scott laughed. "You haven't changed."

I smiled. "Nope."

We talked some more about work for a while, and it wasn't long after that we heard the ute coming back. Ma had put on a lunch spread for our visitors, all different types of our beef: corned, roasted, minced, sliced, all with a bunch of different condiments and warm fresh-baked bread. She must have been run ragged, cooking all morning.

Blake and Travis came in smiling, just as I'd hoped they would. It was funny to watch newcomers sit and eat at our table. Yep, we were co-workers, but we were an awful lot like family. It started off quiet and hesitant, but by the time platters in the middle were empty, there was the usual talk and laughs. Not to mention the trade magazine with my ugly mug on the cover was still the punchline of a few jokes.

Just when we were near finished, Nara stood at the door. She winced apologetically. "Sorry, Mr Sutton. I thought you was finished. I can come back."

I knew it must have been something important for her to interrupt. "What is it, Nara?"

She stepped in awkwardly, holding a fussing Nugget and a still full bottle. "He won't feed. I've tried, and Ma tried. He missed his morning feed and now this one…"

All eyes flickered to me, and a few people fought smiles. Billy just grinned his half-a-face grin, as per normal. I sighed, long and loud. "Hand him over."

As soon as the little bugger was in my arms, he settled, and as soon as I put the bottle teat near his mouth, he fed like he was starving. I shook my head. Someone laughed. "It's not funny," I said, but everyone at the table seemed to think it was.

I looked at Scott. "Don't wanna take a wombat back with ya?"

Scott just laughed, but the vet in him was immediately interested in the little happy guy feeding in my arms. "Wombats aren't too common out here," he said. "How'd you come by him?"

Travis answered. "Found a dead mom by the road." Scott nodded. Unfortunately, it wasn't surprising. Then Travis said, "He's taken to Charlie. Seems he's the only one who can feed him since we got back from Kakadu. Sleeps under his arm too."

"Scratches the shit outta my ribs," I added. "I'll have scars for sure."

Scott laughed. "Seems he thinks you're his new mother." He studied the little guy for a while. "He looks about a year old. He'll be dependent on you until he's two years. You can introduce some grass, grains and special pellets, phasing out the milk over the next year."

"A *year*?" I said probably louder than I should have. It startled Nugget. "Yes you," I said, looking at the offended wombat. "Don't look at me like that. You're not the one who has to get up every three hours to feed you."

I looked back at a somewhat bemused vet and held the baby wombat out to him. "You're a vet. You take him."

He put his hands up like I was gonna shoot him. "I have three kids who would love him," he said, his eyes warmed at the mention of them. Then he sighed. "But my wife would kill me if I brought home another animal."

I looked at Travis and said, "I know exactly what you mean." He laughed, knowing I'd probably mutter the same words about him if he brought home some other critter.

But then Scott sighed. "I can drop him off at a WIRES home, or maybe one of the animal nurses might take him," he said. "If you really want."

I looked down at the little guy in my arms, all wrapped up in a woollen beanie and my old sweater—the same sweater Travis had kept Matilda in. Nugget was back to feeding, his little eyes were closed, his nose twitching as he drank. He seemed to be smiling as he fed. I rolled my eyes and sighed. "Nah. He'll be alright."

Travis had tried to hold back his laugh, but he chuckled and snorted under his breath.

"It's not funny," I told him. "This is your fault."

"Of course it is," he deadpanned, then held his hand out to Blake. "I gotta get back to work. Remember what I said."

Blake smiled as he shook Travis's hand. "No problem."

I looked at my watch, realising we'd have to be leaving

soon to get Blake to the airport on time. I stood up just as Ma came in to collect the now empty trays from the table.

Scott stood quickly. "Good afternoon, Mrs Brown," he addressed her formally. "Lunch was great, thank you."

Ma fussed and blushed a little, the warm pink finally putting some colour on her cheeks. "You're very welcome, boys. Scotty, please say hello to your dad for me."

"Will do," he said with a nod, and with that we walked outside.

I left Scott with Travis and George, taking Blake and the chopper up and heading south-west to Alice. We'd cleared it with the airport and got permission to land and refuel. There was a helipad on the grounds, and it was frequently used by locals and tourists alike.

Our conversation on the flight out was different than the one coming into Sutton Station. He told me he liked what he saw, how our approach to farming was more considerate to the animal—leaving the calves with their mothers for longer than most, less stress, less time held in feedlots, more time in open paddocks—was well above industry standards. He said, "Travis started talking about using the nature of the soil out here to assist, manage, or eradicate disease control problems, or something or other." Blake shook his head. "Don't tell him, but he lost me on that. The beef industry, I understand. The science behind the dirt, not so much."

I laughed, probably a little too long and loud. "That's Travis for ya."

"He's a long way from home," Blake added. "From Texas, or so he said."

"Yep. Calls here home now, though." I shrugged, not wanting to say much more about Travis. I wasn't opposed to people knowing if they had to, but I wasn't about to start blabbing unnecessarily about being gay and what that meant for business deals and proposals. Blake seemed like a fair man, but he was here to discuss business. I had no intention of bringing up his sex life, so why should I bring up mine?

I changed subjects again, pointing off to the right, showing him a line of wild camels. He just shook his head in wonder. "So weird to see them out here."

I nodded. I guessed it was. "Been a pest out here since they built the railroad from Adelaide to Darwin. Afghans brought 'em here a hundred and fifty years ago. Couldn't take 'em home, so they just left 'em, I guess."

"Pests, huh?" he said with a good-natured smile. "Kinda like your little wombat."

I snorted and shook my head. "First it was a kangaroo, now it's a wombat. We'll be a wildlife sanctuary before too long."

"I might be getting a little ahead of myself here," he said, and his voice sounded hesitant in my ears through the chopper headset. "I can't promise anything, and this ain't no guarantee."

I waited for him to get the words right. Wishing and hoping he was about to say what I thought he was about to say.

"Nothing's for sure until our vets do an inspection for themselves," he said. "I just want you to know that."

"Fair enough."

"But I was thinking..." he hedged nervously, "that, gee, my wife would love to see this place."

I barked out a laugh. "Anytime."

BY THE TIME I landed the chopper down on Sutton soil, it was getting on close to dinner time and my mind was frayed. It'd been a big day. Nothing physical, more mental, and spending that long in the chopper, concentrating and navigating, was draining.

I was met by a grinning Travis, who brought with him a hundred questions about how it went. "Pretty good, I think" was about all I said. "Can we talk about it later? I'm beat."

No sooner was I inside than Nugget was shoved into my arms for a feed. At dinner, a full table of leftovers and fresh breads, I told everyone about my conversation with Blake and then fed the bloody wombat again, one more time before bed. I was yawning and my eyelids were heavy, so when Travis led me to our room, I didn't protest.

Not that I ever did.

He held my face and kissed me, softly, soundly, sighing as he pulled his lips from mine.

"I have three hours before I'm on feeding duty again," I mumbled.

Travis lifted my chin. He smiled, dark-eyed and husky-voiced. "I can think of plenty to do in three hours."

As he was peeling my shirt off, I asked, "Is sleep a part of that?"

He shook his head and pulled at the button on my jeans, opening them. "Get on the bed, Charlie," he murmured.

I fell back on the soft, soft cloud-like doona, and Travis grinned as he grabbed my jeans at my ankles and pulled them off me. Then he proceeded to nudge his nose up every inch of my body, followed by a scruffy chin and soft lips. He made sure I didn't miss a minute of the next three hours.

AFTER ALL THE incessant thumping I could stand, I walked outside. Well, it was more like stomped outside, the slamming screen door punctuating my lack of sleep and patience perfectly. I looked up at where Travis was on the roof. "Could you bang any fucking louder?"

Travis looked down at me and grinned. "Yep. Gimme a sec." He held his hand out to Bacon. "Pass me the bigger hammer."

I grumbled. Or growled, or maybe a bit of both. He was re-sheeting the iron roof. Typical Travis, needed something to do and with the still cool weather, he must have figured now was as good a time as any. Of course he didn't want my help. I had an assessment due and financial figures to look over, so he'd barred me from helping, and he had Bacon up there helping instead. They were both smiling now.

"You're not funny."

Travis laughed. "You want me to bang out a tune? What about 'Twinkle, Twinkle, Little Star'?"

I glared at him. "What about 'Shut the Fuck Up'? You heard that tune?"

From somewhere in the house, Ma chipped me for swearing, and Travis threw his head back and laughed. I stomped back inside to my office and ignored him for a while longer, and eventually the thumping stopped.

Only then did Travis call out, "Charlie? Charlie, you need to come see this."

CHAPTER THREE

MORE THAN JUST MEMORIES

TWO CARDBOARD BOXES sat on the kitchen table.

Old, dusty, forgotten.

I had no clue what was in them, and I was almost too scared to look. Obviously put in the roof cavity for safe-keeping—or so no one could find them—these boxes hadn't been touched in years.

My name and date of birth in my father's handwriting on the side of them was what stopped me.

Scared me.

"Charlie," Travis said quietly. He was beside me, as was Ma. Bacon, who had helped retrieve them, was now gone. "Did you want to open them?"

I nodded, then shook my head. "I don't know."

"You don't have to," he whispered. "I can put them in the shed until you're ready."

I thought I was past this. I thought I'd come to terms with my father, his hurtful, no-toleratin' words, his disappointed stare. I thought I'd accepted my past and moved on. Hell, I'd even acknowledged I was as stubborn as my father —even proud of it. I'd dealt with the homophobic comments and stares exactly how *he* would have dealt with someone who didn't agree with him.

I knew that streak of no-bullshit front-foot-leading arrogance came direct from my old man, and I was okay with it.

And yet whatever he kept hidden in these two boxes rendered me back to square one. I was a scared kid again waiting for his words to hurt me.

"I thought he'd said all he could say," I heard myself say. I'm not sure I meant to say it out loud. Trav put his hand on my back, and I looked at him. "What if there's just more 'you're such a disappointment' in there."

Trav lifted his chin, as though the thought offended him. "Charlie, his words can't hurt you anymore," he said. I think he'd said that before. "You know that, right? You have the power over whatever is in these boxes. You decide, not him."

I found myself staring at him. He was exactly right. "How'd you get so smart?" I asked.

"I'm not that smart. I just know how your mind works. I knew exactly what you were thinking, Charlie." He kissed the side of my head. "Did you want to open them?"

I nodded and looked over to Ma, who was smiling at Travis. "You okay, Ma?" I asked.

She still looked tired, but she turned her gentle smile to me as she sat down at the table. "I'm fine," she said. "I just worry when you worry, that's all."

I pulled out a seat, but rested my knee on it instead of sitting down, and pulled the first box over. Without being asked, Travis sat a cup of tea in front of Ma, and they both waited for me to open the first box.

I don't know what I was expecting. Maybe letters, legal documents, maybe even financial documents we hadn't found when we cleared out his room.

What I found made me both smile and frown.

I reached into the box and pulled out the first thing. It was a teddy bear. Old, faded, a bit worn, and it looked like it'd been dropped in the mud. I didn't recognise it.

"Oh, that was yours," Ma said quietly. "Up until you were three, you carried it everywhere."

"I don't remember it," I said, putting it on the table.

Ma picked it up and looked the bear over. "Your father took it off you after your third birthday. Said you were too old to be carrying 'round a stuffed toy."

I shrugged. That didn't surprise me. Not one bit.

"Now this I remember," I said, pulling out a sawn-off plaster cast. It was dirt-brown, frayed and smaller than I remembered. "My first broken arm," I said with a laugh. "Remember, Ma? I came off my motorbike."

Ma glared at me. "Of course I remember. How could I forget?"

Travis took it and looked it over. "That's disgusting. Has it aged, or is that the state you got it in."

Ma huffed. "He wore it in the mud, the dirt, the creek. Then his father ended up cutting it off here, because it stunk so bad."

I snorted. "Yeah, it smelt like roadkill."

Travis looked over the jagged cut down the length of the cast. "Your dad cut it off?"

"Yep, with a pair of shears."

"Dear Lord," Travis mumbled.

I laughed at his expression. "And look, here's the throttle grip to the bike I was riding when I came off," I said, pulling out a motorbike throttle grip that used to fit my peewee fifty. It was black, the rubber now degraded and crumbling. It was an unusual keepsake. "Why the hell did he keep that?"

"Because it was your first," Ma said with a shrug. "And you loved it."

I thought about what that meant. My father hadn't really kept these things for himself. He'd kept them for me.

I didn't know what to make of that.

Next I pulled out an array of things, from a small jar with my first tooth, first pair of baby boots, an old Bunnykins plate and a matching plastic, now cracked cup.

Toward the bottom of the box were books: a scrapbook, a baby book and a photo album. I pulled them out and set them aside and reached in for the last few things in the bottom. It was some laminated certificates from my home-schoolin' days and a plastic bag with folded newspapers.

I moved the first empty box to the floor and looked at all the things covering the table. My childhood mementos. It was shocking and wonderful that my father had kept these things. I ran my hand over my face and tried to collect my thoughts. Still too scattered to put into words, I sighed instead.

But I was smiling.

"Wow," I finally said, sitting down. "I had no idea."

Travis ruffled my hair, then kissed the top of my head before sitting down beside me. He seemed just about to burst. Whether that was out of relief or happiness for me, I didn't dare guess. It didn't matter.

I slid the baby book over first. It was blue, small and had aged yellow. I opened the first page, where in fluid handwriting I didn't recognise was my full name, date of birth, weight, length, hair colour, and also a small square photo of a baby's crying face, presumably mine.

"You haven't changed," Travis joked.

I could only laugh. The next page was recorded dates with weights, heights, milestones. I got my first tooth when I was seven months old, apparently. And it was written very plainly, underlined and everything, that I did *not* like oatmeal.

Ma snorted out a laugh. "Now *that* hasn't changed."

I laughed with her, but the next page made my smile die right there.

There I was, all of maybe two years old, sitting on my father's knee. He was laughing at something, his face all lit up, looking at someone or something the camera didn't show.

He looked so much younger than the man I remembered. Happier, too. He looked so happy. The clothes we wore were indicative of the times—late eighties—the photo itself a Polaroid, yellowed with age.

Travis's hand on my knee made me look at him. "You okay?"

I nodded. "I am." And I was. This wasn't what I was expecting, to find these things from my childhood, and a reminder that my father hadn't always been so angry. I turned back to the photo and absently traced over the picture with my finger. "He looks so happy."

I could feel Ma's eyes on me, and when I looked up at her, she stared at me for a long while. "He *was* happy, love."

"I must remember him differently," I mumbled.

Ma sighed. "He wasn't always so..." She seemed to struggle for the right word.

"Angry?" I suggested. "Bitter?"

"Lonely," she finished.

I didn't have an answer to that. I let it settle over me instead, like a heavy blanket of regret. "I was too busy being a brat to see that," I admitted.

Ma smiled warmly. "You were a teenager, love. You can't be blamed for not seeing, especially when he'd say things he didn't mean." She sighed then and looked as tired as I think I'd ever seen her. "He was a good man, Charlie, up until your mother left. He was never the same after that. Too proud, I think, to admit he wished things were different."

It was quiet then, and I turned the next page. It had tear marks where a photo had once been, but was later ripped out. As did the next page, and the one after that.

I assumed those were of my mother.

The last entry was a picture of me, probably four years old, holding a fish that was half my size, wearing too-big riding boots. I was grinning like the happiest kid on the planet. A kid that didn't know his world was about to be forever changed.

Trav put his hand at the back of my neck and leaned in, not to look at the picture, but to be closer to me. "Do you remember that?" he asked.

I shook my head. "Nope." Then I looked at the photo again. "I think I remember those boots, though."

Travis laughed. "Yep. You're gay alright."

I nudged him with my elbow but chuckled. Next was the scrapbook. It was the same age, pages yellowed and dusty. Pasted inside were newspaper clippings, some photos of me, some just mentions. "You used to do bull riding?" Travis asked.

"Yep. Up until I was twelve and broke my wrist in two places." I'd mentioned to him before that I'd broken my wrist just before my dad was due to go some important meeting. "My dad said no more rodeos after that."

Some of the clippings were about Sutton Station, some were directly about me doing something with the School of the Air. "It wasn't your normal kind of school," I explained. "There ain't no team sports, no after-school activities or anything like that when the closest kid was two hundred and fifty kilometres away. Give or take."

Travis shook his head. "Such a different childhood than me," he said.

"It was pretty great," I admitted. "Riding bikes, horses, chasing bulls... being chased by bulls."

Ma pointed to her hair. "See these greys?" she said, her eyebrows raised. "Every single one of them is from something he did."

There were cut-outs ranging from me bein' little right up to my teen years. The last clipping wasn't stuck in, just folded and pressed between two pages, and was from only a few years ago.

From what I could tell, it looked like it had been cut out of the Beef Farmers Association magazine, just like the one we got the other day with my face on the front. Except this was just text, an interview, it seemed, with my father.

He talked of the last stock prices being a little lower than he'd have liked, but the season had been okay. Then as the conversation turned to family matters, the interviewer noted,

"Charles Sutton spoke of his son proudly, saying he was studying Agriculture in Sydney. 'As much as we can learn from living the land, the future is in education,' he said. 'Charlie will be a better farmer, better than what I could ever be.'

The interviewer had joked, wondering if a young man would come back to the outback after tasting city life. Charles Sutton laughed like it was an inside joke. 'It's a hard life, no one would argue that. But ask any one of us—we wouldn't have it any other way. Charlie will be back. Not because he's obligated, but because he loves it.'

'You must be very proud of your son,' the interviewer

prompted. Charles Sutton answered with one resounding word. 'Very.'"

I read it. And then I reread it. And I swallowed back tears while Travis and then Ma read the article. "I don't understand," I said. "Was he lying when he said that? Why would he lie to them? Why would he say those things? They weren't true."

"Charlie," Travis murmured. "They were true."

I shook my head. "He said the opposite to me. He told me. Ma was there, so was George. They heard what he said."

Ma frowned. "Oh, love."

Travis, undeterred, took my hand. "Charlie, we've gotten pretty good at talking things through, haven't we?"

I nodded. "I'm trying to get better at it."

He smiled at that. "You're doing great." He squeezed my hand. "But do you remember in the beginning? It wasn't easy." He spoke so calmly. "You'd find it easier to lie and say you were fine when you really weren't. You'd struggle so hard, and it was easier to say no and be on the defensive and act like you didn't care than to let someone think, for just one second, that you might be open with them."

I swallowed so I could speak. "But why would he lie to some interviewer? He could have just said I was away at college and left it that, but he didn't. He kept on about it. That doesn't make sense."

Travis shook his head like I was missing the obvious. "He wasn't lying to them, Charlie. What he said to *you* was the untruth. He was proud of you. He just couldn't tell you."

I shook my head. It didn't make sense.

"Just like you, he'd have found it easier to tell the truth to some stranger than it would be to tell the person he loved the very hard truth. It's easier to tell a stranger the truth because there's no risk of rejection. Don't you see? It was easier for him to act like he didn't care to you, Charlie, because with you he had the most to lose."

I looked at Travis then. Really looked at him. Sitting right next to me, holding my hand, with the bluest of blue eyes, was the only person on the planet who really knew me. He knew my every secret, my every mood, dream and need, he'd seen the worst side of me, and yet he still sat beside me.

"You hear what I'm saying, Charlie?" Travis said gently.

Nodding, I swallowed down the lump in my throat and ignored the burn in my eyes. "You're really kinda perfect, you know that?"

Ma snorted, and when we looked over, she was wiping her eyes with her sleeve. "You boys are making me cry."

Just then, Nara walked into the kitchen and stopped when she saw us. "Sorry," she said quickly. "I was just coming in to help with lunch."

Which made us all look at the time. Shit, the morning was almost gone. I stood up and packed everything back into the first box and then realised I hadn't even touched the second box.

"I haven't even started on lunch," Ma said.

"I should have fed Nugget by now," I added, but I looked back at the unopened box.

Ma put her hand on my arm. "Open it, Charlie. Don't waste another day. I can get the bottle ready for Nugget..."

"You know what?" Travis said. "Why don't you two go and sit in the lounge room and go through the box. I'm sure you have lots to talk about. Nara and I can get lunch organised."

I don't know whether he honestly thought me and Ma

needed to talk or if he picked up on how pale Ma was looking, but it was a good idea regardless.

And she didn't argue.

Lookin' back, that right there, that lack of arguin', should have told me something wasn't right.

But I was too engrossed in the box they'd found in the roof space to notice. The box of my childhood memories and the tiny little snippet of hope—the magazine interview clipping that maybe, just maybe, showed that my father didn't hate me like I thought he did—sat at my feet.

Ma sat next to me, and I opened the second box. It was smaller and lighter than the first box, and when I opened it, I saw why.

It only had one book in it.

A small scrapbook. That's all there was. I wondered why it was in a separate box if that's all there was in it. I picked up the scrapbook and set the box down, and slivers of newspaper clippings feathered to the floor.

I picked them up, probably six or seven, and opened the scrapbook. None of them were stuck in, just left loose, like my dad had run out of time or he wasn't too sure what to make of them.

I sat the book between me and Ma and opened the first folded clipping. The paper was old, yellowed and dry. It was an article from a primary school in Darwin talking about some exhibition. The names, the references, meant nothing to me.

I picked up another one of the small clippings. It was an action photograph from the newspaper of some kids playing soccer. I couldn't see any faces, but they must have been five or six years old.

Again, nothing.

I handed that one to Ma, then I picked up another one. Smaller, older, it was a birth notice.

Samuel Jennings, born 4th March, 1983. Mum and son doing well.

I read it. And read it again.

I had no clue who that was and no idea why my father would have kept it.

Frowning, I handed the small piece of yellowed newspaper to Ma. "I don't know anyone by the surname Jennings."

That was when I really looked at Ma. Like *really* looked at her. She was pale, more pale than she had been, the dark circles under her eyes more pronounced. Her breaths were short and quick, and when I took her hand, it was clammy.

I took the newspaper clipping from her, and taking her hand, I pulled her to her feet. "To bed with you," I said. "Don't try and argue with me."

And she didn't.

Very unlike Ma, but she gave a nod. "I don't feel the best."

I led her to her room, past the kitchen, where Travis stopped what he was doing and followed us. "Everything okay?" he asked.

"Ma's okay," I answered, still walking slowly to the bedroom at the back of the house. "Just needs some rest."

"Thank you," Ma said weakly. "I don't want to worry anyone."

We got to her bed, and I pulled back the covers and waited for her to get in. "How about you let us worry about you for a change," I said. "I'll make you some lemon tea and get you some Panadol, yes?"

She gave a nod, and I left the room. I walked into the kitchen, where Travis met me. "Charlie?"

"I'll make her some tea," I said.

"Did something upset her?" he asked. "What was in the second box? I know she hasn't been well, but…"

I shook my head. "She hasn't been herself for a while, weeks even. Remember when she had that head cold?" I asked. "Since then."

I had kind of forgotten Nara was in the kitchen with us. "Mr Sutton," she said quietly and handed me a cup of lemon tea. "I cool it down a little for her, how she likes it."

"Thank you," I said. Nara smiled shyly and went back to getting lunches ready. "Nara? You've noticed a change in Ma?"

The girl looked up at me as though she was almost afraid to answer. But then she nodded. "She gets real tired."

Travis put his hand on my shoulder. "Charlie, yesterday when Scott was here, the vet, he said the same thing."

"What?"

"He said to me he didn't realise Mrs Brown was so unwell. He said the last time he saw her was here, nearly three years ago, at your father's funeral." Travis swallowed hard.

"And?"

"And he just said it was a bit of shock to see her looking so thin and pale."

And so I thought back, like Scott had done, and it was really only when I remembered Ma from years ago, or even six months ago, that I could tell in my mind that no, she didn't look too well at all.

And I could have kicked myself for bein' so damn blind.

Maybe it was just a head cold like she said, but she was pale and she looked tired. She was quieter than normal, and she barely ate much at all, many of her cups of tea went untouched. She was so busy worryin' after everyone else, and we were so busy lettin' her, that I didn't even notice.

Just then the screen door banged and I knew from the sound of the steps who it was. "George," I called out.

He walked into the kitchen, and his eyes flickered with something I didn't recognise. Whether it was the fact Ma wasn't in the kitchen or the look on my face, I didn't know.

"Where's Ma?"

"She's in bed," I said. "George, it's probably none of my business, but I don't think Ma's feeling too good. And I don't mean just feeling a bit crook, I mean she's not very well."

I was expecting a look of surprise or shock, but instead he looked to the floor and sighed. "She hasn't been well for a while."

My body took a step toward him of its own accord. "What has she said?"

He shrugged. "She's good at hiding it."

"Why didn't she say something sooner?" I asked quietly. "To me, I mean. I could have made her take time off, get rested or something."

"You've met her, son. She's stubborn and proud. Don't want to worry anyone."

"I'll call the doctor," I said.

George smiled and shook his head. "I've been saying that for two weeks. She's threatened bodily harm every time."

"George, she's never sick," I said, like I was telling him something he didn't already know. "For as long as I've known her, she's never been like this."

"I know," he said sadly. He tried to smile, but it didn't work. "And she says it's just a cold or a flu or something.

This winter's been hard on her, but she says she'll be right as rain in a day or two."

Whether he was repeating something Ma had said a dozen times or he was trying to convince himself, I wasn't sure. I shook my head. "She said that to me weeks ago when Trav and I went to Alice."

George nodded. "I know, Charlie." He didn't sound mad or even resigned. It sounded like he'd had the same argument with her over and over.

"She's not to work until she's feeling better. I don't care if it drives her crazy, she can yell at me all she wants. She needs rest and she needs us to look after her for a change."

George smiled then, it was small and brief. "I'll tell her."

"We'll keep an eye on her," I told him. "But if she doesn't pick up in a day or two, I'll drive her to Alice myself."

He ducked his head, and as he turned to leave, I handed him the cup of tea and spoke more gently. "I promised her some Panadol."

"I'll get it," he said. He sounded grateful. "Thanks, Charlie."

I turned then to see Travis just standing there watching me. "You okay?" he asked. "You've had one helluva morning."

I nodded, very aware that Nara was still in the kitchen loading trays up with breads and meat. "I'm fine," I told him.

Travis didn't seem to care that we weren't alone. He wrapped his arms around me, and despite my hesitation, I leaned into him. The hug was warm and strong and every-thing I needed. I could feel my worries disappear, and the weight of the morning—finding that box full of my childhood mementos in the roof—didn't feel so heavy when he hugged me.

"What was in the second box?" he asked, pulling back but keeping his hands on my arms.

"Just papers, more clippings," I told him. "I don't know what any of it means. None of it's about me." I shrugged. When the back door squeaked open and the others walked in for lunch, I looked over to see that Nara had already taken one tray out to the table.

I picked up the second tray, full of cut fruit, Travis grabbed the tray of sauces and condiments, and we followed Nara into the dining room. Everyone was sitting there, kinda quiet and waiting. I wondered why no one started eating, and that's when I realised. They weren't gonna start because George wasn't there. I picked up a plate, filled it with sandwiches and fruit. "Um," I started, "Ma's not feeling the best. George is in with her now, so I'll take this for him. You guys, please eat."

I left them kinda wide-eyed and stunned and took George in some lunch. I could hear a low murmur, but when I knocked on the door, their conversation stopped. George was sitting on the bed, and Ma tried to smile. I carried the plate in and handed it to George. "I can make you some toast?" I said to Ma. "All the times I was sick and you made me choke down dry toast, it's the least I can do."

She laughed quietly. "Maybe later."

I left them and went back to the dining room and took my usual seat. It felt wrong having an empty seat beside me. In all the years I'd sat at that table, George was always there right beside me. His quiet, unassuming, stronger-than-hell presence wasn't there.

Suddenly, I wasn't too sure I felt like eating, but Travis

put a plate in front of me. He threw on some bread and sliced meat, and before I could shake my head, he hooked his foot around mine under the table.

Like an anchor or a saving grace, he grounded me. I don't know how he knew, but he always seemed to do, say, be just what I needed. Without a word, he was telling me to stay put and stay strong.

I nodded and looked over at Bacon. "How's the roof going?"

And so the conversation started. Until all the food was gone, we talked about what had been done and what needed doing still. I suggested everyone leave what they were doing and help get the roofing done. I knew it was Travis's project, and he and Bacon would get it done in good time, but I didn't want the house to be losing heat while Ma was in bed sick.

They all understood.

"I don't know how long she'll be off work," I told them. "Could be two days, could be a week or longer. But until then, we all do everything we can to cover her." Everyone nodded. "I don't want her to add feelin' guilty to her troubles, okay?"

Nara poked her head around the door, the corner of her mouth pulling down in an unsure kind of sorry.

"What's up?" I asked her.

She showed me a wriggling blue beanie and a small bottle of milk. Oh shit, I'd forgotten about him.

Nara's voice was quiet. "He won't feed again."

I waved her over. "Bring him in," I said, taking the wombat from her and quickly shoving the bottle teat in his fussing mouth. Then while Nara was still in the room, I continued talking. "We'll have to take it in shifts for cooking," I said. "I know it's not what you're all employed to do, and believe me, no one here wants to eat what I cook, but we need to chip in."

Nara collected a tray off the table. "Um..." She started to say something, but then stopped. Everyone was watching her, and she looked like as nervous as I'd seen her. "Nah, it's nothing." She took a backward step toward the door.

"Nara," I said, stopping her. "Please, say what you wanted to say. Your opinion matters as much as any of ours."

She blinked quickly. "I was just gonna say"—she spoke to the floor—"that I can do the cooking." When I didn't answer, she added, "I help Ma all this time and she teached me what to do. I know I won't be as good as what she does, but I used to cook for my family as well..."

A slow smile spread across my face. Not because she'd just volunteered to cook so I didn't have to, but because she found the confidence to speak up.

"Nara, you are more than capable," I told her. "And I'm very grateful."

"But?" she asked.

"But nothing," I said. "You just scored yourself the job."

Man, her smile was huge. Billy's smile was just as big. Travis's foot nudged mine, he squeezed my knee, and he was starin' at me with that you're-something-kinda-wonderful look in his eye again.

Everyone got up from the table and got busy outside, and after I'd put a now sleeping baby wombat back in his pouch, I helped Nara clean up and took inventory while she organised what we'd be having for dinner. Seeing she obviously didn't need me for anything, I left her to it.

I found myself back in the lounge room sitting down on the sofa. I had meant to just pick up the scattered clippings and I was going to put them away. I dunno how long I sat there, and it wasn't until Travis came in and knelt in front of me that I even realised I'd been reading them over again. I'd even put them in some kind of chronological order.

"Charlie," Trav said softly. "Whatcha got there?"

I handed them over, the birth notice on top. I watched as he read through them, seeing a reoccurring name, looking at grainy, dated newspaper photographs of some kid I'd never seen before.

"Who is this Samuel Jennings?" he asked.

"I don't know."

His brow creased as he knelt back, thinkin'. Then he simply got up. "Come on," he said, walking out of the room. I followed him into my office, where he stood at my desk and opened my laptop.

"What are you doing?"

"See if you can Google any information on this guy," he said, holding up the newspaper clippings.

I took the small papers from him and slowly put them on the desk. "I'm, um..." My voice was quiet. "I'm not sure I want to."

Travis sighed. It wasn't an all-out-of-patience sigh. It was an I'm-sorry-I-rushed-you sound. He put his hand to my face and gently kissed my cheekbone. "I should have asked, sorry."

"Don't apologise," I told him. We still stood so close, so close I could have kissed him if I wanted. But I wanted something else a whole lot more. I dropped my forehead onto his shoulder and leaned into him, waiting for him to put his arm around me. It didn't take long. I breathed him in and let my breath out in a rush, feeling my worries leave me as I did.

He rubbed his hands over my back, spreading his warmth into my body. "You okay?" he asked quietly.

"I am now," I answered. "You have some weird magic power to make everything less heavy."

His voice was close to my ear. "Less heavy?"

I didn't explain what I meant, I just nodded against him. "Yep."

He chuckled, the sound all warm and rumbly. He kissed the side of my head and pulled back. "I'd suggest you come help us out there on the roof, since doin' something manual might clear your mind. But Bacon's telling Trudy that she's not getting on any damn roof and she's calling him a bunch of four-letter words, so if you value your sanity, stay in here," he said with a smile. "Stay close to Ma. I know you're worried about her."

"I am." I nodded. "But thanks for the heads-up on Trudy and Bacon."

Travis chuckled. "It's all good, Charlie. They're fine. Nothing for you to stress over, okay? You have enough to worry about right now."

I leaned up, just a fraction, and pressed my lips to his just as there was a thumping on the roof. "Charlie," Ernie called out. "You've got company. There's a car coming."

"Expecting someone?" Travis asked.

I shook my head. We were too remote to have anyone turn up out of the blue. If someone did come out here, it was usually because someone asked 'em to.

As I walked out into the hall, I almost ran into George. He must have heard what Ernie said. "Expecting some-one?" I asked him.

"Nope. You?"

"No." I gave a nod toward his bedroom. "How's Ma?"

"Sound asleep," he said. Then he gave me a bit of a smile. "She'll be fine. You know how she is."

The sound of the approaching vehicle got closer, so we

walked out the front door to see who it was. They were driving slow. Like real slow. An uncertain kind of slow. "Might be lost," I offered.

"Could be," George said.

The car, a late model Subaru, crawled toward the house, eventually stopping about twenty metres away. If they were expecting to find an empty house, they were wrong. Three men on the roof, one woman holding a ladder at the side of the house, and three men on the veranda stopped and stared.

No one got out of the car.

Travis, being Travis, walked down the steps with a welcoming grin and headed toward them. He leaned his hands on the top of the car and the driver's window opened a few inches so he could see inside.

Travis took a reflexive step back, his eyes were a disbelieving kind of wide, and my instinct was to go to him. I didn't know what was wrong, who was in the car, or what they'd done to scare him, but I leapt off the veranda. "Travis?"

The car door opened slowly, and a woman got out.

I heard George mumble behind me. "Oh my God."

I turned around, wondering if something was wrong with Ma, but he was staring at the woman. Travis took quick strides to stand in front of me.

"What's going on?" I asked him. His eyes were full of worry. "How do you know her, Trav?"

"Charlie?" the stranger whispered, almost like she couldn't believe what she saw. She put her hand to her heart. "Coming here was a mistake, sorry," she said, opening her car door as if to leave.

"Wait!" I called out to her, looking around Travis, who was still in front of me, like he was putting himself between me and this stranger. The woman seemed to stop, so I looked at Travis. "What did you see?"

"You," he whispered, swallowing hard. "All I saw was her eyes. She has your eyes. Charlie, I swear it was you looking back at me."

CHAPTER FOUR

NOPE. THANKS FOR THE OFFER, BUT I ALREADY HAVE ONE.

'AWKWARD' was probably a good word to describe it. Some might call it uncomfortable, drawn-out, painful, or even torturous. Quite frankly, I enjoyed watching her, this stranger, look as out-of-place and outnumbered as she possibly could.

I heard her mutter the word 'mother' like it meant something. Even though she'd said it, there really wasn't a need to.

I'd stood out front of my house, dumbstruck and dazed, as Travis's words told me what I think I probably already knew. At least George had the manners to walk over to her and invite her inside.

There was no doubt about it. This lady, this somewhat familiar stranger that George called Laura, was the woman who gave birth to me.

She wasn't as I remembered.

Not that I remembered much about her at all, if I was truthful. All I could recall was brown hair, and now age and time had changed even that. Her hair was straight, cut-off at her shoulders and greying around her face. She had wrinkles at her eyes and the corners of her mouth. She was well-dressed, looked a little too proper, and she wore a wedding ring.

Travis had been shocked at the likeness of me and this Laura, but I didn't see it.

I sat on the sofa near the door, and Travis stood leaning against the wall beside me with his arms folded across his chest. George sat on the seat closest to the fireplace, and this uninvited woman, Laura, sat on the three-seater sofa by herself. She looked nervous, wringing her hands the way she did and not knowing where to look or what to say.

George spoke first. "Katie would have liked to have seen you," he said. "But she's unwell today. She's sleeping right now." It took me a little while to remember Ma's proper first name. I hadn't heard it years. Katie...

Laura frowned immediately. "Oh, is everything okay?"

"Ma's fine," I answered quickly. I didn't like the way she thought she could act concerned about my Ma. And that's what Ma was. She was *my* Ma. The woman that raised me. The only mother I'd ever known.

Laura smiled tightly at me, then looked back to the floor and went back to wringing her hands.

"She's just having a few days' rest, is all," George added, probably trying to ease the tension in the room.

Laura took a deep breath and looked around the room. "This place is just as I remembered," she said with a smile, more to herself than to any of us.

That was hardly the truth, because really, so very much had changed.

When I still didn't speak, she took another nervous breath, and it was then she noticed the boxes on the floor in front her where I'd left them. I regretted not moving them at first, that she might see what was in them, but when I saw how she reacted, I was glad they were there. The stupid teddy bear was stuffed on top of the bigger box, and I watched as she recognised it: she looked at it, then looked again, blinking as if her memories didn't quite seem real.

"Oh," she whispered. Her eyes shot to mine, confused.

"Found it this morning," I said casually. "Bit of a coincidence, don't you think? Dad must have put it in the roof." She looked at me for a long, searching moment, and I tilted my head and smiled. "I don't remember the teddy bear at all."

Then I watched as it clicked. She got it. She understood. It wasn't the stupid toy I couldn't remember.

It was her.

She looked at the floor again and seemed just about to say something, when Nara stood at the door. She was holding Nugget and his feeding bottle. "Sorry," she interrupted quietly. "I keep tryin', but he won't take it."

"It's okay," I said, standing up and taking him from her. "I've got him, thanks." I sat back down and shoved the teat in the little wombat's hungry mouth, looking up at Laura just in time to see her smile at me.

Travis groaned beside me, like he was strugglin' to bite back words. When I looked up at him, he was still standing with his arms crossed, but his jaw was clenched to near teeth-crackin' levels. "You okay?" I asked him, not caring if Laura heard or what she thought.

"Yeah," he grunted, which clearly meant no, he really wasn't.

I patted the arm of the sofa, indicating he should take a seat, which he did, crossing his long legs at the ankle. I knew Laura was looking at us a bit funny, but I offered no explanation.

I had no reason to. I didn't owe her anything.

Nugget pushed the bottle away, and I sat him up. He looked around, shaking his head. I put him down on the floor, letting him stretch his short, stubby legs. The little guy started to sniff and wander gingerly around our feet, and I let him.

"He's very cute," Laura said with a smile.

"He's a pain in the arse," I told her, not apologising for my language. I had no intention of being someone I wasn't and that included who I was with Travis.

He had his hands folded in front of him like he didn't know what to do with them. I pulled on his arm, the one closest to me, and took hold of his hand. I gave his fingers a squeeze and looked at Laura then, waiting, *waiting, wanting,* for her to say something about it.

She didn't. She looked at her lap and kind of smiled.

I was almost disappointed. I'd have preferred a reaction so I could throw her out, but she seemed to smile genuinely. Not that I'd strictly know. I didn't know her at all. She was now looking at Travis. "Did I detect an accent?" she asked him.

I didn't really like the idea of her talking to him either. "So," I interrupted, looking at her expectantly. She took the hint that the time for small talk was over.

Her question forgotten, Laura nodded. "I, um, I guess I should explain..." she started nervously. "I should have come a long time before now."

Probably, I thought. Then immediately after, I thought, *Probably not.* But still I didn't speak. I truthfully didn't have a great deal to say.

"And I'd apologise a million times, but it would never be enough..." Her words trailed off.

Travis squeezed my hand, and I could almost feel his whole body vibrate beside me.

Her eyes flickered to Travis, and I had no doubt she could see his barely contained anger. "For what it's worth, I am sorry," she said. "So very sorry."

I raised an eyebrow at her, like an apology from her—twenty-two years too late—meant a damn thing.

Biting her lip, she pulled her handbag onto her lap. "But I saw this," she went on to say, unrolling a magazine she'd brought with her. It was the Beef Farmers Association magazine with my face on the front. "And I didn't want to put it off any longer. I should have written or called. I can see that turning up wasn't the best idea." She shrugged. "I was halfway down your driveway before I realised what I was even doing. Can you believe I drove all this way without knowing..." She shook her head and put her hand to her forehead before flattening down her hair.

As far as conversations went, with the supposed rule of two people actually speaking, I knew I was probably oblig-ated to say something. So I did.

"My father's dead," I said flatly. Coldly. A sorry, sorry matter-of-fact.

"I know," she whispered. Her eyes were glassy and sorrowful. "I read about Charles," she said, then cringed. "Your father. I was very sorry to hear about that." She swal-lowed hard and frowned at me. "The day of the funeral... I drove out here."

I raised my eyebrow in a sure-you-did kind of way, and her frown deepened. She near whispered, "I got to the gate, but couldn't drive in. It wasn't the right time. The last thing you needed was me turning up on that day."

That day.

This day.

Travis's hold on my hand was close to bone-crushin', and he took a deep breath.

Laura bit her lip and spoke to her hands. "I just want you to know that I don't expect anything, and I'm sorry for just turning up. I shouldn't have, and I am truly sorry. You have every right to tell me not to come back. I wouldn't blame you one bit."

Nugget came sniffing at my feet again. Peeling my hand from Travis's vice-like grip, I put the woollen beanie down at my feet and Nugget climbed into his makeshift pouch. I scooped him up and tucked him under my arm, where he loved to burrow.

She took out a small notepad and a pen from her handbag. She wrote something down and stood up. "I'll leave now," she said, and Travis exhaled loudly, as if he suddenly found it easier to breathe.

George stood up and followed her to the front door, but Travis made no attempt to move. "Just give me a minute," I called out to George. I stood up and took Travis's hand. He took a deep, trying-to-calm-down breath. I'd never seen him so mad.

"Hey," I said softly. "Talk to me. What's up?"

"What's *up*?" he whisper-shouted, his eyes disbelieving and wide. "Do you even have to ask? Jesus, Charlie, that's your *mother*?"

"So?"

"She just turns up, like she has the fucking right, and it doesn't bother you?" He tried to quieten his voice. "After all this time? What the fuck is up with that?"

I shrugged. "I don't know what she's doing here or why. Or how I feel about it." I shrugged again. I just didn't know.

He groaned, a sound of pure frustration. He ran his free hand through his hair and squeezed my hand in his other. "I swear to God. If this ends badly, if she hurts you..."

I smiled at him. "Trav, for her to do that, for her to hurt

me, it would have to mean that I cared. But I don't, not one bit. She doesn't know me, and I don't know her. That woman out there," I whispered, "might know George and Ma—and George seems to know her. He keeps lookin' at me like he's scared I'll freak or bolt out the door. And you might reckon she looks like me, but Trav"—I shrugged again—"she's nothing more than a stranger to me." Then, not caring if Laura heard me, and kinda hoping that she would, I said, "My *mother* is in bed, asleep in the back room."

He looked flustered. And Travis was never flustered. "Do you want to go?"

"Go where?"

"Anywhere," he said. "We'll take Shelby and Texas, and we'll just go."

"Travis," I stopped him. "I'm fine, really."

He looked at me like I was the most complex, most infuriating puzzle he'd ever tried to solve. "Charlie." He shook his head. "You have every right to be angry, to ask questions. You *should* ask her questions. Go yell at her or something. Jesus, how can you be so calm?"

All I could do was smile. I leaned down and pecked his lips. "Like I said, Trav. She can't give me anything I don't already have."

His eyes softened and he sighed. "Just when I think I got you all figured out..."

I laughed quietly. "I really do love you. You got that figured out, yeah?"

"Yeah," he whispered. Travis finally smiled, and he lightly scratched the fidgeting wombat in my arms.

I kissed the top of his head before I followed the sound of quiet conversation out onto the veranda, and Travis was right behind me. George and Laura stopped talking and both eyed me cautiously, probably expecting me to bombard her with questions or tell her she wasn't ever welcome.

And maybe Travis was right.

I *could* have asked this woman a million questions. And maybe I *should* have. Like why did she leave? How *could* a mother leave her child? Where had she been the last twenty-something years? What life did she have now? Did she ever think of me? On birthdays? At Christmas? Did she even care? Why did she come back? Why now? What was she after?

She handed me the slip of paper, which had a phone number and an address on it. "I'd really like it if we could talk," she said. "When you're ready. Doesn't matter how long it takes. I'm sure you have a lot of questions," she said.

"No," I answered. "I don't really." If she was expecting some profound, happy-tears reunion, she was very, very wrong. "Just one, actually. Just one question."

I could see it in her eyes, that flicker of fear, the bracing for you-are-not-my-mother impact. "Of course."

My question was really quite simple, yet it would change my life forever. "Who is Samuel Jennings?"

CHAPTER FIVE

THE WEIGHT OF WORDS

"BREATHE FOR ME, CHARLIE," Travis said. His hands cupped my face, his voice was close and warm. He was pressing me against the wall in the foyer, holding me up.

I still had Nugget in my arms. I could feel him wiggle between us, and Travis lifted him so he wasn't squashed.

Why was it so hard to breathe?

Then I remembered.

Like it was being played in reverse, in slow, slow motion, I remembered. I remember George telling Laura it might be best if she left. I remembered Travis taking my hand and pulling me inside while I stood there shaking my head, trying to make sense of what she'd said.

How could it hit so hard?

How could it hurt so much?

My mother turns up and I really couldn't have cared less. I had it all under control. She was no more than a stranger to me. She was nothing I didn't already have. I have a mother. I have Ma, so this Laura turning up meant nothing. Just a fill-in-the-blank detail, a face to put to the memory I'd long ago forgotten.

But this? This was different.

"Charlie?" Travis's voice was close, like an anchor, a lifeline. "Look at me, just open your eyes."

I did as he asked, and I don't know what he saw in my eyes, but his face crumpled. His hand touched the side of my face and slid around my neck to pull me against him. My face buried in his neck. "Charlie," he whispered. "Do you trust me?"

I nodded. "Of course."

He snatched up my hand and led me down the hall. We passed the kitchen, and Trav handed Nugget over to Nara, and without another word, he walked me out the back door.

As we crossed the yard, he whistled loudly and Shelby trotted over to the fence with Texas not too far behind. He opened the gate, grabbed Texas by the mane above the withers and hauled himself up onto his bare back. He waited for me to do the same on Shelby, and then with a kick to his horse and a loud "Yah", he galloped out of the yard.

And I followed him.

I leaned low down to Shelby's neck and let her take flight. The feeling of her under me, the rapid three-step galloping thud-thud-thud as her hooves barely touched the ground was a comforting sound. The cool air and warm sun, the isolated and barren, familiar land was absolute, *absolute* mind-clearin', soul-breathin' peace. I'd gone from barely keepin' it together to feelin' like I was free in a matter of seconds.

I don't know how, but Travis just knew what I needed.

Or maybe he needed the space for thinkin'-through-shit too.

Maybe he needed the open air, the vastness, the feeling

of insignificance that only this landscape can bring as much as I did.

The immensity of open desert gave me perspective and room to breathe, and Travis understood that. He understood me.

I let Shelby run herself out before bringin' her to a stop, and Travis did the same. I slid off her back and walked a few metres in the red dirt, finally breathing in gulps of air. I ran my hands through my hair and screamed, "Fuck!"

I had to let it out. The frustration, the anger, the unknown.

I turned around and Travis was right there.

"How could she do this?" I asked. "How can she just waltz in and turn every-fucking-thing upside down?"

Trav nodded, but he never said anything. Like the desert, he just listened.

"Who the fuck does she think she is?" I ran my hands through my hair again. "You know what? I don't care about her—*it's not about her*—I have a mother, and it is *not* that woman." I pointed back toward the homestead, back to where Laura had been. "I sat across from her and felt nothing. But this?"

Travis swallowed hard, his eyes were full of love and concern.

"Do you know how long I spent alone out here?" I asked him. "Do you know how I wished—how I wished so hard—that I had someone? Someone to hang out with, someone to talk to, someone on my side? Jesus fucking Christ," I groaned. "I had to ask one of the station hands or George to play cricket or handball, because I had no one! My whole fucking life."

Travis put his hand to my face, his thumb wiping away my tears. "Oh, Charlie."

I threw my arms around him and hugged him so damn hard. He didn't seem to mind, he held me just as tight. I buried my face into the crook of his neck, and Laura's words replayed in my mind.

She'd gone a bit pale, her eyes wide. "How do you know that name?" she'd whispered.

"I found newspaper clippings in the things my father hid in the roof."

"I didn't want to tell you like this, but I won't lie to you, Charlie," she'd said, more to herself than to me. She'd looked scared as hell and as though she was trying to swallow but her mouth was too dry. "Sam is my son. Charlie, he's your brother."

My world went all quiet after that.

There was a barrage of information. Her words kept spilling out, like a gunshot wound that kept bleeding, darkness seeping from the skin. And all I could hear was my pulse in my ears.

"When I told your father I was pregnant, he made me leave. You have to understand, Charlie, I didn't want to go. He told me not to come back until I got rid of it. He was a troubled man. He was..."

I shook my head. None of what she was saying made sense.

"I stayed in Alice until he was born. I thought your dad might see reason. I tried to see you, Charlie, I tried so many times..."

She'd put her hand out as if to touch my arm, and I'd pulled away quickly, unsteady. Then Travis had pulled me inside the house and George was telling her to leave, and I couldn't breathe.

And there it was, a heaviness that pressed against my chest, a feeling so familiar and horrible.

How could so few words weigh so damn much?

TRAVIS and I sat not far from where we'd stopped. He'd found a bit of a rise, and we sat there until the sun headed toward its western bed. First he listened to me rant and rave, and then he listened to me sayin' a whole lotta nothing. He was just there, so full of patience, that it was clear how stupid I was thinkin' I could possibly live without him back not so long ago.

I took his hand and threaded our fingers together. "Thank you," I said.

"What for?"

"For everything. For knowing what I needed. I needed room to breathe and to think, and you just knew. For knowing when I need silence or a kick in the pants." He smiled at that, and I shrugged. "I dunno how you do it."

He sighed, long and loud, and looked out over the desert. "Some days I think I've got you all figured out, then other days I realise I don't have the first clue."

"Sorry to keep you guessing," I said quietly.

Travis's laugh carried across the open plain. "Don't ever apologise for that. I like that I have to keep guessing," he said. "I thought you once told me that life out here was boring."

I scoffed out a laugh. "My life used to be boring! I can still remember thinkin' nothing ever happened out here. It wasn't that long ago."

His eyes went wide. It matched his smile. "You make it sound like it's my fault!"

"It is!" I told him. "Since you got here, it's been not-boring every day."

Travis laughed again. "Sorry about that."

I squeezed his hand. "You deciding to come here was the best thing to ever happen to me."

"Ah," he said. "I've told you before. I didn't decide to come here. I *had* to come here. Once I saw the list I got to pick from, the name Sutton Station wouldn't let me go anywhere else."

"Like fate or something."

"Exactly like fate or something."

I took a deep breath and closed my eyes. "What do you think he's like?"

He didn't even have to ask who I was talking about. "I don't know. If he's anything like you, he'll be pretty great," Travis said.

"Like me?"

Travis squeezed my hand. "Laura said he's your full brother. Didn't you hear her say that?"

I shook my head. "I didn't hear much of anything..."

Trav took my hand in his other hand and rubbed my back with his other. "She said you could be twins you look so alike."

"I didn't hear that," I said, my voice just a whisper.

"He grew up in Darwin, where they still live. They moved there when he was five. He doesn't know about you," he said, shaking his head. "She said she never told him, or so she said, because he'd only ask questions she didn't have answers to."

"I didn't hear any of that," I admitted. "Is that what she said?"

Travis nodded.

"I don't know what happened to me back there," I whispered.

"That's what you call freaking out," Trav said. "And

freaking out is a perfectly rational response, Charlie. To be honest, I thought you'd freak out before, when you were sitting in the front room with her, but you were so calm."

"You were pissed," I told him. "I ain't ever seen you look so mad."

He shook his head. "I was mad. I'm still mad. She shouldn't have just turned up. That's so outta line, and if she thinks she can just come back after dropping the 'oh by the way, you have a brother' bombshell, I'll gladly tell her otherwise."

I found myself smiling. "You're cute when you're all pissy."

Travis glared at me, which just made me laugh more. It felt good to laugh, like the smilin' muscles hadn't been stretched in too long. Then I remembered something. "Oh shit," I said, jumping up.

Trav got to his feet just as quickly. "What's wrong?"

"Nugget. He'll think he's starvin'. Probably annoyin' everyone, scratching and fussing lookin' for me."

Travis smiled his you-ain't-fooling-anyone smile.

I stopped just before I was about pull myself up onto Shelby. "Trav," I said. "Thank you. For bringing me out here, for... everything."

"You're most welcome," he said with an almost shy smile. He leapt up, swinging his long leg over Texas, and grinned. "Race you home."

"YOU DID NOT LET ME WIN," Travis griped. "I beat you through the gate fair and square."

I held the back door open for him and laughed. "You

had a twenty-metre head start, and we were right on your tail through that gate, which means, speed over distance, we won."

He shook his head and walked inside. "That is the biggest crock of shit I've ever heard."

I followed him in and ran into his back when he stopped suddenly at the kitchen door. Nara was sitting at the table holding Nugget, but Ma was sitting there too.

I walked straight in and put my hand on her shoulder. She was wrapped up in her dressing gown, looking not much better than she did this morning. "How are you feeling? Should you be up?"

Ma gave me a tired smile. "I've been sleeping all day," she said. "I needed to get out of bed."

"Are you sure?" I asked. "Can I get you a cup of tea? Where's George?"

Ma sighed. "Charlie, I'm fine." She studied me for a minute. "I heard you had a visitor, though."

"Something like that." I opened the fridge and did a count of the bottles. There was one missing. I looked back at Nara, seeing Nugget was wriggling in her hold. "Did he feed?"

"Not really," she said, nodding to a half-full bottle on the sink. "But he won't sleep. Keeps running everywhere, gets under my feet."

I sighed. "Sorry about that."

"Oh, it was no problem," she covered quickly. "Just wish he'd take a bottle from someone else."

I snorted. "So do I! Then Travis could do night feeds."

"Like hell," Travis replied, picking an apple up and taking a bite.

"Here," I said to Nara, "let me take him. You're busy

enough without havin' to worry about this little guy too." I picked up Nugget and touched his nose to mine. "You don't need me to feed you, okay?"

Travis laughed. "Yeah, like you'd *let* me do night feeds."

Ma was smiling weakly at us, and I'd guessed I'd put off her question long enough. "You wanna come into the lounge room, Ma?" I asked. "We can talk in there." Then I gave a nod to Travis. "You too, please."

I sat on the three-seater with a now feeding Nugget, and Trav started the fire while Ma took a seat next to me.

"George already told me who it was," she said.

"She just turned up," I said with a shrug. "Same day we found this stuff." I nodded toward the two boxes still sitting on the floor. I shook my head and sighed. "Not that it mattered none, I guess. If George wasn't here, I wouldn't have believed it was her. He remembered her, of course. And Trav says we have the same eyes, but I don't see it."

The afternoon was starting to cool down, and although it wasn't particularly cold yet, Ma looked like she was freezing. With my free hand, I took a blanket off the back of the lounge and put it over her legs. "I didn't recognise her at all. She's not what I remembered."

Ma's eyes softened. "It can't have been easy for you, Charlie. I wish I'd been there for you."

I patted her arm. "I was fine with her. She isn't what bothered me at all. Like I said to Trav, she might have been the woman who gave birth to me, but she's not my mother."

Ma frowned. "She'll always be your mother, Charlie."

"She's not the woman who raised me," I said quietly. "You're the only mother I've ever known."

Ma got all teary then. "Oh, Charlie."

"It's true," I said casually. "Laura sat in here, and it was like I was meeting a complete stranger."

Ma took a little while to talk. "George said she was upset when she left," she said with another frown. "But he said you were more so... after what she told you. I'm really sorry I wasn't here for that."

Nugget finished his bottle, so I put him on the floor. The little guy wandered straight over to Travis. "Don't apologise, Ma. No one knew she was gonna turn up, let alone drop a bombshell like that." I shrugged. "I did kinda lose the plot, and Trav took me out back so I didn't lose my shit completely."

I looked over at him, just as he bit off a chunk of apple and gave it to Nugget. It made me smile.

This time Ma rubbed my arm. I guess she didn't need to tell me how lucky I was to have Travis. It must have been clear on my face.

"What will you do now?" she asked.

"I don't know," I answered her truthfully. "I have no clue. This so-called brother doesn't even know I exist apparently, so I don't know if there's much I can do."

Ma sighed, a quiet, tired sound. "I remember you being no more than five or six, telling me how you wished for a brother or sister." Then she shook her head. "I didn't know, Charlie, if you were wondering that. George neither. We didn't know there was a brother."

To be honest, I hadn't even thought about that. "I didn't think you did."

"If I did know, I would have told you long before now," she said sadly. "All I really remember of your mother leaving is how angry your father was. And in hindsight, maybe your mother looked more scared than sad." She shrugged. "I don't know, Charlie. I just remember trying to keep you busy enough not to notice."

I took her hand. It felt kinda cold and bony.

"I'd forgotten your mother's maiden name was Jennings," she said with sad, sad eyes, "until I read that birth notice, with the date on it. The math ain't exact, Charlie, but that baby was born six or seven months after your mother left. I don't remember the exact date she went away, maybe July or August. I just remember it being cold. I remember you sitting in front of the fire askin' when your mum would be home."

I sighed, feelin' every part as tired as Ma looked. It had been one helluva draining day. "What's done is done," I said. "I need some time to get my head around it all, I guess."

"You take as much time as you need, love."

"Anyway," I said with a smile. "If I did have a little brother, I'm pretty sure you'd spent too many days yellin' at me for throwin' him in a flooded river, or making him ride the poddy calves, or tellin' him to steal your warm scones with jam and cream so I wouldn't get into trouble."

Ma snorted. "I think you're right. One of you was enough."

"I was perfect."

"Every one of my grey hairs is from you," she said, narrowing her eyes at me, smiling as she did.

I laughed. "They suit you."

The sound of Travis snorting made us both look over to him. "Look at this," he said, putting Nugget on the floor with some more apple. The little wombat took a tiny bite and jolted, then did some random jumpy-turning-in-circles thing. Travis laughed again. "I think he likes apple."

Nugget then faced the door and bolted, his little stubby legs moving long before his body, but he scooted out the door and Travis took off after him.

Ma and I both laughed, and it even put a flush of colour

in her cheeks. "How about I get you some broth, and you rest easy."

"Sounds good, Charlie."

But when I bought the soup back out, Ma was fast asleep in her chair.

CHAPTER SIX

WHEN THINGS START TO GO WRONG

IT WAS quiet around the table at first. Everyone sat down for dinner, bein' full aware of what had gone on with Laura. They'd watched her turn up and probably heard most of what we'd said.

I didn't mind, though. I guessed it made it easier. It just meant I didn't have to go repeatin' myself again. Because I would have told them.

Something had changed here. I used to keep everyone at arm's length, keepin' the line between boss and station hand real clear. Now this unruly mob were like family.

I guess it took my mother turning up to show me that family is what sticks by you, not what walks away.

I told them about my so-called brother and how I didn't know what any of it meant. I needed time to process it, let it settle in my head a little. They all nodded but didn't say a great deal, like me, I guessed, not knowin' whether to take it as good or bad news yet.

I told them only time would tell.

There was a very good chance we'd never see or hear

from either of them again. I certainly wasn't itching to make contact again. Not for a little while, anyway.

But I think their real concern was with Ma. They eyed George all cautious-like. Billy didn't smile like normal, and Trudy barely touched her food.

"She's gone back to bed," George said. "She must have needed the sleep, because she's out like a light."

"She looked better this afternoon, but she got tired quick." I wanted to reassure him. "I'm sure after a few days' rest, she'll be fine." Then I added, "I'm sure she misses yellin' at me. If it'll make her feel better, she can do some yellin' at me tomorrow."

George knew I was just joking, but at least it made him smile.

Then looking at everyone around the table, I said, "Please say thanks to Nara on your way out. She did a real good job getting dinner out tonight, so do me a favour and show her some gratitude." The truth was, while dinner wasn't the best I'd ever had, it was easy to forget that Nara was just a kid and this was her first go at doin' it by herself.

All things considered, she did a bloody good job.

When they'd cleared out, Trav and I helped Nara clean up the kitchen, and by the time it was done, the day had taken its toll on me.

It really had been the day from hell.

"Dunno why I'm so tired," I mumbled, barely able to keep my eyes open. I sat on the edge of our bed while Trav pulled my boots off. I just needed to lay down a while before getting back up to do some office work.

Trav shook his head and smiled in a you're-so-oblivious way, before we heard some familiar scratching and snorty-grunting. "Stay here," he said, planting a kiss on my fore-head before walking out, and came back in a minute later with a bundled-up wombat and a bottle of milk. He tucked him in my arm and sat beside me on the bed.

"You've had a pretty big day," he said softly. "Did you want to talk about anything?"

"All of it," I said. "But maybe not right now."

Trav rubbed my arm. "You were great today."

I snorted, too tired to laugh. "I'm pretty sure I'd have fucked everything royally if you weren't here."

He leaned down and kissed me. "You can hardly keep your eyes open."

My blinks were getting longer. I moved onto my side and watched Nugget as he drained his bottle. "Apparently baby wombats don't care if I'm busy or tired." I gently scratched his forehead and told him, "You just seem to think it's all about you, doncha? I hate to break it to ya, little guy, but the position of me, me, me has been filled."

Travis laughed and raked his fingers through my hair. "Out of all your jobs here, that is the one you excel at."

I took his hand from my head and kissed his palm. I held his hand then, feeling the warmth of his touch on my hand somehow fill my chest. As much as I wanted to watch him, my eyes finally closed and slow-blinkin' became deep-sleepin'.

When I woke up to a needed-to-be-fed-again wombat, Travis was shoving Nugget into bed with me in the crook of my arm. He mumbled something about 'the little shit won't let me feed him' and got back into bed.

For the next feed, I got up, warmed a fresh bottle, grabbed the bloody wombat and took him back to bed with me like I used to do with Travis's baby kangaroo. Some days I was just too tired to fight it.

I put Nugget in between us and closed my eyes as he

fed, but sleepin' was useless. Because after his breakfast, it was playtime apparently.

This was getting ridiculous.

"You're a pain in the butt, you know that?" I asked the wombat. The little bugger seemed to smile. He bounced a bit, burrowing under my pillow and out again, rolled and bounced some more. I laughed as quiet as I could. Until he burrowed under me and scratched my ribs. "Ow."

"Oh, for fuck's sake, Charlie," Travis mumbled. "Really?"

I picked Nugget up and put him in front of Travis's face. "But he wants to play."

"It's too early," he whined, still half sleepin'. Nugget sniffed his face, and his whiskers must have tickled Trav's nose, because he pulled back and scrubbed his hand over his face. The glare he gave me told me he was now, much to his distaste, wide awake. "I'm starting to regret bringing him back here. I should have left him out there to die."

I gasped and pushed his shoulder. Nugget went back to doing happy-bouncy-circles in between us, making me laugh. Travis hid his smile by pulling his pillow over his head, but his shaking shoulders gave him away.

"I'm building him a playpen tomorrow," he said, muffled by the pillow.

"You mean today," I said. Then the little bugger scratched me again. "Ow!"

Trav pulled his head out, half-concerned, half-amused—until he saw my ribs. "Jesus."

I looked down at the red, welted scratches across my ribs and under my arm. "How have you not seen these?"

"Well, the last few times we've been naked together, I've been face-first in the mattress."

I snorted out a laugh. "Are you saying our sex is boring?"

"Far from it," he said with a slow-spreading smile. "So far from it."

"I'll have to remember to turn you over tonight."

Travis chuckled, but then ran his hand over the scratches in my skin. "You know, I hear semen helps heal abrasions."

I snorted. "Is that right?"

"Yep. Something to do with vitamins and proteins."

I scooped up Nugget and his woollen beanie pouch and sat both in the hall. "Sorry, little man, but you know, priorities." I pulled the door shut and Travis laughed as I jumped back into bed. "How much trouble can an unsupervised wombat possibly get into?"

THE ANSWER to that question is quite a bit, actually. A bored, curious, somewhat disgruntled wombat can get into quite a bit of trouble.

In the time it took to test Travis's theory about skin remedies, there was poop in the hall, one of Travis's boots was missing, and the bigger boxes in the lounge room had been knocked over, the contents—my childhood mementos —were strewn across the floor and a rather-pleased-with-himself wombat was rumbling with the teddy bear.

I'd have been pissed off if he wasn't so damn cute.

Travis helped Nara with breakfast while I cleaned up all the mess and searched for the missing boot. I found it, somewhat chewed, under one of the sofas. I went into the kitchen and held Nugget under one arm and the boot up with the other.

Travis's eyes went wide. "He ruined it!"

I looked again at the teeth-marked leather and frayed elastic. "He gave it character," I amended.

Travis snatched the boot from me. "Why the hell didn't he chew yours?"

"Mine were in our room, where you took them off last night," I reminded him. "Yours were in the hall at the front door. See, I put my things away, not like you, who just leaves his stuff all over the floor."

He ignored me completely and huffed. "I'm making some sort of enclosure today where he can't chew on my stuff. And the little turd"—he leaned down and looked in Nugget's face—"no matter how cute he is, is stayin' in it."

And right after breakfast, Travis went straight out into the shed, and I followed him out. "You're not really pissed off at him, are you?" I asked.

"No, not really." Travis smiled and shook his head. "I'm surprised how taken you are with him, though."

I shrugged. "He's a cute little fella. I dunno, he's got character."

Trav lifted his foot. "He has taste. In three-hundred-dollar boots."

I sighed. "I'm sorry I made you give Matilda away," I told him. "I'm not sure how I'd feel about doin' the same. I shouldn't have made you do it. I'm sorry."

Travis put an old crate down. "You didn't make me," he said. "Charlie, it was the right thing to do. I know that. She couldn't have stayed here; she'd hurt someone, and if we'd let her go, if the other kangaroos didn't kill her, then she'd probably end up getting shot. Taking her to the kangaroo refuge was the safest option for her."

I knew what he said made sense—it was the same logic I'd told him, after all. "I still feel bad about that."

Travis eyed a bunch of old boxes in the mezzanine at the end of the shed. "Are those empty?"

"Nope. But you can empty them. It was my father's stuff. We went through it all after the funeral. There's nothing in them, really. Maybe combine some boxes, or throw it out, whatever."

"You can't just throw it out," he said.

"It's nothing, really," I said. "It's mostly old clothes. There's no papers or anything personal. It's mostly just junk. I didn't really know what to do with it after he died, so I shoved it up there."

He frowned and I could tell he was tryin' to decide on how to say something by the lines in forehead. "Charlie, did your father have a will?"

"Yep. I was there when the solicitor read it out."

"Never mentioned Samuel?"

I shook my head. "No. Or my mother. He left everything to me. Why?"

Trav sighed. "I just wondered, that's all."

"Do you think that's what Laura came back for?"

The way his eyes shot to mine before he spoke told me yes, that's what he thought. "Well, it's just that turning up out of the blue for no reason..." He shrugged.

"They can try all they like," I said simply. "But it'll be over my dead body."

Travis kind of smiled. "It won't be *your* dead body," he said, jokingly. "Billy and I have seen *Wolf Creek*, remember?"

I laughed at that. "Thanks. It's comforting to know you'll massacre people just for me. It's kinda sweet."

Travis laughed this time, but then he sighed. "How do you feel about it now?" he asked. "About Laura and knowing you have a brother?"

"I'm still not sure," I answered honestly. "It'll take some time, but I'm okay with it, I think. It's certainly not Samuel's fault. Don't see why I should hold it against him."

"What about your mother?"

"Jury's still out on that," I said. "If anything, I'm mad at how she handled everything."

"You should be mad," Trav said. Then he corrected himself. "Okay, maybe not *should*. But if you were really pissed, it'd be totally understandable." He rummaged through a crate of plumbing bits and pieces. "Here, hold this."

I took the length of pipe. "I'd hate to think how I would have handled it if I didn't have you."

Trav handed me a pipe coupling. "You would've done just fine."

"I doubt that. With everything else going on right now? I'm pretty sure I'd have flipped my shit. I'd have no employees, no business, and no fucking clue."

He looked at me and smiled. "Actually, that's probably true." He put the crate of pipes back on the shelf and took the one I was holding from me. "You have a lot on your plate right now, Charlie. Don't be too hard on yourself. I actually think the way you're talking things through out loud and not just in your head is a pretty good sign that you're doin' okay."

"Yes, but that's only because of you."

"Well, lucky for you, I'm not planning on going anywhere," he said with a smile.

"Did you notice Trudy hasn't been eating much?" I asked. "Yesterday and this morning, she was just pushin' her food around her plate." I shrugged. "I thought Nara's food was pretty good."

"Nara's food is just fine. Charlie, Trudy hasn't been eating much these last few weeks. Haven't you noticed?"

I shook my head. "I guess I've been busy," I said, a poor excuse for not noticing one of my staff being unwell. "I've been watchin' Ma like a hawk."

"She's not well, Charlie," Travis said. "Ma, I mean."

"I know," I agreed. "George was quiet this mornin' at breakfast." I handed over the coupling and nodded to his pile of plumbing pipes. "What are you gonna do with that? You gonna build Nugget a bathroom or something? That pipe is too big for water, unless you're planning on damming some harbour I don't know about."

Travis snorted and held up the pipe so I could see his face through it. It was ten inches round and about a metre long. "I'm gonna make the little boot-chewing brat a tunnel."

Someone cleared their throat behind us. It was George. He didn't have to say something was wrong, it was written clear on his face.

"George?" I asked. "Is it Ma? What's wrong?"

He swallowed hard. "She's not getting any better, Charlie," he said. "I've called the doc. He's on his way."

CHAPTER SEVEN

THERE ARE NO WORDS...

I STOOD AT THE DOORWAY, too scared to go in, too scared to walk away. "Come in, Charlie." Ma's voice was weak.

"We just heard from the doc," I said, walking in. "He'll be here soon."

"I told George not to call him, but he wouldn't listen. I just need some rest and I'll be fine."

She didn't look fine. She looked so small in her bed, and her face was pale and dark around the eyes. She didn't look fine at all.

"Then the doc will tell us that," I said, trying not to whisper. "He might just say that all the bloody men in your life need to stop stressing you out."

Ma smiled. "Probably."

I sat down on the side of the bed. "I'm worried about you."

"No need to be, love," she said. "How's Nara going? Everything okay with you? You had a rough day yesterday."

"Would you stop worrying about anyone else?" I patted her hand. "We're all just fine."

Then because the silence was too hard to bear, I told her all about Nugget chewin' on Travis's boot and how Travis was making a jail for Nugget.

"A jail?"

"Well, it's more like a playpen, with a bed and this tunnel-type thing. You know Trav. Over-engineers everything."

Ma smiled again. "Doesn't do things by halves, does he?"

I shook my head. "Nope. Don't know where I'd be without him, really. Like yesterday, he was so good to me, Ma. Keeps my head on straight like you do," I told her. "All those lectures about talkin' and honesty must have sunk in."

Ma laughed quietly. "They weren't really lectures. They were more like a friendly heart-to-heart."

"Well, if that's what you call an arse-kicking that I needed to hear, then yep, a friendly heart-to-heart works."

"Just glad I could help," she said.

"You did. I need remindin' sometimes, that's all. That's why you need to get yourself better," I told her. "If someone's gonna kick me in the pants, I'd prefer it be you."

Ma was quiet then. She looked so damn tired.

George was at the door, and I ain't ever seen him look so lost. Both our heads turned at the sound of a four-wheel drive. "That sounds like the doc," I said, standing up. I walked to the door and tapped George's arm on my way out. "I'll go meet him."

By the time the late-model Land Cruiser pulled up at the house, everyone was there waiting. To say the news of Ma bein' so unwell affected us all was an understatement.

Doctor Hammond was the same doc who'd been treating me since I was born, and he was the same doc who treated Trav when he'd spent a day and a night in the summer desert with a busted knee.

The man collected his black doctor bag from the back seat and walked over. He addressed me first. "Charlie, good to see you again," he said, shaking my hand. Then he looked at Travis. "Ah, the American Agronomy student. How's the knee?"

"It's doing just fine," Trav answered.

Doctor Hammond acknowledged everyone else with a nod and smiled grimly at me. "Where's the patient?"

"Come through," I said, walking up the veranda steps. "I'll show you the way."

I led him down the hall to the bedroom at the back of the house. George stood up when he saw the doc, and I pulled the door shut to give the three of them privacy.

I walked back out to find Travis waiting in the lounge room. He was holding Nugget. "The others are waiting outside," he said quietly. "I think it's feed time for this guy." He handed him over. "I'll just grab a bottle for him."

I dunno whether Trav was just tryin' to keep me occupied, but it worked. Every minute waiting for the doctor to get here had just about drove me mad, so I think Travis knew keeping me busy was the key. Instead of pacing and asking 'how much longer' every five minutes, I sat on the lounge and fed Nugget.

The wombat was finally done just as George walked out. I put Nugget on the floor and stood up. The man looked like he'd aged ten years.

"He's just doing an examination," George said quietly. He sat down on the sofa like his whole body was numb.

"What did he say?" I asked.

"Not much," he shrugged. "Took her blood pressure,

looked in her ears and eyes, that kind of thing. Asked her a bunch of questions... personal-type questions. Woman's kinda stuff."

I nodded. "You want a cup of tea?" I asked him. "Can I get you something?"

He looked at me then and gave me the best smile he could manage. "Nah, I'm fine. Thanks anyways."

If waiting for the doc to get here was bad, then waiting for him to do his thing was pure torture.

And after we'd been waiting for what felt like forever, as soon as the doc walked out with a sullen look on his face, I realised that waiting wasn't the worst of it.

It wasn't the worst of it at all.

Me, George and Travis all stood up, and Doctor Hammond gave a loud sigh. "Joseph," he said, looking at George. "Can I speak to you alone?"

"You can say it in front of these boys," George said. He cleared his throat. "They'd only hound me 'til I told 'em anyway."

"There's no real easy way to put it, so I'll just come right out and say it," the doc said, his face still stern. "I've done a pelvic exam, and it looks like endometrial cancer."

Cancer.

Who knew one small word could stop the world from turnin'.

Ma had cancer.

After a long just-starin', no-breathin' moment, George swayed. Travis and the doctor helped him sit down.

Doctor Hammond patted his shoulder. "I'll need to run further tests to confirm it, but I'm confident in my diagnosis."

I was still just standing there staring. This wasn't happening. He had to be wrong. This was my Ma he was talking about. "She has cancer? What does that mean? More tests? How can you know what it is if you need to run more tests?"

Doctor Hammond smiled kindly. "Charlie, I've seen it before. Mrs Brown's case is quite advanced. She's actually rather ill." He sighed, letting his words sink in. "The loss of appetite and tiredness is a little unusual, I'll admit. She's very worried about everyone here, and the stress is probably contributing to that."

"What do we do?" I asked, trying to keep the panic under the surface. "Just tell me what to do, and we'll do it."

"She needs to be hospitalised. Today." The doctor looked at George and put his hand on his shoulder. "Joseph, I need you to understand something."

George looked up at him, all lost and hopeless.

"This isn't a death sentence, not by a long shot," he said firmly. "But you need to get up. Your wife is going to need you, so no wallowing, you hear?"

George nodded weakly.

"You need to go pack some of her clothes and get your wife to the hospital. Come on, get up," he said, all no-nonsense.

But George did exactly as he was told, and no sooner had he walked out than Doctor Hammond turned to me and smiled. "Sometimes I need to be a drill sergeant more than a doctor. Young Joseph just needed a little kick-start to get going."

I swallowed hard. "Doc, will Ma be okay? I mean, is that... what you said she had... type of cancer." I couldn't even remember what he'd called it.

"Endometrial," he said again. "Or uterine cancer."

"Is it bad?" I ran my hand through my hair. "I mean, no cancer is good, I get that. But what does that mean... for her?" God, I couldn't even think straight. "Prognosis. What's the prognosis?"

He pressed his lips in a thin line and sighed. "Like I said, I need to run more tests. But out of all the cancers that affect women, this isn't a bad one to have. It's not good, by any means, but survival rates are high."

Fuck. *Fuck.* Survival rates?

I never mentioned the chances of fucking dying.

"It was just a flu," I told him. "She told us it was just a bug and that winters got colder as you got older. She told me to shut up when I asked her," I said. Travis was beside me then, his hand on my lower back. I looked at him. "I asked all the time if she was feeling okay, and she'd rip my head off and tell me to mind my own business."

"I know you did," he whispered and kissed the side of my head. "I know."

Doctor Hammond looked at us both, unable to hide his surprise in seeing Travis console me like that. I'd had him run tests for STDs, and I guess he just figured out why. "It's not your fault, Charlie. I'd say she's been ill for some weeks," the doc went on to say. "And she knew something wasn't right, she just didn't want anyone to worry."

I shook my head. "She's so busy worryin' about everyone else."

"Well, the thing is, we need to stay positive in our thinking," the old man said. "We have a pretty good idea of what we're dealing with, and then we can deal with treatments and getting better. But first things first, we need to get her in to town."

"Can you take them?" I asked. "Are you heading straight back to the Alice now?"

"Well," he said, blinking. "I am, yes."

"Your four-wheel drive will be more comfortable for Ma

than our old ute," I said. "If that's okay. Then Trav and I will follow as soon as we can."

The doc smiled. "I guess I best take them, then. Let me make some phone calls."

I offered him the use of our phone, but he pulled out his mobile and hit a number in his contacts. In a very quick, all-business kinda call, he'd told whoever it was at Alice Springs Hospital that he was on his way with an emergency patient, expected arrival time in three hours, and would require x-rays, MRI and pathology for a range of names I didn't understand.

And while he was talking, all I could think of was cancer.

My Ma had cancer.

"Jesus," I whispered, making myself take a deep breath.

Trav pulled me against him, kind of side-on and quick, but for just one second, just one perfect it-will-be-okay second, he centred me.

George appeared at the door with his arm around Ma. She looked tired still, and embarrassed. I walked over and took the overnight bag from George. "Doctor Hammond can take you guys in now," I told them. "Trav and I will get things organised here and follow."

"You don't need to be fussin' over me," Ma said, trying to smile.

"I'll fuss all I damn want," I told her, taking her arm. "Come on, we'll get you in the car."

"I can walk myself," she snapped.

"You could," I said, helping her walking out the front door. "But we're helpin' ya so you'll just have to deal with it."

"I'm not so sick that I can't give you a clip behind the

ears, Charlie," she said, as we helped her gingerly down the veranda steps.

"You'd have to catch me first."

She snorted quietly. "Yeah, you'd always come home when you were hungry. And you, Charlie, were always hungry."

I opened the back seat of the doctor's Land Cruiser, and George helped her climb up. He ducked back inside to grab something else, and I looked up at Ma. "We'll be right behind you."

She held out her hand, which I quickly took. All joking was gone from her now. She looked worried, but most of all, she looked scared. "Thank you, Charlie."

George came back with another bag and a pillow, and got in to the back seat of the Cruiser beside his wife. Doctor Hammond gave me a nod and started the engine. I looked up at Ma and said, "See you soon," before closing the door.

And I stood there and watched the Cruiser drive away. We all stood there. All of us: Billy, Trudy, Bacon, Ernie and Nara. Travis stood by the front door. No one said anything, just watched Ma and George leave in a cloud of dust. I had to say something. They hadn't heard what the doc has said, so maybe their shock was in the not-knowin'. I had to be the one who told them.

I cleared my throat, and they all watched me and waited.

"The doc seems to think Ma has cancer," I told them. Their faces dropped, and Trudy put her hand to her mouth. "Uterine cancer, he called it. Said her chances were good, but he needs to run more tests and work out what needs doing."

No one said anything. Not a word.

"Travis and I are going in to the hospital now," I added.

"We'll probably just be a day or two. Until they get her settled in and we know more of what we're dealing with."

This time I got nods.

"Billy, you're in charge while we're away. Just do what you can to make the roof waterproof. I'd prefer it if none of ya fell off trying to lay iron while I'm not here." The truth was, I didn't care about the roof. I didn't really even care about the house right now. But I certainly couldn't deal with any of them getting hurt. "I'll let Greg know you guys are here by yourself, so if you need him for anything, just call him. He can be here quicker than me."

"Sure thing, boss," Billy said.

"We're expectin' the first calving any day," I told them. "Please do the rounds, check on the mothers a couple of times a day." I looked at each of them and shook my head. "Dunno why I'm tellin' you guys this. You all know what to do. I trust your judgement, but call me if you're not sure."

I looked to the youngest of the lot. "Nara, you just keep doing what you're doing. Don't take crap from anyone, okay?" The girl nodded, but she looked worried, scared even.

Lookin' at each of them, I realised they all did. "Ma will be fine. The doc said it was the best kind of cancer to get, if there is such a thing, and that now we know what's wrong, we can fix it." I went to walk up the veranda steps and stopped. "I'll call tonight and let you know what I know."

I walked inside then with Travis right behind me. I pulled out the big duffel bag and threw some clothes in it. It didn't matter who they belonged to, since we seemed to share our wardrobe. The bathroom was next. I collected razors, toothbrushes, deodorant and shoved 'em all in the bag and threw it by the door. Then I went into my office, typed out a quick email to Greg explaining my station hands were on their own and to keep his ear to the ground for me. I told him I'd call him to explain when I could and signed off. I shoved my laptop in its carry case, and when I looked up, Travis was in the door.

He was just kinda standin' there, lookin' all sorts of lost. "Trav? You okay?"

He nodded quickly, then slowly, and then he shook his head. "Are you?"

I rounded the desk quickly and threw my arms around him. I didn't stop to think how he might be affected by all this. "God, I'm sorry," I said, pulling back. "Are you okay? Trav, say something."

He nodded with his eyebrows all furrowed. "Just a bit shocked, I think, I dunno. I'm fine, really. I am." He swallowed hard. "We need to go."

"We do," I agreed. I walked back to my desk, grabbed my laptop bag and handed it to him to carry. "We've got three hours to talk in the car."

He smiled, kinda sadly. "You're taking this whole talking about everything to a whole new level, huh?"

I pecked his lips with mine. "Someone once told me I had to, or he'd leave me. So yeah, take it to a whole new level I did."

I waited for him to smile then I turned around and, stepping into the hall, tripped over a fucking wombat.

"Ugh, you," I said, picking Nugget up. "What am I gonna do with you?" I sighed, which was more like a groan. I knew what I had to do, so I stomped back into our room and found an old camping knapsack in the top of the wardrobe.

With Nugget under my arm, I held the bag open and huffed and grumbled as I shoved his beanie pouch and the old half-a-blanket we wrap him in into the bag. I considered kicking the used-to-be-mine, now his-rumble-teddy-bear across the lounge room, but instead picked it up and stuffed it into the bag as well.

I shook my head and cussed at him as I shoved his bottles into the bag and I even threw in an apple or two.

Trav eyed me cautiously from the kitchen door. "Charlie, what are you doing?"

"Packing his stuff." Which was stupid, because the bloody wombat didn't have *stuff*.

"You can't give him away," Travis whispered. "You just said this morning you didn't think you ever could..."

"Give him away?" I asked. I shook my head. "No, he's coming with us."

"Charlie..."

"I can't expect anyone else to look after him," I explained. "Nara has enough to do without worryin' about night feeds and all that. Not to mention the fact that he's decided to not let anyone but me feed him."

Travis sighed, long and loud, but he rolled his eyes. "I'm pretty sure the motel we stay at won't let you keep him."

"They won't know."

Travis walked up to me, patted Nugget on the head and kissed my cheek. "If you just don't want to leave him here, just say it."

"I don't want to leave him here."

He smiled. "I'll go load the truck."

Maybe it was stupid takin' him with us, but the idea of him not feeding for however long we'd be gone for made my stomach twist. So the three of us piled up into the old ute; me driving, Trav on the passenger side and Nugget perched up like he was something special right in between us. And we headed into town, to the hospital more specifically, to be with Ma.

I WASN'T TOO FAR wrong about talkin' for the three hour drive into town. Normally Trav would put his head on my shoulder and his feet on the dash, but not this time.

He'd taken the bottles and apples out of the bag and put Nugget into it. It must have done alright as a pouch, because the little guy was soon asleep.

And then we talked.

I admitted to bein' scared, and thinkin' that maybe we should have called the doc a long time before now. Travis thought the same. Cancer was such a hard-hittin' word, and as soon as the doc said it, everything changed. I apologised again for not stopping once to ask if he was okay. His scared-as-hell face in my office reminded me that I wasn't the only one anymore. I should have thought about him first, and I was sorry. I was so used to him bein' the strong one, the one who held me together, that I just didn't think.

Of course Travis laughed at that. He told me I was stronger than I gave myself credit for, and that I was doing the right thing—the very best thing—by dropping every-thing and going with Ma to the hospital.

"She must be so scared," he said.

We did a little less talkin' and a bit more hand-holdin' after that.

WE DECIDED it was probably a better idea to find a place to stay first, feed Nugget and get him all settled then we could head to the hospital and spend some uninterrupted time with Ma and George.

It was gettin' on late afternoon, and it wasn't strictly

visiting hours yet. But the lady behind the desk must have taken pity on me, whether I looked nervous or something, but when I asked what ward Katie Brown was in, her answer damn near made me cry.

Oncology.

CHAPTER EIGHT

HOSPITALS ARE JUST A DISINFECTED KIND OF HELL.

I HATED HOSPITALS. I hated the smell. The acrid scent of sickness, industrial disinfectants and horrible food burned in my nose and the back of my throat.

But most of all, I hated seeing Ma in the hospital bed. It confirmed everything that the doc had said—that she really was this sick. She looked so small and frail in the impersonal bed, and of all the things my Ma was, frail just didn't fit.

But as bad as she looked, I think George looked worse. He was sitting beside the bed, holdin' her hand.

It was easier to look at Ma, as sick as she was, than it was to see the sadness in George's eyes.

It almost took my breath away.

Or crushed my lungs. I couldn't decide which.

"Oh, Charlie, Travis," Ma said. "Come in, boys. I told the nurses you'd be coming. Didn't have any trouble getting in to see me?"

I shook my head and put my hand on the foot of the bed. "No. They let us straight up."

"We've only just got into this room," she said. "Had all sorts of tests, but I can rest now they said."

"Did they tell you anything?" I asked quietly. I wasn't sure I wanted to know.

"The doc's gonna come back when he has the blood tests and biopsy results back," George said. "He was hoping it would be first thing tomorrow."

"Well, that's good," I said, not really sure what else there was to say. "We're stayin' at a motel not too far from here. Same one we stayed at before, so we'll be back nice and early. How about you, George?"

He barely took his eyes off Ma. "They said I could stay here. Told 'em I could sleep in the chair here, but they were gonna bring in a fold-up bed or something."

"Good," I said, knowin' he had no intention of leaving any time soon. "It'll be dinner time soon, I'm guessing. George, you want us to go get you something? You too, Ma. I don't know what kinda special diet they'll have you on or nothin', but I'd be thinkin' whatever it is ain't gonna be all that great. We can bring you back something better."

Ma's blinks were getting longer. "I might just have a sandwich and a cup of tea later. I'm not that hungry."

"Okay," I whispered. "George? What about you?" He was about to protest, but I added, "That way you won't have to leave."

He nodded. "That'd be good, thanks Charlie."

"We'll be back," I told George. Ma was already asleep. I pulled Travis by the arm and it took every ounce of will power I had not to run as fast as I could out of the hospital.

"GOD, THAT WAS AWFUL," I said, finally breathing in fresh air. "Fucking hospitals."

Trav rubbed my arm. "You okay?"

"Yeah. Just a bit of a shock, ya know?"

He nodded. "Yeah, I know." He took the keys. "Come on, I'll drive."

We climbed into the ute and Travis drove, only mumbling under his breath once or twice about what side of the road he was on. I thought we were headed to find something to eat, but he pulled up at a pet store.

"What are we doing?"

"You'll see," was all he said as he was getting out.

I followed him into the pet shop, past the puppies, fish and birds down to the kennels and produce. When he stopped at cat beds, I shook my head. "Oh, no no no. We're not getting a cat. We used to have one, it lived in the shed and the bloody thing was feral."

He didn't even look at me. "It's not for a cat, Charlie." He picked up a cushion-box looking thing with a hole in the front. "It's for your damn wombat."

"Oh," I said brightly. "Well, that's okay then."

He pushed Nugget's new bed into my chest. "So he sleeps in *his* bed, not ours."

A sales guy, about eighteen years old, walked up and was looking at us funny. He probably just heard what Travis said, and I didn't care. I just shrugged, guessin' that I'd come a long way in the last six months. "How did I know he'd think it was playtime?"

Travis sighed and turned to the sales assistant. "Do you have any feed pellets for wombats?"

He raised his eyebrows. "Wombats?"

I nodded. "Yep, you know, 'bout this big"—I held up my hands to show him—"shape of a brick, cute little thing."

Travis took a God-fucking-help-me breath. "About a year old, pain in the arse, stubborn as hell, gets into everything type of wombat."

The poor kid blinked. "Um, well, we have pellets for rabbits and guinea pigs, kangaroos…" he said, walking in what I assumed was the direction of what we were after.

After I used my phone to Google what the hell kind of pellets wombats should eat, we bought a bag of pellets, some maize and some bedding hay.

We took it straight back to the motel and watched as the little wombat sniffed around his new bed, not too impressed by any of it. Trav threw his blanket and rumble-bear in there, and then he threw Nugget in there as well.

Once he'd figured out how to get in and out of it, he loved it. It was like a dark and cosy wombat hole. We fed him some apple and added a few pellets and bits of hay, and then we left him doing jumpy, burn out circle work on the carpet.

When we got back into the ute this time, I was smiling. I reached over and took Trav's hand and kissed his knuckles. "Thank you."

He smiled, all smug and knowing, like it was his plan all along to make me forget about Ma, even just for a little while.

"Now, we'll go and find some human food," he said. "And flowers for Ma, and we better make sure she has some of her favourite brand of tea."

I looked at him and smiled. "You're kind of wonderful, you know that?"

"You can thank me later," he said, starting the engine.

"Oh, I plan to."

"Twice."

"Deal."

BECAUSE WE COULDN'T DECIDE which flowers she'd have liked—I said the yellow ones with the 'You're a Star' balloons, and Travis said the pink ones with 'Get Well Soon' balloons—and because people in the supermarket were starting to stare at us as we argued, we ended up getting both.

I know she liked mine better, she just said she loved them both the same, just so it wouldn't hurt Travis's feelings.

We took some barbeque chicken, chips and salad for George, and even Ma ate a little. She was still dozing on and off by then. They'd given her some drug that helped with pain and made her sleepy, George told us.

So we stayed for a while, made sure she was comfortable and made sure George ate something, then we said goodnight, promising to be back first thing in the morning.

I LOVED a lot of things about Travis, but at the top of that list right now was how he gave me thinkin'-time silence. Ma and George both knew sometimes I just needed thinkin' space and a little time to get thoughts right in my head. Maybe Travis learned from them, maybe he just knew me well enough, but when we got back to the motel, even despite the antics of a happy-to-see-us but give-me-all-the-attention baby wombat, Trav didn't push me to talk.

He knew I would. He just knew I needed time.

He fed Nugget some more pellets and cleaned up after him, while I lay on the bed, starin' at the ceiling. It was an awful reminder of the brevity of life, seeing someone you love be so sick. All the what-if's weighed in, adding to the mass of guilt for not makin' Ma see a doctor when we all knew she wasn't well. So what if she'd yelled at us, or gave us the silent treatment for taking her to get a check up? Bein' full-named and cussed at would be a walk in the park compared to seeing her where she is now.

My phone interrupted my thoughts, and I sighed when Greg's name scrolled across my screen. I assumed he'd just read the email I sent him, telling him my farm was bein' manned by my staff alone. Sure, there'd been times when I was away or George, but never both at the same time.

So Trav would know who I was talking to, I answered the call. "Greg."

"Hey, Charlie, what's up?"

"George, me and Trav are all in town," I told him. "I told the guys back at the farm if it was an emergency to give you a call. Hope you don't mind, but you'd be quicker flying than me driving."

"'S no problem," he said. "Anything the matter?"

"It's Ma," I said. "She's not well."

"Oh, man."

"We'll know more tomorrow. The oncologist is running tests." I swallowed hard. "But they're optimistic."

I guess the word 'oncologist' told him all he needed to know. "Oh, Jesus. Charlie, I'm sorry to hear that," he said.

"I don't know how long we'll be away for," I said. But I told him I'd send him a quick email when we were home, and if he needed me to look over any details of reports or whatnot, just to send it along and I'd look at it when I could.

When I'd clicked off the call, before I put my phone down, I called home. I didn't even know if anyone would be in the homestead—it was a little after dinner time—but luckily Trudy answered the phone.

Travis took my boots off while I told her all I knew about Ma and that I'd let them know what the doctor said tomorrow. "How are you feeling?" I asked. Then, realizing I didn't know if I was supposed to know she wasn't feeling well—Travis had told me, not Trudy—I squeezed the bridge of my nose and added, "You weren't too well apparently."

"I'm fine," she replied, a little too quickly and a little bit snappy.

If I ever understood one thing about women, about Outback women, it was that they didn't like being fussed over. Well, they didn't like us to think they weren't strong enough to handle anything they were dealin' with. Even if, just like Ma, it landed them in hospital.

I made a promise to myself that I'd make a doctor's appointment for Trudy myself if I had to, but bein' so far away and with them out there on their own, I left it alone. For now. I sighed. "Okay. I'll call tomorrow."

I disconnected the call, threw my phone onto the bed and dug the heels of my hands into my eye sockets.

The foot of the bed dipped, and I could feel Travis crawl up my body without even moving my hands from my eyes. He lay on me, his legs between mine, his weight on top of me feeling so damn good, and peeled my hands away. The look on his face was one of concern and so much fucking love. "You okay?"

I smiled despite my mood. "I have you. I will always be okay."

He closed his eyes and kissed me softly, as though my words soothed him, pleased him.

"How's Nugget?" I asked.

"Asleep."

"Greg was worried, and I think I pissed Trudy off," I said.

Trav shook his head. "Stop worrying about everyone else. Just for tonight." He leaned up on his elbow and touched my face—soft thumbs traced lines and long fingers tracked through my hair. He scanned my features, and when his eyes finally met mine again, they were warm and deep. "I want to take care of you tonight," he whispered, kissing me again. "Will you let me?"

Normally I took control. I always saw to his pleasure before my own, whether we fucked hard or made love. I wanted him to know I would put him first, his needs before mine, in everything I did.

But tonight it would be different.

I didn't know what he meant by 'take care of me', whether he would just make me come or he would top me. And I realised it didn't matter. I'd let him do either—or both. I cupped my hand to his face, and before I pulled him in for a kiss, I nodded.

He kissed me deeper, tasting me, tilting my head so he could kiss me deeper still. It made my head spin, and my blood warmed through, and when he ended the kiss with a nudge of his nose, all coherent thoughts scattered.

I let him have his way with me. I couldn't have stopped him, even if I'd wanted to. My body wouldn't have let me. Along every inch of skin, every nerve ending, he was all sure hands and strong mouth. And when he cleaned me and prepped me, all gentle fingers and warm breath, I wanted it.

I'd never wanted anything more.

Travis lay me on my back with my legs open, and he gently pushed my knees up to my chest as he leaned down and kissed me. He kept his eyes open, watching me for what, I didn't know. Pain? Doubt?

There was neither.

I gave myself to the sensation of being penetrated. Every cell, every synapse in my brain belonged to Travis as he pushed inside me. Slowly, he filled me, and I revelled in the stretch, the feeling of being joined with him—being one with him. He touched my face and held my hand; he kissed my lips, my jaw, my neck.

He made me lose myself. With every thrust, with every groan, he made the world disappear, he made everything but us disappear. He made me his.

Travis leaned up on one hand, taking my cock in his other, and he pumped and squeezed, thrusting and stroking me to orgasm. My whole body flexed as I came, shooting thick between us, and Travis let go of my cock to hold me, burying his face in my neck as waves of aftershocks tore through me. I'd never come like that before—so hard, so intense.

I'd never felt so loved.

It was only then that Trav let himself go. He held my face, kissing me hard, so hard, as he thrust into me until he came.

Travis had always said sex was better without condoms. I usually topped, and I agreed with him. It was better. But feeling him come inside me was something else.

It was more than just a convenience and more than extra sensitivity. It was a freedom, a complete giving. A statement that said "yours forever".

It felt like a gift.

Travis didn't move until he slid out of me. "Do you want a shower?" he murmured.

I was sticky, slicked in lube and could feel his cum in my arse, but I shook my head. "No." My voice was a mix of croak and groan.

"Do you feel okay?" he asked, sounding alarmed. "Are you sore?"

I snorted at that and rolled onto my stomach. "Yes, I feel okay. No, I'm not sore. I want you to do it again," I told him.

I lifted my hips off the mattress, raising my arse. "Just like this. You, on top of me."

He chuckled and kissed my shoulder. "I might need a few minutes."

Spreading my knees a little, I raised my hips even more, slipped my hand beneath myself and started to jerk myself in long, languid strokes. "I'll start without you."

He groaned out a laugh and manoeuvred himself between my thighs. I could feel the weight of his balls on my arse as he started to pull on his own cock. It wasn't long until he leaned over me, one hand beside my head, the other guiding his cock into my hole. His voice was hot and gruff in my ear. "You won't start anything without me."

He slid in easily, every fucking inch of him, and he kissed the back of my neck, the shell of my ear, the skin along my shoulder. He pressed his full body weight on my back and wrapped his hands around my fists, and I asked him to fuck me, harder, deeper, faster.

So he did.

I wanted Travis to have me, to take me, to make me his. I wanted to give him what he gave me, and I wanted him to know I belonged only to him. He grunted and groaned in my ear, fucking me until he came in my arse one more time.

He collapsed on top of me, inside of me, breathing my name over and over. I was sore, sated and smiling. "Jesus," he mumbled, kissing the back of my neck. He pulled out of me slowly and got off the bed. I heard the shower turn on next, and then he was pulling me off the bed and dragging me to the bathroom.

The water was steaming hot over my tired muscles, and Travis soaped me up and washed me down. He never stopped touching me: soft hands, soft kisses. There was a quiet reverence in the way he took care of me, how he stood under the spray of water with me, how he kissed me.

He held my face in both hands, and his eyes were closed, his lips barely moved against mine in an almost kiss. He nudged my nose with his, making my knees go weak, and I chuckled. "It still gets me," I whispered.

Travis opened his eyes slowly, as if he was drunk and completely unaware of what he'd done. "What gets you?"

"You and your nose nudges," I answered. "I don't think I'll ever get sick of it."

Smiling, he shut the water off. We dried off, got dressed and Travis ordered Chinese for dinner. With a full stomach, I crawled into bed, content and sleepy.

I fell asleep wrapped up in Travis with him tracing circles on my back. I dreamt of blue eyes, smug smiles and Southern drawls, and even in my dreamin' sleep, I'd never felt so loved.

Well, until a won't-wait-for-nothin' wombat declared it was midnight-feedin' time, then three-o'clock-it's-too-damn-early feedin' time and by breakfast time, a new day started.

Something had changed last night, for me at least, like I'd fallen in love all over again or something I couldn't place. I don't know if it was the uncertainty of Ma's health or the reappearance of my estranged mother or the intimacy of what we'd done last night, but something was different. I needed to be near Travis. I needed him close, and by the way he hugged me and kissed me oh so softly before we left for the hospital, I figured he felt the same.

He held me close and his eyes searched mine. "You ready to go see Ma?"

Today was the day we would find out if the cancer had spread. I leaned into him and tightened my arms around him, yet it was still not close enough. I shook my head. "Not really," I answered honestly. "But we should go."

AS FAR AS WE KNEW, the doctor would be giving us results today and, subsequently, the best course of action. It was all routine, apparently. It's just what they did. Then everyone could make informed decisions about which options were best. George had said today would be decision-making day, and I was fully expecting to help them do just that.

But when we walked in to Ma's room, her bed was empty and George wasn't there. It was a god-awful sinking feeling, and when I backed out into the hall, a nurse grabbed me. "Are you Charlie?"

I nodded.

She was maybe thirty-five with short blonde hair. She smiled kindly. "George said you'd be here early," she said. "He said for me to tell you they've taken her into surgery."

I couldn't seem to make the words come out. "Where is he?" Travis asked beside me.

"Come this way," she said, leading back toward the elevators. "First floor. Turn right, you'll see surgery waiting rooms to your left."

The second the doors were closed, Travis took my hand. He held it until the elevator stopped and tried letting it go when the doors opened. I kept a hold of it, probably too tightly, but too scared to let it go. I didn't care what anyone else thought. I didn't care if I was hand-holding in public with a guy. Because I was pretty damn certain that if he wasn't near me, if I wasn't touching him somehow, I'd fall apart.

We found the waiting rooms just like the nurse said, and then we found George.

Nothing like his normal self who stood tall and walked proud, he was sitting in the far row of seats with his elbows on his knees and his head in his hands. He looked every one of his hard-workin' years, and he looked so terribly sad.

It was like an equal mix of wanting to know and wanting to run the other way. I wanted to know what the hell was going on, but wasn't sure I could deal with bad news. George looked so damn broken, and that scared me the most.

Still holding my hand, Travis led me over to George. He let go of my hand so I could kneel down in front of the man who was like a father to me. "George? What's going on?"

When he looked up, he had tears in his eyes, but he tried to smile. "They've taken her in for surgery." He shook his head. "I was doin' okay 'til they wheeled her away," he said, the tears finally brimming over. "Don't know what I'll do if something happens to my Katie."

I put my hand around his neck and pulled him against me. I ain't ever seen him cry before. Not even close. He was absolutely the strongest man I knew, and having him cry on my shoulder just about killed me.

And when I looked up at Trav and saw he was fightin' his own tears, I stopped fightin' mine, and I cried with George.

He pulled his head back and wiped his face on his sleeves, cursin' at himself for being foolish.

I sat in the seat beside him and put my arm around his shoulder. "We're all scared, George."

Trav sat beside me, and when I offered him my other hand, he was quick to take it. For a few minutes the three of us just sat there takin' deep, thought-collecting breaths. Eventually, I asked, "What did they say?"

"They're doin' a full abdominal hysterectomy," George said. "And they'll take a look to see if it's spread."

"And if it has?" I asked.

"Then she'll need chemo, or some such thing."

I swallowed thickly. "If that's what it takes," I said.

He nodded and patted my knee. "Yep. Whatever it takes."

"How long will the operation take?" I asked.

"They said about two hours."

"Have you eaten?" I asked. "Come on, we'll go find the cafeteria and have a cuppa. We'll be back before she's out, I promise."

We found the cafeteria and I ordered some tea for me and George, a coffee for Trav, and some toasted sandwiches and scones. When I put the tray on the table, George's eyes widened at all the food.

"You need to eat," I told him.

He sighed. "You sound like Ma."

I laughed and handed Travis his coffee. "I doubt it's very good," I told him.

"That's why you should drink tea," George said with his usual slow-talkin, dry-as-the-desert sense of humour.

"Even bad coffee is better than tea," Travis said with a smile. He bit into a scone with jam and frowned. "Good Lord, don't let Ma eat one of them." He looked back at the cafeteria counter. "Or someone'll be gettin' fired."

This time George laughed, and I hooked my foot around Travis's in a kind of thank-you. And for the next half an hour or so, we talked of all the things Ma would chip us for and laughed at all the times she's threatened us, scolded us, clipped us behind the ear, or just yelled at us for the sake of yellin'. "'Cause really, we all know I didn't ever do anything wrong," I said, and George laughed so hard he almost choked on his sandwich.

By the time we walked back to the waiting room, we were all in a much better frame of mind. We sat back down, and Travis picked up a few magazines. He snorted laughing when the Beef Farmers magazine with my face on the front was among them.

"Ugh, I'm really regretting that bloody thing," I grumbled.

Travis opened it and turned it on its side like it was a centrefold. "I dunno," he said, shaking his head. "I'd date him."

George chuckled, and I snatched the stupid magazine and tossed it back on to the table with the others.

There was a nurse watching us from the door. I didn't recognise her at first, so I didn't really pay her any mind. Until she spoke, anyway. "Charlie?"

We all turned to face her.

"George?" she asked. "I just read the patient names at handover this morning," she said.

She looked different. She was wearing nurse scrubs, her hair was pulled back and she had a clipboard in her hand. It took a long second for me to realise just who it was. I wasn't expecting to see her any time soon—if at all—and I certainly wasn't expecting to see her here.

It was Laura.

CHAPTER NINE

I'VE DECIDED THAT I LIKE GOOD NEWS

THERE WAS A LONG SILENCE—I couldn't quite place seeing her here. Even if I'd expected to see her again, I certainly didn't expect to see her at the hospital—and I was thankful a doctor walked in behind her. Laura stepped to the side, giving the doctor centre stage.

"Mr Brown?" the doctor asked.

George stood up with me and Travis right beside him. The three of us took off our hats in unison. "Yeah."

The doctor, a guy about the same age as George, looked questioningly at me and Trav, then back to George. "Should we talk in private?"

I swear I could feel the hope drainin' from George. I put a hand on his back, but he shook his head. "You can tell these boys," he said, his voice just a whisper.

"The operation went well. It would appear that the adenocarcinoma was contained in the endometrium," he started, but quickly clarified. "That means the cancer itself was contained within the uterus. We've done a complete hysterectomy, so it looks like we got it all."

We all finally breathed.

The doctor smiled a little, but put his hand on George's arm. "While this is good news, you need to be aware that we'll need pathology to confirm this, and more than likely, there still will be follow-up treatments."

I don't think George heard any of that.

I think he was still stuck on 'looks like we got it all'. He was just nodding and smiling and teary, and his was breathing kind of laboured. "Can I see her?"

The doctor smiled. "Briefly. She's in recovery. I can only take one of you, though."

I practically pushed George forward. "Go."

Trav and I watched him disappear through some doors. Then he put his hands on his hips and breathed like he'd just run up a few flights of stairs. "Man, that is good news."

I rubbed his back and kinda leaned into him, just a little bit, still unable to shake the need to have him near. "It really is."

He turned and put his arms around me, pulling me close. I didn't care if anyone saw. I needed him, he needed me, and they could just fucking deal with it. He kissed the side of my head. "We need to call home and let them know. They'll be worried sick."

I nodded, then I remembered something. Or some*one*. I pulled back and looked around for Laura. She looked like she was torn between wanting to give us space and wanting to stay. Travis turned and huffed when he saw her. She gave a sad, tired smile. "I didn't know Katie was here," she said. "I saw her name on the surgery list when my shift started at seven this morning."

My head was just about spinning. "What are you doing here?" I asked. I looked her up and down, taking in her uniform. "You're obviously staff. I thought you said you lived in Darwin?"

"I do," she said. "I rotate as part of the Northern Territory Health's regional training program. I'm a surgical nurse. It gives other nurses here a chance to do training and work in bigger hospitals in Darwin. I'm here for another six weeks..."

I didn't know what to say to her.

"I'm sorry about before, Charlie," she said. "About just turning up unannounced. That wasn't fair on you."

"No, it wasn't," Travis answered defensively.

Laura smiled sadly again. I don't think she minded Trav's biting tone. She probably considered it a win that it came from him and not me.

But Travis, being Travis, fully owned his feelings and wasn't afraid to show them. I, on the other hand, was still on the I-don't-know-how-to-feel side of the fence.

"I called Sam," she said quietly. "When I got home after seeing you, it was the first thing I did." She sat down in the seat closest to the door. "I told him everything. I should have done it years ago."

My head kept spinning. Considering the events of these last few days, this was all too much. "Now isn't a very good time. Ma just had her operation..."

Laura nodded. "I know. I'm sorry. I seem to have worst timing. I didn't know she was so sick."

"None of us did," I replied. It occurred to me then that I didn't want to see Laura. I wanted to see Ma.

Another nurse walked past and I called out to her. "Excuse me?"

She stopped, looked at Laura cautiously, then to me. "Can I help you?"

I nodded. "I'd like to see Katie Brown. She's in recovery. Her husband's with her right now, but I'll just be real quick."

"Are you a relative?"

"Yes," I said without hesitation. "I'm her son."

"Let me see what I can do," she said, then looked back at Laura. "You all right?"

Laura nodded. "Yeah. I'm fine."

I replayed in my mind what I'd just said in front of her. That I was someone else's son. And I opened my mouth to apologise.

But then I realised I wasn't sorry at all.

MA WAS STILL all dozy and drugged when they took her back to her room, and George had hold of her hand like it was the only thing keepin' him alive.

Figurin' we'd be doing a whole lotta sittin' around watchin' her sleep, I told George we'd be back in an hour or so. The truth was I needed some fresh air, and by the way Travis kept clenchin' his jaw, I figured he did too.

We went back and checked on Nugget, and seein' that Trav hadn't relaxed any, I remembered something he'd done once. "Come on, let's get him packed up. I wanna take you both somewhere."

We found a cafe in town and ordered burgers and drinks to go. When I then pulled the ute up to a local park, Trav snorted. "You wanted to bring your wombat to a park? I think he's a bit young to be using the slide, Charlie."

I laughed at him. "I didn't come here just for him. I came here for you too."

"I'm a bit over slides too. Kinda have been since, ooooh, I dunno, the fourth grade," he said with a smile.

"Shut up and bring that, will you?" I said, nodding to

the bag as I got out of the ute. I carried Nugget and his bag of belongings while Trav carried lunch.

I walked over to a spot, far enough from the road and the play equipment, where the grass was kinda long and the spring sun was warm. I put Nugget down first and watched as he sniffed the grass, not sure what to make of it.

I sat down and patted the ground. "Sit down. Take your boots and socks off, Trav."

If he had wondered what the hell I'd brought him here for, now he knew. It wasn't too long ago, he'd sat in the small park near the supermarket and ordered me to do the same. He said he missed the feel of it and that it was kinda great—not that I agreed too much—but if it helped him de-stress a little, then I could sit in the park all damn day. He smiled and, sitting down, pulled off his boots and socks. He wiggled his toes in the long grass, his smile now a grin.

We ate our burgers and watched Nugget as he wandered, not too far, sniffing and running. He'd come back to us every minute or so, then scoot off to some new patch of very important-smelling grass.

If the morning hadn't been so stressful, it would have been a perfect day.

When we'd eaten and Nugget was annoying Travis for a belly scratch, I lay down in the grass and stared at the sky. We were only a metre or so apart, and although I wasn't touching him in any way, just being with him right then was enough. The memories of last night—and the still lingering ache in my arse—made me sigh.

"You feel okay?" Travis asked. He frowned. "You're not sore, are you? I was pretty rough, and—"

"Are you kidding me?" I cut him off before he could apologise. "You were everything I needed last night. It was fucking great, so don't you dare say you're sorry."

He snorted out a laugh. "Right, then. No apology. But if you're sore..."

"Well, I have an ache in my arse. I can't decide if it's an unpleasant ache or an I-need-you-to-do-it-again kinda ache."

This time he laughed. "You're starting to sound like me."

I sighed again, still starin' at the sky, and my smiled faded. Of course Trav knew something was on my mind. "You wanna talk about whatever's botherin' you?" he asked. "You've got a lot on your plate right now."

"I didn't really mean to say that I was Ma's son in front of Laura," I said. "But once I'd kinda realised what I'd said, I was glad I'd said it. Should I feel bad about that? Because I don't."

"It was the truth," Travis replied, looking at me. He was lyin' down on his side, one arm supporting his head, the other scratching Nugget's belly. "I was glad you'd said it too."

"You don't like her," I said. It wasn't a question.

It was his turn to sigh. "I don't know her, so I can't say if I do or not. But I don't like how she thought she could just turn up. I don't think she realised the ramifications of her actions, and I think that says a lot about her."

"Such as?"

"She only thought of herself. She didn't once think 'what if he doesn't want to see me?' or 'how will this affect him?'. It was more about her needs and wants, not yours. And that doesn't wash with me."

I smiled at him, but he didn't see. He was looking at Nugget, lost in his thoughts.

"I don't mean to make things difficult, and I don't want to sway your decision in any way," he went on to say.

"You won't."

"I don't doubt that she's had it rough. I know she has," he said, looking at me now. "She had a terrible time because of your old man, just like you did. I think maybe he pushed her away, just like he did with you. And I should be able to sympathise with that, because I get what you went through, I really do. I've seen what rejection can do to kids, Charlie." He shook his head and frowned. "But I guess I'll never understand how a mother could leave her kid."

I thought about that for a little while. "I think you're right."

"Which part?" he sat up. "I kinda said more than I probably should've."

"All of it," I told him. "I think she did have a tough time, and she had another kid to think about too by then. I can't dismiss that. I know what a bastard my father could be, so I can certainly sympathise with her on that."

"Do you blame her for leaving you?"

I sighed. "Nope."

Trav shook his head, the way he did when I made him I-don't-understand-you mad. "How can you not?"

"Because I don't remember her. How can I miss something I don't remember having?" I answered simply. "Anyways, I look at it like this: if she hadn't have gone and left me, I wouldn't have had Ma. So really, I should be thankin' her."

He sighed, long and loud. Eventually he said, "You know, I appreciate your way of thinking. It's a point of view I wouldn't have seen, and I think it makes you a bigger man than me to say that."

"But?"

"But I swear to God, Charlie. I don't think I will ever understand you." He shook his head and his smile faded.

He looked at me for another long second. "What else is bothering you? I can tell, you know. You're not as good at hiding shit from me as you think. I don't understand you some days, but I can always tell when you've got something on your mind."

That made me chuckle. "I don't really know, to be honest. I'm not keeping it from you," I told him. "I just don't know what to think of it."

"Think of what?"

"That stuff we found in the roof, the mementos my father kept," I said. "Well, it made me kind of think maybe he wasn't so bad, you know? I mean, maybe he just struggled with life and didn't deal with shit very well, but he kept those things, and he did that interview where he said he was proud of me. It wasn't just that he said it, it was the fact that he cut it out and kept it." I shrugged one shoulder. "And just when I thought maybe he wasn't the bitter, angry man I remember, then along comes my birth mother and we learn all over again that yes, he was just as cruel to her as he was to me."

"It's confusing," Trav agreed. "You wanna know what I think?"

I nodded.

"I think maybe he was cruel on the outside, because he thought that's how he had to be to survive out there," he said, pulling at the grass. "I think he struggled with it, but didn't think he had an option."

I thought about that, what it meant, not just for my father or for Laura or even for the teenaged version of me that got shipped off to Sydney to learn how to be not-gay, but for the adult version of me. Because if it wasn't for Travis, I'd be a mirror image of my old man.

I'd be angry and bitter, and very, very much alone.

"You kind of saved me, you know," I told him quietly. "You bein' a stubborn arse and refusin' to get on that plane, stayin' here and fighting for me, even though I was a jerk. Well, you saved me that day from bein' just like my father. Did I ever tell you that?"

Trav looked at me for a long few seconds, searchin' for what, I didn't know. He eventually smiled, with shy lips and crinkles at his eyes. "No you didn't, but thank you. I don't know if that's exactly true, but thank you for saying it."

"It's been a crazy few weeks, hasn't it?" I asked. "We get back from at week at Kakadu—which was great, by the way —we have that meeting with the biggest supermarket beef buyer in the country, we found that stuff in the roof, Laura turns up, and then Ma gets sick." I sighed just thinking about it. "No wonder my head's spinning."

Trav grinned. "I thought it was my awesome topping skills last night that did that."

I snorted, and Nugget came barrelling over to me. He headbutted my chest and did his little playful jumpin' thing, making Trav and me both laugh.

"You ready to go back and see how Ma's doing?" I asked.

"We'd better get George something to eat," he added. He started to pack up the bag and asked, "Did you want to go home tonight or tomorrow?"

"How about we see what the doc says," I said, getting to my feet. I picked up Nugget and tucked him under my arm. "But we should take this little guy back to the motel first."

WHEN WE GOT BACK to the hospital, Ma was sleeping.

Seeing that we'd brought him lunch, George suggested we go to the visitors lounge so as not to wake Ma.

There were rows of chairs, small tables with magazines and a wall-mounted TV, which thankfully was on mute. George sat down, groaning as he did. I figured he hadn't been this still in forever and his body probably felt like it was seizing up. "The doc came back," he told us. "Said we was real lucky. The cancer didn't spread."

"Oh thank God," I whispered, more relieved than I ever remember feeling. It was like a weight had been lifted with just a few simple words. "When can she come home?"

He gave me a tired smile. "She'll be in here a week," he said. "So I guess I will be too."

I wouldn't have expected anything else. "George, you take as much time as you need. I don't care how long that is, we just need to know she's okay."

George ran his worked-hard fingers through his hair. "We're about to get real busy," he sighed. "Calving soon, if they haven't started already, then there's the—"

I put my hand up to stop him. "George."

"I can't leave her," he said.

I smiled at him. "I would never ask you to."

Travis handed over the white sandwich bag and juice we brought in for him just as my phone rang.

I'd forgotten to turn it off when we walked in, and I was going to disconnect the call, but then I saw the number. "I probably should take this."

I left Trav with George and went straight to the men's room, then answered the call. "Charlie Sutton."

"Hi, Charlie, it's Blake Burgess."

"Blake, how you going?" I asked. "You'll have to excuse the acoustics."

"Sounds like you're in the bathroom," he said with a laugh. "Need me to call you back?"

I laughed with him. "Nah. I'm at the hospital. Figured if I hid in the bathroom, no nurses could yell at me about bein' on the phone since they can't see me."

"True," he said. Then he got to the point of his call, the call we'd been waiting for, to see if we could secure a fixed income for a few years. "Charlie, I have a proposition for you."

***

WHEN I WALKED BACK into the visitors lounge, Travis stood up. He looked worried. "Everything okay?"

I grinned, slow and wide. "That was Blake Burgess, the buyer from Woollies."

Trav's eyes went wide and he started to smile. "And?"

"And he was impressed. We made the cut."

Travis threw his arms around me, almost tackling me. "Oh thank God," he said with a laugh. "Some more good news. First Ma and now this!"

George was standing now, and when Trav let go of me, George shook my hand. He was smiling too, genuine, relieved and even a little bit proud. "That's real good news, Charlie."

"Not as good as Ma's news," I said. "But good news, nonetheless."

"What else did he say?" Travis said.

"He's sending through a proposal," I told him. "It'll have all the details, but he's talking a thousand head of cattle in the first intake."

Both Travis's and George's mouths fell open.

I laughed, still shaking my head at the impossibility of it

all. "I can't believe it. He's organising for their vet and inspector to come see us when they do the rounds in a week or so. And a contract for our solicitor to look over."

"Jesus," Travis mumbled, running his hand through his hair and blowing air through his puffed-out cheeks. "They don't muck around. We have a lot to get ready between now and then, and you've got an assessment due."

Shit. I'd not given that a second thought. But the last thing I wanted was for George to be stressing, when his priority was not at home. "We don't have to worry about that right now," I said to Travis, flickering my eyes toward George.

Trav must have caught on, because he didn't argue. But George saw it too. "Charlie," he started.

I shook my head. "George, I need you to be right here." I put my hand on his arm. "But it does mean me and Trav will have to go home today. I was hoping we could stick around until tomorrow, or even 'til Ma can come home, but we should be goin' back."

He nodded. "That's fair enough. Just wish I could do more. Feel a bit helpless if I was tellin' the truth."

I guessed he wasn't just talking about home, but about being here and not bein' able to help his wife. "You've done more than your share over the years. Let us pick up the slack for a change, huh?"

We went and checked on Ma, but she was still asleep. I told George we'd go pack up our gear at the motel and come back on our way out of town.

It'd been one helluva day.

We packed up the room as quickly as we could, including giving little Nugget a bottle before we left. He sat in his new box bed between me and Trav in the ute, and when we pulled into the car park, Trav moved the box so the entrance hole was facing the roof so Nugget couldn't climb out.

"So the little shit can't get into trouble or chew the crap outta anything while we go inside," Trav explained when I questioned what he was doing.

Nugget grunted and squeaked, not liking this development at all. "We can't just leave him," I said. "He can't get out, he can't even see!"

Travis raised one you've-gotta-be-kidding-me eyebrow. "Well, we certainly can't just carry him into the hospital, Charlie."

I looked at the backpack full of the wombat's things. "No, we can't just *carry* him in," I agreed. "But that doesn't mean he can't still come with us."

MA WAS MUCH BRIGHTER when we walked back into the hospital. She was at least awake and smiled at us as soon as she saw us. George was happier too. Maybe it was relief, maybe it was pure fucking joy, but the man was looking at Ma like she was the best gift he'd ever been given.

To him, she probably was.

I was wearing the backpack, though it was heavy. And moving. Luckily no one stopped or even questioned us when we walked into the ward. I carefully put the backpack on the bed and kissed Ma's cheek. "You look so much better," I said. "How are you feeling?"

"I'm fine," she said quietly.

"How are you really?" I asked, giving her the don't-lie-to-me stare that she'd used on me for years.

She gave me a small smile. "Sore. Tired."

I squeezed her hand. "Then lucky you're here to rest."

Travis leaned over us and kissed her cheek. "Can we get you anything?"

"No, love," she said. "They're looking after me." She was understandably weak. Her blinks were getting a little longer, but she was fighting it. "George was telling me you got some good news from that buyer."

"We did," I said with a nod. "It's great for the station, Ma. But it means we have to go back today."

"That's fine, Charlie," she said. She smiled at me and Trav. "I'm just grateful you boys were here at all."

"Where else would we be?" I asked, gently putting the backpack on the bed.

Nugget wanted out of the backpack right that moment. Checking there were no nurses in sight, I pulled back the zipper and lifted the little wombat out of the bag.

"Oh, Charlie," Ma said, half-amused, half-scolding.

At the same time, George said, "Don't think he'd be on the visitors list, Charlie."

"Well, I couldn't just leave him at the ute," I told them, giving him a scratch under the chin.

"Charlie's smitten," Travis said. He sat down in the chair along the back wall of the room. "He won't admit it, but he is."

"I'm not *smitten*," I countered. "He's just little, cars get hot, and he would've been lonely..."

"Mmhmm," Travis hummed. The three of them were looking at me like I'd lost my freakin' mind.

"He stayed at the motel with you?" George asked.

"Well, he still won't feed from anyone but me," I said, giving Nugget a scratch. "I couldn't leave the little guy to starve." When I looked at Travis, he was smiling at me. "Don't look at me like that," I said. "It's your fault for bringin' him home."

Travis laughed. "Sure."

"Travis bought him a new bed and everything," I told Ma, not that she was overly interested right then, but I wasn't the only one spoiling Nugget.

Trav snorted out a laugh. "I bought him that so he'd sleep in his own bed, not ours." He lifted up one of his legs. "The little shit chewed on my boot."

Ma chuckled and immediately winced, her hand going straight to her lower stomach. "Oh, don't make me laugh."

George and Trav jumped to their feet, and the three of us were quick to fuss all over her. "Are you okay?" we all asked at the same time.

Ma was still smiling. "I am," she told us. "I love that nothing's changed."

A nurse walked in and went to Ma's side, near George. She read some machine, checked the fluid bag, and then she looked at me and her mouth fell open. "Is that a wombat?" she asked in disbelief.

"It's not what you think," I said, giving her the best smile I could. I held Nugget under one arm, pulled his beanie-pouch out of the backpack and helped him into it. I carefully put him back into the bag and zipped it up.

The nurse was still staring at me when I leaned down and kissed Ma on the forehead. "We'd better get going."

Trav walked over to Ma, and leaning down, he kissed her too. "I'll look after him for you."

Ma smiled, and although she was tired, it was the best she'd looked in a long while. Then she remembered something. "Oh, Charlie. George told me Laura was here. I wasn't sure if you knew..."

"I spoke to her yesterday, just for a minute," George said quickly. "She works here, for the time bein' anyway." He looked at me. "She just asked how Katie was going, and that was all. She didn't say anything else."

I smiled at George and squeezed Ma's hand. "I saw her yesterday too," I told them. I didn't want Ma to worry about any of that. "But she's not my concern right now. You are. So you just worry about getting better. We'll be back in five days to get you, yes?"

"If you've got time," George said. "You'll be busy, so we can work something out if need be."

"We'll be here," I promised him. Travis helped me put the backpack on carefully, and even with the still stunned nurse staring at us, I gave him a quick kiss. And if she wasn't shocked before, she was then. It was a true testament to how far I had come—the old Charlie Sutton would have never done such a flippant thing. But this Charlie Sutton didn't care what anyone but Travis thought.

We said goodbye to Ma, and I told George I'd be calling every day for updates. He told me he was real glad we'd been here with him, and I told him it was about time I made up for all the times he was there for me. With a slow-spreading smile and fatherly hug from George, we left.

Walking out of the hospital that time was a much better feeling than it was walking in the first time. We were both smiling as we crossed the car park and headed toward the ute, when someone a few rows of cars over called out to me. "Charlie?"

It was Laura. Again. She was getting out of her car, dressed for work. She was right about one thing. She had the worst possible timing. Travis groaned, and I knew it wasn't just my mood that took a nosedive.

She walked toward us and looked at her watch. "I start in twenty minutes," she said. "You guys heading off?"

"Heading home," I corrected her. "Ma has another five

days here, and we've got a lot going on right now back at the station."

"Well, I'm glad I saw you," she said. Then she looked at Travis. "Both of you."

I nodded and smiled, not really sure what else there was to say. Travis said nothing.

Clearly uncomfortable, Laura looked at a passing car and tried to smile when she looked back at me. "Can I call you?" she asked. "I told you that I told Sam about you. Well, after the shock of it all, I guess, he said he wanted to know more about you, so if you're interested…"

"I don't know," I answered reflexively. "Maybe. I'm really busy right now with work and home, and now Ma."

She nodded, but the disappointment was clear on her face. "I understand."

"I'm not saying no," I told her. "But you can't just dump this all on me and expect me to deal with it on your time schedule. I'm sorry for sayin' it like that, but it's how I feel."

"That's fair enough," she said. She almost seemed pleased by my answer.

"How long are you here for?" I asked. I knew she'd told me but I couldn't remember.

"Another six weeks."

"Then let's work on that," I told her. "We'll talk again before you leave. That's all I can do right now."

She smiled. "Sounds great."

We left her at that. After we got back into the ute, I put Nugget into his bed box, and when I looked up, Travis was starin' at me. "What's up?"

"I'm so proud of you," he said quietly.

I sat back in the seat, letting my head loll back, and sighed. "It's all I can give her right now."

Trav held out his hand, which I took immediately. He

sat kinda side-on. "It's more than enough, Charlie," he said. "You're getting good at this whole talking about feelings and stuff."

"I had a good teacher," I told him.

Trav leaned halfway over and licked his lips, wanting a kiss. I leaned in, of course, and his eyes closed as I almost pressed my lips to his. But instead of kissing him, I gently nudged his nose with mine and pulled back. His eyes shot open. I laughed at him before I leaned over and kissed him for real.

He scowled at me, clearly trying not to smile. "Take me home, Charlie."

We hadn't got too far out of town before he'd leaned against my shoulder, put his feet up on the window and closed his eyes.

CHAPTER TEN

FOUR BEATLES, ONE NUGGET AND A
RUMBLE BEAR

THERE REALLY WAS no feeling quite like coming home. The smell of my house, the sounds of the creakin' floorboards in the hall, being inside familiar, comforting walls. There wasn't anything like it. Hell, even the feel of Ma's worn wooden table in the kitchen felt like home.

After we'd told everyone everything we knew about Ma and then of the news Blake had given me, we ran through what had been happening at the station for the last two days.

The roof was covered and secured, just like I'd asked. Some cows had started calving, though with four check-ups every day, all was well so far. "No abandoned calves yet, none stillborn," Ernie said.

Nara was doing okay as the station cook. She said the food wasn't nothing special, but it kept 'em fed. She kept Ma's veggie garden watered and only harvested what she needed, and there was a confidence in her as she moved around the kitchen. By the way she kept about her work, dismissing us by saying dinner would be in about an hour, I knew she was gonna be just fine. Some people might have called me crazy for takin' on some troubled kid at the station, but in hindsight, I was real happy I did. Nara had found her feet here, and I was proud of playing a part in that.

I'd already put Nugget's things in the lounge room and fed him, and when he was happy to wander and play, I took our bag into our bedroom and started to pull clothes out of it.

Everything was just as it was, as it should be. The station had been not just without Travis, but without Ma, George, and me. And everything was still perfect. Not one thing went wrong, and if it did, it was dealt with quickly and rectified. I sighed loudly.

"What's up?" Travis asked. I hadn't heard him come in behind me.

I shrugged. "I dunno. I just..."

"You just what?"

"We've been gone for two full days."

"So?"

"Not just us," I said. I threw some dirty shirts into a pile on the bed. "But George and Ma as well. This place has never been left without one of us, at least."

"And..." He trailed off, waiting for me to finish.

"They did a good job. Everything ran smooth without us."

"That's because you run a good business," he said, putting his hand on my back. "If the wheels fell off the whole show, it would mean otherwise. You should be happy and proud."

I pulled a rolled-up jumper out of the overnight bag, not really wanting to say what was on my mind.

Travis took the sweater from my hands and put it on the

bed. He lifted my chin and made me look at him. "Charlie, tell me."

I took a deep breath. "I just thought maybe..." I shrugged because it was stupid. "Maybe something would've went wrong."

Confusion flickered in his eyes. "What?"

"I just thought this place couldn't run without me or George. But it can. If I were to disappear off the face of the earth tomorrow, this place would still run."

"Charlie," he said quietly.

"Like it wouldn't matter, you know? If I were gone, it wouldn't make a difference." I felt stupid for saying it. "It's silly, I know. I should be happy. And I am. I'd really expected nothing less of those guys, because they're the best. I just thought—" I shrugged again. "—maybe one thing would stop if I were gone."

Travis held my face. "I would stop," he said. "It would matter to me."

I closed my eyes and leaned my cheek into the palm of his hand, taking comfort in the warmth. "Thank you."

He lifted my chin again and kissed me. "Charlie, you've got a lot going on in that head of yours right now."

"I do," I said, looking at him. "I guess I just thought I'd have more to take care of when I got home. I mean, we have enough to do, don't get me wrong, but I thought I'd have to fix something or redo it or just... something." I shook my head and rolled my eyes at myself. "I told you it was stupid."

Travis chuckled, a deep throaty sound. "It's not stupid," he said and kissed me again before pulling me against him. "How about I do all this laundry and you make a start on your office work."

I pulled back and looked at him, shocked. "You? Do laundry?"

He pushed my shoulder. "Shut up. It's a one-time offer, so take it or leave it."

He didn't have to tell me twice, I almost ran out the door, but I got to the hall and stopped. I walked straight back into our room, grabbed his face and kissed him. "Thank you."

He was surprised, but happy. "What was that for? It's just laundry."

I shook my head. "Not for washing clothes. For listenin' to me prattle on with the bullshit in my head and for not makin' me feel like a dickhead."

Travis laughed. "Well, you're still a dickhead, but I'll listen anyway."

"I was being nice to you," I said, pushing his shoulder this time.

He laughed some more, then with that Travis-is-horny kind of mischief in his eyes, he lowered his voice. "You can be real nice to me later. Twice, if you want."

"Not sure I should, " I teased. "You know, After the dickhead comment and all."

He smiled that damn smug smile of his and scooped the dirty laundry off the bed. "Yes you will," he said with a casual certainty. He leaned in and whispered slowly, "Like you could ever say no to me."

I was about to argue the point, I most certainly could say no, but the aching draw in my balls said otherwise. I tried to say something, but in the end, I gave up and shrugged.

He chuckled all the way down the hall.

I LOST of track of time in my office. By the time Nara called me out for dinner, Travis had the fire going, Nugget's bed was set up in the lounge room, and all the washing was done.

There wasn't much chatter around the table as we ate. The food was good, and even though Trudy was quiet, she ate everything on her plate. I assumed she was feeling better, and when I had a moment alone with her, I'd apologise for oversteppin' that boss-worker-mind-your-own-damn-business line I seemed to have crossed when asking her if she was feeling okay.

It was different now. Twelve months ago, there'd been no line-crossin' at all. I was just their boss. If they had problems or weren't feeling well and needed time, I gave it. I didn't ask questions, I didn't dare tread that personal-information tightrope. I never saw a reason to.

But now, since Travis got here, this station was run more like a family. And while that was great in some regards —I loved them like I would a family—I couldn't help but wonder where the boss part of me began and where it ended.

Just something else to add to my already full mental list of things to get through.

After dinner, I went back into my office. Taking a deep breath and trying to clear my head the best I could, I started at the beginning. Again.

I sorted the mail, putting most of it in a will-get-to pile and binning the rest. Next were emails. I prioritised the work-related ones, read through the two from Allan regarding the upcoming Beef Farmers Association meeting, printed off some invoices and statements, and confirmed an order of feed through the co-op. I didn't even bother opening the two emails from the university about my upcoming assessment.

"You look stressed," Trav said, leaning against the door frame.

"I'm okay," I told him.

"Everyone's gone, the fire is stoked, your wombat is asleep," he said, walking around to my side of the office and leaning against the edge of the desk. "I've just spent the last twenty minutes in the bathroom, if you know what I mean." He leaned down and kissed me. "And you look like you need some stress relief."

"Is that right?" I said, liking where this conversation was going.

Trav sat back on my desk, his legs spread wide. "Remember when I introduced you to the guy who gave Sutton Station a buyer's contract? And you said you owed me something big?"

"Yeah?" I answered cautiously.

"Remember when you said you'd never had desk sex?"

I smiled. "I think I recall..."

"We have the whole house to ourselves."

"Travis..."

He let his head fall back, and he groaned. He was totally acting it. "Yes?"

I considered telling him no. I thought about telling him we really shouldn't fool around in my office; we had a big, comfy bed for that. I even considered just rolling my eyes and not answering him at all.

But then he pulled the travel-size bottle of lube from his pocket and put it on my desk. He palmed his dick, his jeans doing little to hide the bulge. I looked up at his please-fuck-me eyes, and instead of telling him no, I said, "Lock the door."

Trav grinned and, like he had all the time in the world, got up from my desk and walked over to the door, slowly closed it and slid the lock in place.

By the time I'd moved my laptop and the piles of not-doing-tonight paperwork and cleared the desk, Trav was standing in front of me. Then, not taking his eyes off mine, he slowly sat on my desk, pulling himself back so the backs of his knees were at the edge and his feet were off the floor.

He was playing this out, getting off on it, savouring every second.

I stood between his legs, put my hands on his arse and dragged him forward so our hips met. I leaned over him, half pushing him backward, my face just an inch from his, our hardened cocks pressed together through the denim of our jeans. And then I kissed him.

Trav's body jerked under mine, and he groaned into our kiss. His hands were over my sides, my chest and then—finally—undoing my jeans. He slipped his hand around my length, causing my breath to stutter against his mouth.

Both my hands were framing his face, holding his head as I kissed him. Tasted him. Consumed him. Trav fumbled with his own jeans until he had both our cocks in one hand, sliding them together.

"Oh fuck," I gasped. It was too much, and I was going too fast. "I'll come if you keep doing that."

Trav grinned, his lips swollen, his eyes dark and heavy-lidded. "Not until you're inside me," he said.

I stood up straight, and fisting his shirt, I pulled him upright. When he was on his feet, I spun him around and pushed his shoulder down toward the desk. Then I pulled his jeans and briefs down over his hips, exposing his arse. Trav groaned when I grabbed the lube. He knew what was coming. He wanted it. Like me the other night when I craved his dick in my arse, that burning need was rolling off him. He gripped the top edge of the desk with both hands, spread his legs a little, and whispered, "Please, Charlie. Just do it."

I slicked his arse first, then my fingers and slid first one, then two inside him. He knew I'd never rush this part—I would never hurt him—but it wasn't what he wanted. He pushed back a little and groaned, but it was a frustrated sound. He was too full of need and all out of patience. "Fuck me, just fuck me."

My jeans were still around my hips, his were around his thighs, too impatient to undress any further. I poured more lube up the length of my cock and some more over his hole, gripped his hips and pressed my engorged head against him. "Is this what you want?" I asked.

All he did was nod, and I pushed inside him. He groaned out, long and low, pressing his forehead against the desk.

I eased into him, then slowly back out and in again, and soon picked up rhythm. I buried myself to my balls in his arse with each thrust, and he moaned every time. He was so tight and so hot, so wanting, all I could do was fuck.

It was rough and fast and so fucking good. A familiar warmth spread from my balls to my belly, up the backs of my thighs and across my chest as my orgasm built and built and coiled, and then I couldn't stop it. I slammed into him once, twice, three times, and pleasure ripped through me, unloading into his tight heat.

I didn't even try to be quiet. God only knows what fucking sounds I made as I came, an orgasm so intense, I collapsed on him, my face between his shoulder blades. "Jesus," he panted. "You all right, Charlie?"

I slowly pulled out of him and stood up as the room still spun around me. I couldn't even speak. I just pulled his jeans up over his arse, took his hand, leading him to the door. I fumbled with the lock until he laughed at me and unlocked the door himself, and then I led him through the darkened house to our room.

This time, I lay him on our bed, pulled his boots off, then his jeans, kissing up his thighs. "I'll go get a washcloth," I said.

"No," he said, his voice husky and deep. He took his half-hard cock into his own hand and started to stroke himself. "Your work here isn't done yet."

I stripped off and crawled up his body. "Are you okay?" I asked him. "I was a bit rough."

He barked out a throaty laugh. "That was fucking hot," he said.

I blushed, embarrassed by my lack of control in my office. "Oh."

Even though the bedroom was dark, I knew he could see the flush spread over my cheeks because he put his hand to my face. "Don't be shy now," he said. "You certainly weren't shy before."

"Are you sure you're not sore?" I asked, dreading that he would say yes.

He snorted. "What I am is ready for round two." He still stroked himself, his accent distinctly slower and sexier. "Now you can do me again, slower this time, and I come first."

I laughed at his forthrightness. He always just said what he wanted. And I was happy to oblige, of course.

I SPENT the whole next day with Ernie and Billy checking calving cows. Bacon and Travis finished re-sheeting the roofing iron while Trudy was the one on the ground, passing stuff up to them.

It was a three-day plan. Me, Ernie and Billy would be out all day, but home every night, and Trav, Bacon and Trudy would do work at the house. I'd specifically chosen the teams to give me and Trav some space. We'd agreed some time ago that space was a good thing, and considering we'd just spent every day together for three weeks straight— three weeks I'm certain I wouldn't have got through if he hadn't been with me—a few days apart would do us good.

Billy was on a motorbike, Ernie in the old Land Rover and I was on horseback. And man, it felt good to be in the saddle again. Shelby was a bit pissed at me for being unridden so long. She nudged me into the fence post and stomped her foot and huffed a bit, but as soon as we were out in the paddock, she settled right into our usual rhythm.

The sun was warm, the breeze was cool and the desert looked particularly pretty. If Trav thought sex was the best way to de-stress me, this was a very close second. Okay, well maybe not that close. But I loved it. It reminded me of who I was, why I was here, like it was just me and this beautiful and cruel country, and even if just for a few hours, I could forget the responsibilities back at the house.

Before lunch, we found three abandoned day-old calves, one dead and another too far gone to save. I took my .22 from my saddle holster, put the end of the barrel to the poor thing's head, and pulled the trigger. It was an awful part of my job, but it would be worse to let the dying calf suffer.

It was an unfortunate fact of life farming cattle.

By the time we called it a day, we'd found four calves that would need around-the-clock feeding. That number would grow over the next two to three weeks. As a kid I used to love this time of year, but as I got older, feeding so many calves got old real quick.

We'd no sooner got the newborn calves into the holding yard back at the homestead when Travis walked across to meet me and shoved a fussing Nugget and a bottle of milk in my chest. "This little shit still won't feed."

I had Nugget on his back, tucked in under my arm and a bottle in his mouth in less than two seconds.

Travis growled and threw his hands up. "I give up."

I laughed, which, of course, was the wrong reaction apparently. He raised one it's-not-fucking-funny eyebrow at me.

"I got you something," I told him, nodding toward the calves we'd brought back with us. "Four somethings, actually."

Travis looked then, seeing the newborn Brahman calves with their knobbly knees, big brown eyes and floppy ears. He watched them for a long second and a slow-spreadin' smile lit up his face. I knew he'd love them.

"Ernie's getting the poddy feeder from the back shed," I told him. "He'll show you how it works, how much to feed 'em, how often. We'll try and get surrogate cows for 'em, but it doesn't always work."

Trav nodded, still smiling. Then he walked over to me and prodded a still drinkin' Nugget lightly on the tummy. "At least these guys'll let me feed them," he said. "Not like you."

Completely oblivious to Travis's rant, Nugget didn't give one fuck. He just kept on taking his bottle. "He can't help it, Trav," I said low enough only he could hear. "He thinks I'm his mum. Or his dad. Or whatever."

Travis looked at me, rolled his eyes and sighed. "I'm not really pissed at him," he said with a soft smile.

Just then Ernie and Billy carried the poddy feeder around the side of the homestead, each holding one end. It was a long plastic frame with twenty teat slots. Trav's eyes widened. "What the hell?"

I snorted. "Feeding four by hand with bottles is fine, but feeding thirty at the same time will get you trampled," I told him. "We hook that on to the outside of the fence, the teats go on the inside of the yard for the calves, and viola! Instant poddy production line."

Once we got it all set up and installed the new teats, we got the formula mixed up and all the while, little Nugget dug in the dirt and got under my feet, almost tripping me a couple of times. I picked him up, again, and looked into his little blinking eyes. "What the hell am I supposed to do with you?"

Travis was in the holding yard with the calves. He grinned at me. "Maybe I could get you one of those baby papoose things that you strap on like a backpack, but it carries the baby at the front."

I stared at him with my mouth open. "Shut the fuck up."

Ernie and Billy both laughed, just as Nara called out from the front veranda that dinner was ready.

Walking inside, I put Nugget back in his bed box and went and got cleaned up. I helped Nara finish carrying everything to the table, and by the time I sat down, Travis had named the four calves.

John, Paul, George and Ringo.

And nope, he wasn't even kidding.

Laughter broke around the table, and there was the usual chatter during dinner, though Trudy was still quieter than normal. She ate well and even smiled a little, but something was wrong. I didn't want to say anything in front of anyone else, and then I wondered if her and Bacon were fighting, then I wondered if I wanted to know at all.

I didn't need more things to add that ever-growin' list of things to worry about.

After dinner when the others had gone and Travis was out checking on the Beatles, I called George. He said Ma was doing better every minute of the day. She was up and walking, assisted of course, but she tired easily. George said they were still waiting on results from more blood tests and ultrasounds, and he'd let me know if anything else went wrong.

The boxes we'd found in the roof of my childhood mementos were still in the lounge room, so I packed them on top of my filing cabinet in my office. I didn't want to think about any of that right now. I had enough to worry about. Instead, I re-tidied up the mess of papers in my office that got discarded last night during Travis's insistence on desk sex, smiling as I opened my emails.

Sitting nice and pretty in my inbox was the proposal and contract from Blake. I'd opened the contract and got as far as page three before I realised I hadn't understood a single fucking thing. Why did legal documents need to be written in old English. I'm pretty sure Shakespeare himself wrote this fucking thing. It was a hundred pages of I'm-too-dumb-to-read-this-shit legal jargon, which just added to my list of frustrations.

I closed the document and emailed it directly to our solicitor. I quickly explained the situation and how I wanted him to read through the pages of legal crap and to break it down into words I understood.

I just happened to look up when Nugget raced past my office door and then, ten seconds later, raced back.

Sighing, which was probably more of a groan, I followed him into the lounge room. He had his nose shoved under the sofa, so I grabbed him. "Oh no you're not," I said, picking him up. "You're not scratching the shit outta the furniture or the floor, you hear?"

He wriggled in my hold, scratching me on the stomach until I put him back down again. "Where is Rumble Bear?" I asked, more to myself because fuck knows wombats don't speak English.

The teddy bear wasn't anywhere. "Did you carry it somewhere?" I asked stupidly. I'd seen him pick it up in his mouth and move it around, but not from room to room.

I scouted the room, looking behind the door, in the hall, then I upended his bed. It wasn't there.

I heard the front door open, and knowing Travis would be in the hall taking his boots off, I called out, "Hey, Trav, have you seen Rumble Bear?"

He didn't answer.

"The stupid teddy bear he rumbles with," I explained. "Have you seen it?" Then it twigged. I remembered where Nugget was trying to burrow himself. So, getting down on all fours, I looked under the lounge, and lo and behold, there it was wedged in at the back.

"How the hell did you get him in there?" I asked. Nugget just twitched his nose in a what-a-stupid-question way.

I reached in and pulled the bear out, and then sitting back on my haunches, I said, "I think we're gonna need to Nugget-proof this house. He's worse than a bloody baby."

I looked up, expecting to see a smiling Travis in the

doorway. But it was Trudy. I'd been meaning to talk to her all day, but it had got away from me. She looked at me, at the wombat I was holding, then the teddy bear, and burst into tears.

CHAPTER ELEVEN

WHEN SECRETS AND BLOOD SPILL OUT

"TRUDY, WAIT!" I called, chasing after her. I passed a very surprised and shocked Bacon in the hall. I grabbed her arm, and immediately pulled my hand back, because I'm sure there are employer/employee rules about improper touching.

But there are no rules for friends, or sisters even, because that's what Trudy was to me. She was more a sister than an employee, a fact I hadn't realised until I saw her in tears.

Thankfully she stopped just near the kitchen doorway, and she groaned, a sound that was pure frustration. "Ugh. Fucking hormones," she said, running her hands over her face and up through her hair. "I'm sorry," she said. "Just forget it. I shouldn't have come here, sorry."

I'd never seen her cry. Not ever. I'd seen her angry, I'd seen her threaten to punch people, I'd even seen her laugh so hard she had to pee. But I ain't ever seen her cry. Hell, she didn't even cry when, three years ago, she broke two fingers when baling wire fought with gravity and she instinctively tried to stop it.

Now truthfully, I didn't have experience in the female mind. If movies and television shows were any kind of guide, I figured the emotions of hormonal women was like a cross between a kitten and a grizzly bear.

But this was Trudy, and havin' her standin' in my hallway clearly upset was different. And Bacon was just standing there looking more sad than helpful, giving me no clue as to what the problem was. So I stuffed the stupid teddy bear I was still holding in the same arm with Nugget, took Trudy's hand and led her into the kitchen.

She sat down, wiping her eyes on her sleeve, and shook her head. I sat down too, and with an almighty sigh, Bacon sat down as well. "You know the rules of the kitchen. Anyone is free to speak their mind," I said softly, looking between both of them. "Something's obviously wrong..." They wouldn't be here talkin' to me if it weren't.

I looked at Trudy, waiting for her to speak. But she didn't.

"Look, if you two need some time off, together or alone," I started. "You just have to say."

"Trudy's pregnant," Bacon said quietly.

Oh. *Oh.*

She glared at him and more tears started to fall. "I told you not to say anything," she snapped at him.

He shook his head and smiled sadly. "Trude, if you weren't gonna tell him, then what did you come here for?"

She shrugged. "I don't know."

I was still just sitting there blinking, like a rabbit in a spotlight.

And then the pieces all fit together. Bacon didn't want her climbing on the roof, she hadn't been eating much, she said she wasn't feeling well, the tears, the hormones.

I was such an idiot.

I should have seen it before now.

"I don't know," she said again, shaking her head. "I don't know what I'm doing. My head's all over the place, I can't think straight." She scrubbed at her face. "I guess I had to tell you. You're my boss, and you should know for medical reasons and all that."

I nodded, and I needed to think of something to say. I assumed because of the tears and tension between them that this news, this unexpected news, was not welcome. I had to tread carefully. "Um, I appreciate you telling me," I said. Then, because I'm a simpleton, I kept talking. "I have no idea about these things. I mean, I know how it all works —I'm not stupid, I'm just gay. And me and Trav don't have this problem, with the whole hormones and pregnancy thing. I mean, pregnant cows yes, but..."

Trudy's mouth fell open and Bacon looked at me like I was the village idiot. Which I was, apparently. "And I have this problem where, when I don't know what else to say, I say really stupid things and can't shut up. Like now." I swallowed hard. "Sorry."

Like I hadn't just spieled a torrent of nonsense, Trudy sighed. "I don't know what I'm going to do." She looked at me with such sad, sad eyes. "I don't know if I'm gonna keep it."

Bacon groaned and ran his hands through his hair, but he looked at me. "She doesn't want to get rid of it," he said, leaning forward and waving his hand toward Trudy. "She just thinks she doesn't have a choice."

Just then, Travis walked into the kitchen and stopped. "Oh. Sorry," he said, clearly surprised to find us in there. He started to back out. "I was just..."

I stood up. "Trav, can you take him?" I asked, handing over Nugget and his teddy.

Travis nodded quickly and took the little wombat without another word. When he'd gone, I looked over to Bacon. "Can you give me a minute with Trudy, please?"

He stood up, the chair scraping against the kitchen floor as he did, and walked out. If I had to pick one word to describe Bacon right now, it would be 'desperate'.

When it was just me and Trudy, I pulled my chair over to hers and took her hand. I had probably crossed a dozen employer/employee boundaries, but I didn't care.

"You're allowed to be scared," I whispered.

She nodded.

Then something occurred to me. "Are you worried about your job?" I asked.

Her eyes flashed to mine, and after a long second, she nodded again. "You can't afford to be payin' staff you don't have."

The fact that she was worried about that was ridiculous. And heartbreaking. "Trudy, listen to me. You have the right to paid leave and for your job to be held for you. That's the law," I told her. "But besides that, Trudy, you're a part of this Station. It's not just your job, it's your home."

I don't know if that was the right or wrong thing to say, because she started to cry again.

I squeezed her hand. "Now, if you don't want to keep this baby, then that's between you and Bacon. But remember, in the end, it's your choice. No one will hold it against you. Hell, no one else even has to know."

And there were more tears.

"You just need to know," I told her, "that whatever decision you make, you will have a job."

"Craig wants to keep it," she croaked out, wiping her nose on her shirtsleeve.

I kept forgetting Bacon's real name was Craig. It took me a second to catch on. "What do you want?"

She started to cry again, instant tears. "How can I be a mother?" she asked.

I blinked. "What do you mean?"

"Me?" she asked. "I'm not maternal. At all. The poor kid wouldn't stand a chance with me as a mother. I work cattle and horses. I can't cook. But I watch you feeding your baby wombat and it fucking kills me."

Oh.

"He's so little and he depends on you, and you just take it in stride," she said, wiping snot on her sleeve again. "I mean, you bitch and whinge about it, but you do it, and I don't think I could."

I wasn't quite sure what to say to that. "For what it's worth, Trudy, I think you'd make a great mum."

Well, that was the wrong thing to say apparently, because she stood up and walked to the sink. She was taking deep breaths, and just when I was about to apologise, she turned to face me. She held out her hands and started to cry again. "How can I be a mum? Look at my hands. Mothers don't have hands like this."

I stood up quickly and took both her hands in mine. Her hands were hard-working and callused, the knuckles on two fingers were flat and gnarled, her nails were cut short and dirty. But this wasn't about her hands. Not at all.

My voice was just a whisper. "A mother doesn't love with her hands, Trudy. She loves with her heart."

Trudy sobbed, and I did what felt right. I put my arms around her and hugged her as she cried. Whether Bacon heard my telepathic cries of what-the-hell-do-I-do-now, or he just heard her crying, I don't know. But he appeared in the doorway. I waved him over and he quickly took my place.

He wrapped his arms around his girl, and she held on to him and cried even harder. "I'm scared," she told him.

He kissed the top of her head. "I know."

I clapped my hand on his shoulder and mouthed, "You okay?" He nodded, so I mouthed, "Goodnight," and left them there, finding Travis in the bathroom. He leaned against the vanity and smiled at me, and he held his arms out. God, I almost fell into him with a sigh, leaning right into him. He put his arm around me and kissed the side of my head. "You're kind of amazing, you know that?"

I closed my eyes. "Did you hear all that?"

"Most of it." He rubbed my arm. "Bacon told me, just now, about the baby."

I sighed again, and pulling back a bit, I rubbed my forehead. "Fucking hell. My head feels like it's going to explode. Or cave in. One or the other."

Travis pulled me against him again and chuckled, the sound rumbling in my ear pressed against his chest. "You need a hot shower," he said. "It will help you unwind."

"What about them?" I whispered. I didn't have to tell him I was talking about Bacon and Trudy. "Maybe I should go check on them."

"They need some time to figure things out," he said. "And so do you." He let go of me, only to pull my shirt over my head and undo my jeans. Then he turned the water on in the shower. "You get in."

He was right. The hot water was heavenly on my shoulders and the muscles in my back. I didn't realise how tense I was. I quickly washed myself and was shutting the water off as Trav came back in.

"They're gone. Kitchen's empty," he said, pulling his

shirt off. I tied the towel around my waist, and when I glanced up, he was about to start the shower again, completely naked.

Normally I'd take my time looking over his body—the way his back moved, how the muscles in his forearms flexed and bulged, the broad lines of his shoulders—but my eyes drew straight to his hips.

Travis had bruises.

Purple lines marred the pale flesh across his hip bones: deep, blotchy, painful.

"Jesus, what's that from?" I asked, instinctively reaching out to touch them.

Travis snorted. "Like you can't guess."

I stared at him, not understanding. "What?"

"Your office," he said with a smile. "More specifically, your desk."

Oh sweet mother of God. When we'd had sex on my desk... He was bruised from where I'd slammed him into the edge of the desk. "I did that to you?" My voice squeaked.

"Well, rest assured I wouldn't be letting anyone else," he said with a laugh, turning to start the shower.

He thought they were funny.

I, on the other hand, did not.

I wasn't amused at all. I was fucking horrified.

"I am *so* sorry."

Travis rolled his eyes. "They're just bruises, Charlie. It's not like I have internal bleeding or anything."

"That's not funny."

He sighed his oh-for-fucks-sake sigh and, abandoning his attempts to start the shower, turned around to face me. I imagined he was counting to ten in his head before he spoke. "I'm fine, Charlie."

"I didn't mean to hurt you." The fact that I had done

exactly that made me feel sick. Maybe he was gonna argue the point with me, until he saw I was looking a little ill. I exhaled sharply and breathed out slow, trying to quell the nausea.

"Oh, Charlie." He put his hand to my face, then wrapped his long fingers around the back of my neck and pulled me against him. He kissed the side of my head. "You didn't hurt me."

I pulled back to look in his eyes, hopin' he'd see the sincerity in mine. "I am really sorry."

He smiled sadly at me. "I know you are. I know you didn't mean to, it was the desk, Charlie. Not you. You didn't do this deliberately. It was just the wrong angle or something. I certainly didn't feel it last night."

"I should have thought of that. I should have known it would cut into you."

He lifted my chin. "So next time we put a folded-up towel across it or something."

"Next time?" I shook my head.

He smiled and kissed me. "Hell yes, next time."

"Travis," I started. "There's no way—"

"It was the hottest thing we've ever done," he said with a smile. "Seriously, Charlie, they're just bruises. They don't hurt." Before I could argue further, he turned me around so I faced the mirror. He wiped the steam away, and standing behind me, he lifted my arm. "Look at those," he said.

He was looking at my side in the reflection, and when I followed his gaze, I saw what he saw: long red lines, scratches really, crisscrossed the skin under my arm and down my side and even across my stomach.

Oh.

I looked at where Nugget had scraped his way across my skin. I'd known I had scratches, but I hadn't really taken much notice. After a while, I didn't notice them at all. "He doesn't mean to scratch me."

"Of course he doesn't," Travis said. "It's just what happens, right?"

I could see the point he was trying to make. "It's not the same," I said.

"Well, not really, but it kind of is," he said. Then he kissed my shoulder. "What about all the times I've given you hickeys?" he asked. "I've put love bites on just about every inch of your skin."

"That's not the same," I said.

"It's exactly the same," he countered softly, kissing my shoulder again. "Love bites are bruises, and in the course of lovemaking, sometimes we get marked."

Resigned, I sighed. He turned me around, and with the gentlest of touches, he kissed my lips, my nose and my closed eyelids. I was too tired to argue. My head was spinning.

"Oh, Charlie," he whispered, kissing my cheek. "Go to bed. I'll be right in. I'll just take a real quick shower." He stepped back and gave his dick a squeeze. "A cold shower."

I snorted, too tired to even laugh. But I left him to shower alone. I put some boxers on, got into bed and closed my eyes, though my mind was racing. My mental list of shit to worry about was getting longer and longer. And now I worried for Trudy and Bacon.

It was their choice to make, it was their lives. Trudy was scared, and I didn't blame her one bit. It was a life-changing decision, whichever path Trudy decided to follow, and it certainly wasn't my place to say anything.

Travis slid into bed, all shower-warm and clean-smelling, and firmly pulled me against his chest. "You okay?" he asked in the darkened room. "I can feel it in your body how stressed you are."

"I hope they make the right decision," I said.

Travis was quiet for a long second. He knew who I was talking about. "I'm sure they will. Bacon wants her to have the baby, Charlie. He's worried he'll lose both of them. That's what he told me tonight."

All I could do was sigh. "I think Trudy does too. She's just scared."

"What do you want them to do?" he asked.

"I want them to be happy."

He tightened his hold on me. "What do you really want them to do?"

"I want them to have it. I want them to have the baby," I blurted out. Then, because we had a tellin'-the-truth-policy, I said, "But only if they want it one hundred percent without any doubt. Because if they don't, I don't want them to have it at all."

Travis was quiet, his body still. "What?"

"I know that sounds horrible. But I also know what it's like to not be wanted," I said quietly. "I know what it's like to have parents who walk away or who sent me away. I know what that's like, and no kid, whether they're four or even when they're eighteen, should know what *that* feels like."

Trav tightened his hold on me, his arms wrapped around me so completely. "Oh, Charlie."

I didn't say anything after that. Trav just pulled the blankets up around me and went right back to tight-holdin' me. I couldn't remember a time when he'd held me that close.

I fell asleep and only woke up when Travis shoved a

fussing wombat into my arms and said, "The little shit *still* won't let me feed him."

BOTH TRUDY and Bacon looked a little happier at breakfast. Well, they looked like they'd gotten some sleep at least. When I'd gone to the stables, she thanked me again on the quiet for last night, to which I said she was more than welcome. I told her to take as much time as she needed and to take it easy.

"I'm not handicapped," she replied, a bit snappish. "I can still work."

"I never said you couldn't. In fact, I insist that you do," I said. "It's what I'm payin' ya for, isn't it?"

"Sure is, boss." She smiled, like I'd hoped she would. I figured she just wanted me to treat her like I would any other day. So I did.

"Good." I led Shelby out of the stable. "Stables need mucking out, Ma's garden could do with some mulch, help with the poddy calves, or you can service the quad runner. We're not using it today," I told her as I tightened the girth on Shelby's saddle. "The others will be workin' on the roof again, so if they need a hand, give them one. But stay off ladders and no gettin' up on the roof."

Trudy rolled her eyes. "You sound like Bacon."

"Well, his concerns are different to mine," I said. "You've got a lot on your mind right now, and that leads to stupid mistakes. I'd prefer you not be five metres off the ground, okay?" I smiled at her. "I don't have time to be fillin' out all the worker's compensation forms if you were to fall."

She smiled now, knowin' full well what I really meant. But as she turned to leave, she stopped. "You know, same could be said for you." She looked like she'd said too much already, but must have figured in for a penny, in for a pound, because she kept on talking. "You've got a lot on your mind too, with Ma, and George not being here. All that meeting stuff with Greg, and now the buyer's contract. Not to mention your mother and a so-called brother, and now with me addin' to your worries."

I smiled. "You forgot to mention a uni degree I won't be able to finish and a certain wombat who keeps me on three-hour shifts." I gave Shelby a pat on the neck, scratched behind her ear, and let out a long sigh. "That's why I'm taking Shelby. I was gonna take the chopper, but Travis wouldn't let me. Said troubled minds often make aircraft fall outta the sky."

Trudy looked at me like I was pulling her leg. As if Travis had any say in what I, the boss of this station, could do.

"True as I stand here," I said. And it *was* the truth. Travis had done his I'm-being-serious eye-staring-thing along with his don't-fucking-argue jaw-bulging-thing, and I didn't have the fight in me. "He knows spending the day with Shelby helps clear my head," I said with a shrug. "So maybe if I can listen to him, maybe you can listen to Bacon and not go climbin' on the roof."

I lifted my foot into the stirrup and hauled my ass up into the saddle, giving Trudy a smile before pulling Shelby around and moving out. It wasn't like I could tell her that Trav had wanted to come with me but I'd said no. I'd reasoned that I needed him at home fixin' the roof and making sure everything ran smoothly. What I didn't say, though he saw straight through me, was that spending the day in the saddle would only aggravate his already bruised hips.

He took a deep breath, and pinching my chin between his thumb and finger and pushing me against the bathroom counter, he kissed me hard. "I said the bruises don't hurt."

I laughed because he knew me well enough to know what I wasn't saying, and then I groaned because he was pressing his dick against mine. Even through our jeans, the sensation made me buck into him.

He grinned wickedly. "I'll stay here today, but just so you know," he whispered gruffly, "tonight you're adding to those bruises. Either over your desk again or by your thumbs digging into my hips when I skull-fuck you."

Then he stepped back, and I almost fell forward, out of breath. I palmed the heavy ache in my dick, and he threw his head back and laughed as he walked down the hall.

"Ugh," I groaned, squeezing my hardening cock. "I'm gonna have this all damn day."

"That's why I did it," he replied, and I could even hear him laugh as he walked out the front door. He obviously didn't want to stay here while I rode out on horseback, but he would do it because I'd asked. He was just going to make me pay for it.

As I rounded the house on Shelby, heading out for the day, Travis was already on the roof of the homestead. He looked up and grinned when he saw me, so I glared at him, which just made him laugh some more.

With Ernie on a motorbike and Billy in the old ute, I spent the morning inspecting the herd of cows. After the winter muster, we'd sectioned off the pregnant cows into the closest western paddock. It made birthing easier come springtime. The paddock itself was still big—some thirty square kilometres—but there were only two bore-fed watering troughs so it basically localised the herd into two smaller areas.

I had said I'd be back around lunch time, but it didn't quite go to plan. We found three more abandoned calves, no older than a day or two. But there were also two cows whose calves hadn't survived, so the trip home was longer than I had anticipated.

We'd radioed the homestead and told them we were walking the calf-less cows home, so it would take twice as long to return. If nature would have it, these cows who lost their calves would be surrogates, but we'd need to keep a close eye on them.

It was mid-afternoon by the time I got back. I left Shelby's reins hanging over the fence, knowing she wouldn't go far, and I headed straight inside. Being three hours late, I knew that Nugget would think he was starving and would make everyone's life hell.

I raced inside and found Nara and Travis in the kitchen. Travis was holding a sound-asleep Nugget and there was an empty bottle on the table.

"You got him to feed?" I asked.

Trav grinned. "I didn't, Nara did. This is his second bottle since you've been gone. Nara fed him the first time, and I got to do it the second time."

I was stunned. Literally stunned and almost speechless. I looked at Nara and it took a second for my brain and mouth to kick into gear. "How?"

Nara smiled shyly. "I didn't know how long you'd be gone, and I had to do something—he was makin' me mental." Then she did a mix of frownin' and cringin'. "I thought maybe if he could just smell you, he'd eat, so I found your shirt in your bathroom. I checked the laundry first, but couldn't find nothin'. I didn't go into your room, I promise."

I hadn't even noticed the silly wombat was wrapped up,

all happy and smug, in a different-coloured pouch. It was the shirt I'd worn yesterday.

I don't know if she thought I'd be mad that she went into my bathroom—and truthfully, I didn't particularly like the idea of anyone but us goin' in there—but all I could do was smile.

"Nara, you don't need to apologise. It's a great idea!" I said, rubbing my finger on the little wombat's forehead. "Man, if I hadda known that's all it would've taken, I'd have done it weeks ago. Then Travis could help me do the night feeds."

"Pfft," he scoffed. "Not likely."

"You got up to him last night," I countered.

"Only because you didn't," he said. "But I couldn't get him to even look at the bottle." Travis stared down at the little sleeping baby wombat. "But now that he thinks I'm you..."

Travis just looked a dozen different shades of perfect sitting there with Nugget all cosy and sleepy in his arms. "So you don't hate him so much now that he'll let you feed him?" I asked, unable to stop the smile.

"I never hated him," he said defensively. "It's just that he... preferred you, and you were all caught up in him, and..."

Holy shit. "Trav, please tell me you weren't jealous of Nugget."

He narrowed his eyes at me. "No."

Oh my God. He so was. "Well, give him to me and then you can go sort out the other three poddy calves we bought back with us today."

"Three more?" Trav asked.

"And two cows. Hopefully they'll surrogate for one or two of the newborns."

Trav sighed and stood up, and reluctantly handed Nugget over like he was the most precious thing. I hadn't noticed Trudy behind me, and when I turned to see her, she was watching us. I know how it must have looked—with me and Trav treating the baby wombat like it was human—but that's not what it was.

Trav must have felt the same, because he lightly touched her shoulder as he walked out. I quickly put the bottle in the sink, and when I turned to face her, she smiled sadly. "You don't have to pretend," she said quietly.

Nara walked out of the dry-store pantry with ingredients to make dinner, so I nodded toward the hall and Trudy followed. I went into the lounge room and put the still sleeping wombat in his bed box. "I'm not pretending," I told her. "You mentioned before that it was hard to see me treating Nugget like an infant. That's not how I see him. I don't. He's more like a puppy. A boot-chewing, furniture-scratchin', pain-in-the-arse puppy."

Trudy smiled. "It's okay, Charlie," she said. "You don't have to try and justify anything. Nugget's cute. He *is* like a puppy."

"A pain-in-the-arse puppy," I corrected her.

Her smile faded as she sighed. "Just seems like everywhere I see babies. Baby wombat, baby calves, baby bottles for feeding. I know it's spring, but I guess I never took notice before. Now it's all I see."

"You've got a lot to think about," I said. I wasn't any good at these kinds of conversations.

"It's *all* I think about," she amended.

I wanted to ask if she'd made a decision, but not only was it not my place to ask such a personal question, I figured she'd tell me when she was ready. So instead, I said, "Take as long as you need. It's not an easy decision.

Just know that your job here is yours for as long as you want it."

She smiled a little easier this time. "Thanks. It helps to keep busy."

Then I remembered that she'd come into the house, probably to tell or ask me something. "Was there something you needed?" I asked.

"Oh," she said. "Yeah, just wanted to let you know I've done what you asked."

Geez. I think I gave her a list of five things to do. "Everything?"

"Stables are done, garden's done, I fed the calves once, Travis did the other feed, and I did a basic service on the quad runner: grease and oil change, cleaned the air filter and spark plugs."

I looked at my watch. It wasn't even three o'clock. I smiled at her. "And that is why I'd have you on my team any day of the week." I walked toward the door. "Come on, let's go see how these calves are going. Travis has already probably named them."

It turns out he had. He pointed to each individual calf as he told us, "Stills, Crosby and Nash."

Leaning my forearms on the fence, I put my head down and let out a good-lord-help-me sigh. "Are you serious?" I asked, finally looking up at him.

"I couldn't think of any other three-people bands," he answered simply.

"What about the Bee Gees?" Ernie asked.

Travis looked horrified. "Uh, no."

"What are you gonna do if we bring back ten calves tomorrow?" Bacon asked.

Travis was looking over the small Brahman calf, and he

looked up, confused. "Yeah well, I'll have to Google bands for that."

Not believing that this was actually a serious conversation, I put my head back down. Trudy patted my shoulder and laughed as she walked away.

———

TRAVIS DRAGGED me from my office when it was too-damn-tired o'clock. The house was quiet after dinner, where Travis's taste in music and subsequent calf-naming ability was still a topic of conversation. He reminded me that he'd made a promise of sorts this morning—that I could add to those hip-bruises tonight by taking him over the desk again or by holding onto him as he skull-fucked me, I believe was the term he used.

I refused the desk option point blank. So he sat me against the headboard of our bed, knelt over my chest, and holding my face in his two hands, he fucked my mouth.

I worked my fingers into his arse, and it wasn't long before his thrusts got quicker, his groans got lower and he shot into my throat. He slumped against me, heavy and pliable, squirming and chuckling, so I pulled him down onto the mattress. I clambered off, stood at the side of the bed, and pulled him by his legs over to me.

He was on his stomach, bent over the bed with his feet on the floor and his arse at the perfect height.

I poured lube down his crack and smeared it inside him with my fingers, stretching him even further, then slicked my length as well. Trav groaned and lifted his arse for me in a hurry-and-just-fucking-do-it-already kind of way. I leaned over him, pressed against where he wanted me most, and kissed his shoulder. "The bed's much softer," I murmured.

He gripped the bedcovers in his fists, his knuckles white. "Charlie, I swear to God, if you don't fuck me—"

His words stopped dead when I pushed into him, and he pressed his forehead against the bed as he moaned.

I eased the rest of the way into him, giving us both time to adjust, until he beg-beg-begged me to move, to just "hurry-up-and-fuck-me-please-please-Charlie", so I did.

I gave him everything he demanded, and when he pleaded with me to come deep-deep-deeper inside him, I gave him that too.

He was almost asleep before I'd finished cleaning him up, and when I pulled him against me, he snuggled right in. I dragged the covers over us and ran my fingers through his hair, and he mumbled something I didn't quite catch.

"What was that?"

He sighed contentedly and mumbled, "Just said that if I were a cat, I'd be purring right now."

I fell asleep smiling, until Travis pushed me out of bed to go feed Nugget. Just because he now *could* feed him, didn't mean—at 1am—he wanted to.

IT WAS THURSDAY, the day before Trav and I were going to head back to Alice to pick up Ma and George. I'd gone out again on Shelby, checking the herd. Calving season was relatively short. Normally the majority were born within a two-to-three week period, but not always. With a herd of pregnant cows approximately a thousand strong, there was always enough to keep us busy.

Travis and Bacon would finish re-sheeting the roof today, or so they said, so Ernie and Billy went on motorbikes, Trudy took the ute and I went on horseback.

The days were clear and warm, the breeze a bit cool, but springtime in the desert was my favourite season. Actually, I corrected myself, I loved all seasons out here. Whichever we were in at the time was my favourite. I made a mental note to take Trav and camp out for a few nights one of these days when things settled down and we weren't so busy.

But for now, with him fixing the roof and me spending the days out in the paddocks, the few hours of separation were a good thing. I wouldn't let complacency and taking shit for granted ever get between us again.

We found another two abandoned sick-but-still-alive calves, one already dead. But there were a good fifty-odd newborns with their mothers in the paddock, so even with the losses, the ratios were pretty good. So, because I was slower on Shelby than the others on bikes and the old ute, I told them to do a sweep up to the northern end of the paddock, figurin' I'd check the bore while I was there at the southern end.

I dismounted from Shelby to check the water trough first and, very stupidly, put my hand on the edge of the metal rim—like I had done hundreds of times—and sliced the palm of my hand.

The cut was on my right hand, in the crease on my palm from under my middle finger to under my little finger. It was about four centimetres long and about half a centimetre wide. It just kinda pulled right open, the skin went all white, and when it didn't bleed at first, I knew it was deep. It wasn't life-threatening, more of a pain in the arse than anything. I pulled the small first aid kit from my saddlebag, cursed at myself for being so stupid, shoved some cotton swabs over the now fast-bleeding cut and bandaged it the best I could.

Gettin' back on Shelby without using my right hand wasn't particularly easy, and by the time I had both feet in the stirrups, the blood was dripping off my hand.

Now, blood's never bothered me. God knows I'd seen enough of it—not always mine—to be immune to the sight and smell of it. I wasn't dizzy or anything, but bein' so far out and bein' alone, with the others already a good forty kilometres away and Ma's *Don't do anything stupid* ringin' in my head, I headed for home.

There was no point in busting Shelby for twenty kilometres to get home—I wasn't dyin' or anything—so I wasn't too surprised to see the Cruiser and bikes back in the yard already.

"Was gonna send out a search party," Billy called out with his usual grin as I rode in.

"Just enjoyin' the view," I said, swingin' my leg over and sliding down off Shelby, giving her a good pat on the neck. The truth was, despite the throb in my cut hand, those few hours alone out there in the desert with Shelby were the best head-clearin' hours I'd had in a long time.

As it turned out, they hadn't been home long, but they already had the two new calves in the yard tryin' to get 'em to feed. Bacon was with there with them, and when I looked over at the roof, I could see it was finished.

"Where's Travis?" I asked.

"He was finishin' something off in the shed," Bacon answered.

"What'dya do to ya hand?" Ernie asked, which, of course, made everyone look at my hand.

I held my palm upward, lookin' at the dirty, bloodied bandage. It had stopped bleeding some time ago, but my fingers, hand and arm were stained with old blood and so were my jeans where it had obviously dripped onto my thigh. I shrugged. "I thought I'd check out the water trough, and sliced it open. It's not that bad."

Billy looked at my hand and arm, then my bloodstained jeans, and he laughed. "Just a scratch, huh, boss?"

I smiled at him. "Yep."

They seemed to have everything under control, so I headed toward the shed in search of Travis. I led Shelby over to the stables first, taking off her saddle and bridle and giving her a scoop or two of her favourite oats before walking in to see Trav.

He glanced quickly over his shoulder. "Oh hey, gimme a lift with this?"

This was a large wooden frame, about a metre square and covered on all sides and the bottom with thick cardboard. "I used the packing boxes like you said I could," he said. We each took a side of the box, my left hand on the top, my right hand on the bottom, and lifted. "I made sure everything's packed into other boxes, though."

"Where are we taking it?" I asked. I was pretty sure it was a little playpen for Nugget, but Travis was running this show. I was just helping.

"Inside," he said. "The living room. That way he can't get into shit he shouldn't be gettin' into when we're not there."

It wasn't all that heavy, just awkward to carry, but we got it through the back door and into the lounge room, putting it under the window next to the TV. I hadn't even thought about the cut on my hand until I went to pick up Nugget's bed box and blood was again dripping down my fingers. "Shit," I mumbled, pulling my shirt under my hand so more blood didn't drip onto the floor.

"Jesus Christ, Charlie," Travis cried, his eyes wide and staring at my favoured hand. "What the hell did you do?"

"I cut it."

"No shit." He quickly pushed me into the hall, through the kitchen and over to the sink. He grabbed a tea towel and applied pressure to the cut with it. "Why didn't you say something?"

Nara was making bread at the table. "Oh, you okay, Mr Sutton?"

I sighed, hating to be fussed over. "I'm fine. It's just a cut," I told her, and then I looked at Travis, who was holding my hand to the point of pain and glaring at me. "I didn't mention it because I forgot about it, because it's just a cut."

He made a sound at me that was strictly more growl than huff. He pulled the cloth away, then shook his head at the bandage. It was now a dirty mess of horse sweat, dirt and blood. He unwrapped it slowly and gasped when he saw the actual cut.

I turned the tap on and stuck my hand under the cold stream of water, letting it flow over the open cut. I had to admit, it wasn't pretty. Not even a minute later, Nara had packed up her bread-making stuff and I was sitting at the kitchen table next to the big first aid kit, a bowl of water and some pine-smellin' bacterial wash. The bleeding had stopped again, but Travis had his serious face on. "How did you do it?"

"I put my hand on the edge of the water trough at the first bore," I told him. "I was gonna get in it and just make sure the pump was clear."

"The corrugated iron?" he asked. "When did you have your last tetanus shot?"

I had to think for a second. "Um, I can't remember."

"This needs stitches," he said. He inspected it closer

and grimaced. "And proper cleaning." He looked closer again. "There's *stuff* in it. It's kinda gross."

He was dabbing delicately around the wound like I was made of glass. "Seriously, Trav, I'll die of old age before you're done." I took the cotton swab and cleaned it myself. In the end, I just stuck my whole hand in the bowl of water, cleaned off as much dried blood and dirt as I could, and then just poured undiluted disinfectant over the cut. It looked better, but still too open to heal on its own. It had all but stopped bleeding, except for faint a few diluted red swirls in antiseptic.

Travis shook his head at me and my Outback way of gettin' things done. "You're covered in blood," he said, looking at my shirt and jeans.

I looked down at my clothes. "I've had worse." Then I nodded toward the medical kit. "Can you get the sewing needle?" I asked him.

Travis's eyes widened. "The what?"

"A needle," I repeated. "I'm sure Ma keeps it in a sterilised pack in there somewhere."

"What for?"

"Oh, I'm gonna knit some socks," I said, rolling my eyes. "What do you think I want a needle for?"

"Oh, hell no," he said. "You are *not* gonna sew yourself up."

"Well, no. I'm not. You are," I told him. "How's your sewing skills?"

He paled and shook his head. "Nope. Not... I can't even... just, no."

"Well, I can't. I mean, normally it'd be fine. I've done it before," I told him. "But that was in my leg, not my hand."

He frowned and swallowed hard. "I'm sure we could call the doctor for stitches? Or take you into town."

"All that way just for a few stitches?" I asked. "Hell no. And Doctor Hammond would bust something laughing if you called him for stitches... Actually, you should call him, but put him on speakerphone. I wanna hear him laugh."

"You're not funny."

I rolled my eyes again. "The needle, Trav," I repeated. "I need it. It looks like a fishing hook and real thin fishing line."

He found the needle and screwed up his face.

I held out my hand for him to sew me up.

He looked horrified. "There is no way—*no way*—I can do that."

"Trav, it's my right hand. I can't do anything with my left hand."

He was just staring at my injured hand and missed the opportunity for the best wanking joke ever.

I sighed. "Well, can you at least thread it for me?"

Trudy huffed into the kitchen. "Oh, for fuck's sake. You two are like two old women." She snatched up the needle and threaded it easily. Then without another word, she sat herself down, grabbed my hand, and putting the point of the needle right next to the cut with a familiar precision, she pierced my skin.

Travis winced the whole time like she was doing it to him, whereas I looked on, studying Trudy's sewing skills. "I thought you hated needles?" Travis asked.

"I do."

"But not getting stitches. With a needle. With*out* anaesthetic?"

I shrugged one shoulder. "Different kind of needle."

Travis shook his head. "Not really."

"It's totally different," I argued. "One closes cuts and wounds, the other drains blood out or injects stuff in."

"They're both pointy, metal and go into your skin."

I hadn't even noticed the pulling on my hand had stopped. When I looked at Trudy, she was staring at us. "Are you two done? Do you argue like this all the time?"

"We're not arguing," we answered in unison.

She must have found something funny, because she smiled.

I looked at my newly sewn palm, and Trudy gently pulled my fingers down, touching lightly around the wound and inspecting her handiwork.

"You've got the hands of a surgeon," I said, since I knew her callused, hard-working hands bothered her.

From her smile, I could tell she understood the reference. "Yeah," she snorted. "With my brains, it was a real toss-up for career choices: surgeon or muckin' out stables."

I laughed. "And here you get to do both."

Smiling, she looked again at my hand. "Try to keep it clean and dry." She stood up and walked out without another word.

"Thanks, Trudy," I called out.

"No problem" came her reply followed by the sound of front screen door closing behind her.

Travis was studying my hand. "Well, we're going to the hospital tomorrow. They can have a look at it, and you'll need another tetanus shot."

"I don't need a tetanus shot."

He raised one are-you-serious eyebrow. "Well, you cut your hand on a rusty piece of metal, so you're getting one."

"Is that your I'm-being-serious voice?" I asked.

Trav exhaled slowly. "You scared the crap outta me with all that blood," he said. "I thought something bad had happened to you."

I held up my hand. "Something bad did happen."

"I meant something *really* bad."

"If it was really bad, I'd have radioed for someone to come get me."

Trav kept staring at my hand and frowned. "And you were on Shelby. You should've been on a bike or something."

I put my good hand on his knee. "Trav, it wasn't a big deal. And anyway, a horse will always bring you home or come home without you. Like how Shelby did with you that time. If you'd been on a motorbike, we wouldn't have known you were missing 'til later." Then I remembered, "Oh, I'll need to brush her down too. I didn't get back to do it."

"I'll do it," Trav said quietly.

"I can do it. I have a perfectly capable left hand," I told him.

The corner of his mouth lifted in a sly smile. "Had a lot of practice with it, huh?"

I snorted. "If you hold it in your left hand, back to front, it looks like someone else is holding it."

Travis burst out laughing just as Nara came back in. Thank God she hadn't heard what I'd just said. Trav patted my leg and we both stood up. He packed up the first aid kit and said, "I'll go out and make sure Shelby's settled in. I'll brush her down."

"I'll go check on Nugget," I said, walking up the hall.

"Shouldn't you be studying or something?" Trav said.

I stopped and turned to face him. "Well," I started, knowing this probably wasn't going to be well received. "I spent some time thinkin' about that when I was riding back on Shelby."

From the look on his face, I think he already knew. But he asked anyway. "And?"

"I'm not gonna finish it," I told him. "I won't be getting my degree."

CHAPTER TWELVE

SOUNDS LIKE HOME TO ME

THE DRIVE into Alice was kinda quiet. We left at six, after the dogs and horses were fed, breakfast was done and everyone had their jobs for the day. Everyone was excited, myself included.

Ma was coming home today.

Driving with my cut hand was too awkward, so Travis was behind the wheel, which I knew he hated, but he didn't argue. Not once. He never once bitched about what side of the car he was sitting on, what side of the road he was driving on. It was so unlike him.

He'd been a little quiet since I'd told him I wouldn't be finishing my uni degree. He'd said he understood—I was just too busy, and he reasoned that of all the things I was dealing with, if one had to go, then it was the sensible choice.

He'd *said* he understood. But his silence told me otherwise.

So, with a three-hour trip ahead of us and our new rule of talkin' shit through, I started the conversation. "You wanna tell me what's bothering you?"

Trav glanced from the road, to me, and back to the road. "Nothing really."

I snorted. "You can't lie for shit. And, I might add, was it not you who insisted on the complete-disclosure rule?"

"Complete disclosure?"

"Yeah. You know, talking about stuff. I mean, if I can do it, anyone can. There is still shit I'd prefer not to say out loud, but I do. Because you told me I had to. We have a complete-honesty thing happening, do we not?"

He smiled at me. "We do. And what shit do you say out loud that you'd prefer not to?"

I shrugged. "Most everything."

He laughed. "Well, you're getting very good at it. For someone who just twelve months ago didn't speak to anyone about anything—unless it was work related—I think you're doing pretty good."

"I tell you everything."

He smiled at me. "And I am very grateful."

"So tell me what's bothering you."

Trav sighed. "I just... I just feel like I pushed you into finishing your degree."

"You did," I said. He quickly turned his head to look at me. I laughed at his expression. "You re-enrolled me without telling me. That's not pushing me to finish it, that's throwing me right in."

He seemed stuck for words for a second. "I did, didn't I? I'm really sorry, Charlie. I hate knowing that I made things worse for you."

"*Worse* for me?" I scoffed. "Trav, you're the *best* thing that ever happened to me. Ever."

He smiled at me this time, almost shyly. "You're the best thing that ever happened to me too, Charlie." Then, because he's a funny bastard, he added, "Ever."

"Shut up," I grumbled.

"Will you reconsider?" he asked. "I mean, I know I pushed you into it and all, but don't just quit. I'll help you do it, or something. I'd just hate to see you throw it away when you're so close to being done."

When I didn't say anything, he added, "Just think about it. Don't tell them you're quitting and if by the end of it we didn't get it finished, then you can defer. But don't quit."

"You just said you were sorry for pushing me into starting it," I reminded him. "Now you're pushing me into finishing it. Just how sorry were you?"

He shrugged. "Well, obviously not *that* sorry."

God, he made me laugh. Then, doing what he normally does to me, I leaned against him and pulled his arm over my chest so I was kinda tucked in against him, put my feet up on the window and pulled my hat over my eyes. "Just shut up and drive."

It was about twenty minutes later that Travis said, "Um, Charlie?"

"Hmm," I mumbled.

"Uh, this is a pickup."

"Well, we call 'em a ute," I said. "We've been through this already. But yes, this is a pickup or a ute, whatever. Great observation, by the way. You should be a cop or something."

His arm was still across my chest, and he tried to stick his fingers in my sides. "Don't be a smartass."

I laughed, but kept his hand in mine. A little warm-hand-holdin' felt kinda nice. "What's your point?"

"Well, we're going to pick up George and Ma! There's just two seats! How are we all supposed to fit?"

I snorted out a laugh. "And you just thought of that

now?" I asked. "I take back my comment about you bein' a cop, Trav."

"What the hell are we gonna do?"

"Well, I got to thinkin' about that when I was riding Shelby home yesterday too."

"I'm starting to think you bein' out there alone with too much thinkin' time is a bad idea."

WE PULLED the old ute up at the front of the car dealership and got out. "I can't believe you're just gonna buy a new car!" Trav said, shaking his head. "Just on a whim. Most people buy shirts or a burger on a whim, not a car."

"Well, it's not technically a car," I corrected him. "It's a new Cruiser." I pointed to the rows of new seven-seaters and started to walk toward them. "And it's hardly a whim. We haven't bought a new vehicle in years. It's long overdue. And I don't want Ma travellin' home for three hours in a bumpy old ute."

He didn't argue after that.

In fact, he got a bit excited about it. I mean, it wasn't something we did every day, so checking out and sitting in a bunch of different models of SUVs, as Trav called them, was fun.

I popped the hood on one and shook my head. "What's wrong?" Trav asked.

"No engine should be this clean," I told him. "It just ain't right."

He laughed at that. "And the inside is all leather, very clean. Dunno how long it'll stay that way."

"It'll be your job to clean it," I told him.

"Oh, whatever," he scoffed. "I'm pretty sure the job clause said boyfriend, not slave."

"Job clause?" I asked. "Is that all I am to you?"

Travis laughed, and someone behind cleared their throat. When we turned around, the salesman was behind us. He was about forty, wearing a suit, and although he tried to smile, he looked less than pleased with us. At first, I figured all he saw the twenty-year-old ute out the front and us in worn jeans, dirty boots and old hats. But then I realised from the contempt on his face, it wasn't how we looked; he'd heard our conversation.

"Can I help you gentlemen?" he asked.

Trav spoke first. "Well, I was hoping for something with the steering wheel on the left-hand side of the vehicle," he said, his accent thick. "Got anything on the lot like that?"

The salesman was thrown for a minute. "Uh, no."

I chuckled, and careful of my bandaged hand, I lowered the bonnet of the Cruiser and pushed it shut until it clicked. Trying to lighten the mood, I added, "And then he just needs to change the law to make us all drive on the other side of the road, ain't that right, Trav?"

He laughed and opened the passenger door and climbed into the new car. "Yep. That's next on my agenda. Right before I abolish words like ute and fair dinkum."

I cracked up laughing, then turned back to the salesman. He wasn't smiling. Ignoring his blatantly poor service skills, I said, "Tell me, what's the warranty like on these."

His answer was short and clipped. "Four years."

Taking a deep breath, I climbed in behind the wheel and shut the door so the salesman couldn't hear me. Trav frowned. "What's his problem?"

"Don't think he liked our conversation about being boyfriends."

Travis glanced quickly back at him, and he frowned. "He's lookin' at us like we're dirty."

"Don't worry about him," I said, taking his hand over the console, not giving a fuck if the guy could see us or not. "You like this one?" I asked. "Colour? Interior? It's like Doctor Hammond's."

He nodded. "It's very nice."

"Okay. That was easy," I said, opening the door and getting back out. I smiled at the salesman. "I wanna buy one of these."

The man smiled in a sure-you-do kind of way. "Well, this a ninety-five-thousand-dollar vehicle."

I looked at the smug fucker and glared for good measure. "You know, I actually can read." I pointed to the price in the front windscreen. "What? Is there an age criteria? Are we too young? Not dressed fancy enough for ya? Oh wait, let me guess. Too gay for ya?"

He tried to laugh it off, but he swallowed like something tasted foul in his mouth. "What in particular are you looking for?"

"What am I looking for?" I asked. "Your boss, actually."

He blinked. "What?"

"You asked what I wanted, and what I want is to see your boss."

He swallowed hard. Twice. "Oh, uh, well, I don't know if he's in right now."

"Well, let's go inside and find out," I said. Then I sneered at him, because fuck this guy and fuck his attitude. "Come on, Trav," I said, looking back at a wide-eyed Travis, and nodded toward the showroom.

Of course the boss was in. I walked right up to the counter and asked to see the owner. Not the manager, not the supervisor. The *owner*. The receptionist took one look at the now flailing, sweating, pulling-at-his-tie salesman and said, "Just a moment."

So I waited, just a moment.

Another man walked out, taller, business shirt on, sleeves rolled to his elbows, no tie. He was probably sixty years old, with short grey hair and soft, pen-pushing hands. He looked concerned. "Can I help you?" he asked. "Is there a problem?"

"I want a four-point-eight litre fuel-injected, turbo diesel GXL Cruiser. That blue one out there, specifically," I said, nodding to the one we just got out of. "I want roof racks, a towbar, extended warranty, I want it registered, and I want it ready in an hour."

The owner blinked, twice. "Right. I'm sure we can arrange that," he said, clearly confused as to why I was talking to him and not the salesman who was still just a few metres away.

"I'm going to be honest with you...?" I trailed off, waiting for him to say his name.

"David. David Campbell."

"I'm going to be honest with you, David," I started again. "Your sales staff could do with some work on customer service. Now, given you're the only Toyota dealer in town—and I want a Land Cruiser—my options are quite limited and I'm short on time. Though I'm not opposed to flying to Darwin, and spending a hundred grand in someone else's car yard. And I reckon I could *still* drive back here before your homophobic piece-of-shit salesman has shut his fucking mouth."

We turned to look at the sales guy, whose name I still did not know. He looked like he had a fishbone stuck in his throat. The owner, David, blinked again, but the look he shot at his employee told me he wasn't happy. "Not a problem, Mr…"

"Sutton. Please call me Charlie."

He turned to the receptionist, who was standing there staring with wide eyes. "Can you start the purchase papers please?" Then David looked at me. "Will you need finance for the vehicle? It might take more than an hour, that's all."

"No, no finance. I have the cash," I said. "I can write out a cheque or call the bank and get them to transfer it."

David smiled, almost relieved, and I turned around to give the salesman one last fuck-you smile. It didn't look like he was having any luck with that fishbone.

David spoke again to the lady at the counter. "Call through to the boys out the back, tell them to take the blue Cruiser off the floor, fit roof racks and a towbar." He looked at me and Trav. "Please, come to my office."

I signed all the necessary paperwork and wrote out a cheque on the spot. He had to call the bank to get it cleared first, which took all of five minutes. He asked for my business banker, spoke to him directly, said my name, the amount in question, nodded twice, hung up the phone and smiled.

And that is how this Charlie Sutton, just like my father, got things done.

We did have to wait for the extras to be put on to the vehicle, which was fine. I told David we'd wait outside, the spring sun was too good to miss.

I leaned against our old ute, and Trav eyed me cautiously. "You okay?"

"Yeah, apart from being ninety-five-thousand dollars lighter."

"No, I meant from that other guy."

I smiled. I knew what he meant. "Yeah."

"You were a little scary back there," he said, shaking his head.

"Scary?" I asked. "Far from scary. But I ain't ashamed of who I am, Trav. Not anymore. Anyways, it's easier to be layin' down the law when I'm holding the money. That wasn't really a shot at that arsehole bein' homophobic, that was more me bein' pissed off with his shitty customer service." I shrugged. "And nobody treats you like that."

"What? Like a 'nobody puts baby in the corner' type of thing."

I had no clue what that meant. "Huh?"

He smiled and shook his head. "Never mind."

It was literally one hour almost to the second when some guy in overalls drove the brand-new Land Cruiser out and handed the keys to David. He gave them straight to me. I held up my bandaged hand. "Sorry I can't shake your hand," I said.

"No problem," he said, opting to shake Travis's instead. "I'm sorry your experience with us wasn't one hundred percent perfect. I've included a full tank of fuel at no extra cost."

After we'd waved him off, I threw the keys to the brand-new Cruiser to Trav. "You can drive it."

He looked at me like I'd just sprouted a second head. "Oh, hell no. I am not."

I held up my injured hand. "I can't drive. Well," I amended, "I will drive the old ute, because if I run into something or sideswipe somethin', I'd prefer it not to be the new car."

He looked horrified. "What if I run into something?"

I snorted. "You won't."

He shook his head, almost violently. "Uh-uh."

"Come on, George and Ma will be wonderin' where we

got to," I said, looking at my watch, seeing it was just after ten. "The doc was gonna come see her around now and discharge her. You can follow me to the hospital."

I didn't give him time to argue, I just walked around to the driver's side of the old ute and got in.

He followed me and spoke through the open window as he walked past. "Just so you know, I hate you right now."

I turned the key and the old ute rumbled to life, loud and rattling. I grinned at Trav and shook my head. "No you don't."

I watched as he stalked off looking like he was mumbling the whole way. He followed me to the hospital and was still mumbling at me when we met in the hospital car park. He threw the key to me, making me catch it with my left hand. "How was it?" I asked.

"Horrible," he said, still pouting. Then he rolled his eyes. "And beautiful."

I laughed. "You're welcome."

"I was terrified I was gonna dent it or something." He pushed me toward the hospital. "Now come on, Ma's been waiting a week."

And wow, what a difference a week meant.

She looked so much better. Gone was the pallid skin and the dark circles under her eyes. Her cheeks had colour, her eyes had shine and she smiled so hard when we walked in.

"Look at you!" I said, kissing her cheek.

She was sitting on the edge of the bed, dressed and ready to go. She gave me a hug. "Oh, Charlie, I've missed you," she said. "And you, Travis," she added.

He leant in and gave her a kiss. "Jeez, Ma. You look great. You need a week in the hospital more often."

She snorted. "Not likely." Then she noticed my hand. "What did you do?"

"I cut it," I told her. "It's no big deal. Where's George?"

"He went looking for the doctor. He's just about gone crazy in here," she said. "Show me your hand."

I rolled my eyes and held my palm out. The bandage was now blood stained. "I bumped it when I was driving in just now," I explained. "Trudy sewed it up for me yesterday."

Ma was frowning already.

"You're not allowed to worry," I told her. "I'm sure the doctor said you weren't to be stressin' over nothin'."

"He needs a tetanus shot," Travis said, throwing me right under the fucking bus.

"Oh, thanks a lot," I griped at him.

He grinned. "You're welcome."

"Is that payback or something?" I asked.

"Yep," he said, still grinning.

I narrowed my eyes at him, but Ma intervened. "Boys, stop that," she chided us.

I found myself smiling at her. "Never thought I'd miss the sound of that," I admitted.

Ma smiled right back at me in a knowing moment; she'd missed scolding us just as much. "So," she said. "Where's your little wombat? Didn't bring him today?"

"Trav built him a little pen to stop him from runnin' amok through the house, and Nara found a way to feed him without me bein' there," I told her. "So he stayed at home."

"Cows calving yet?" she asked. "How many poddies are we minding so far?"

"Enough of the work interrogation, Ma," I snorted. "You still need to rest you know."

From the look on her face, I knew she was about to

reprimand me again, until George and the doctor came into the room.

George never looked happier to see me. "Oh, Charlie, Travis," he said, "boy, is it good to see you two."

"Likewise," I said with a smile. "Good timing. Ma was just about to give me a lecture."

George grinned at that. Like me, he knew that Ma's temper and quick tongue-lashings were a sign of her improved health. "The doc here wants to just give one last check over, then we can go," he said.

Taking that as a cue for privacy, I walked to the door, expecting Travis to come with me, but he stopped. "Doc?" Travis asked. "Where can we get a tetanus shot?"

I groaned. "I don't need one."

Trav didn't even look at me. He just kept his eyes on the doctor. "Yes, he does."

The doctor stuck his head out the door, called for a nurse and asked her to take me down to see some doctor in the A&E and get it looked at. Like she probably didn't already have enough to do. She smiled at me nonetheless, and we followed her out.

We came into the emergency department through the hospital and not through admissions, and I guess the nurse asking for some specific doctor made it all happen quicker, because within five minutes, I was sitting on a gurney bed and some guy built like a brick shit house who looked too damn big to be a doctor had the bandage off my hand and was poking and prodding at the stitches in my palm.

"Do you have a pain kink or something?" I asked him. "Because that hurts, and you look like you're enjoying it."

He laughed at me, and I knew I was right. Yep, definitely a pain kink. "I'm not surprised that hurts. It's jagged as hell, stitches are rough."

"I won't tell Trudy you said that," I said. "She'll come in here and kick your arse."

He snorted. "Well, on that note, you can tell *Trudy* that her tapestry skills are stellar."

I nodded. "You're gonna give me a needle, aren't you?"

He grinned. "Yep, sure am. You don't like hospitals, do you?"

I shook my head quickly. "Hospitals are okay. Needles not so much."

Travis sighed his all-outta-patience sigh. "Seriously?" he said to the doctor. "He wanted to sew his own hand yesterday, but he had one of his workers do it for him, no anaesthetic, no nothing. He didn't even flinch. He wrestles Brahman, does death manoeuvres in a helicopter, for God's sake, but mention a needle and he whines like an infant."

The doctor laughed again. "Sounds familiar." But then he held up the needle and said, "You might wanna look away, son."

But it was too late. Because I'd seen it. Blood started to pound in my ears, and I might have swayed a little. "Jesus," Trav said, jumping in and pulling my face against his chest. "You *really* don't like needles." I think he laughed.

"Told you I don't," I mumbled into his shirt.

The doctor jabbed my arm, and I could feel the hot swell under the skin as he pushed the liquid in. Trav ran his fingers through my hair, a much-needed distraction.

"All done," the doctor said.

I looked at him, and thankfully, he had the needle out of sight. I felt stupid for being a grown man who powdered and wanted to puke when he saw a needle.

Trav pulled my chin up. "You feelin' okay? Not gonna fall in a heap if I let go?"

"I'm okay," I said, trying to shake off the fuzzy feeling in my head.

The doc had a baffled, amused look on his face. I guess he wasn't expecting two guys to be so touchy-feely. Just then, a familiar face appeared at the door. It was Laura. She was dressed in her nursing gear, and she acknowledged the doctor with a nod.

"Heard you were down here," she said to me. "I've just been up to see Katie and George before they left, and they said you were getting your hand looked at." She walked into the cubicle. "You're looking a little pale. You feel okay?"

"I'm fine," I replied.

The doc swung his chair around and took my hand, inspecting the cut again. "You want me to redo those stitches?"

I shrugged. "Um..."

"I'll need to give you a local—"

I cut him off. "Nah, it'll be alright."

"I'm going to clean it, though. Might sting a bit," he said.

The doc set about his work on my hand, and Trav still stood near the bed and kept his hand on my knee. I know he had an issue with Laura, but I dunno... it was kind of good to see her.

"How's things?" I asked her.

Her smile was instant. "Good. Been busy here, but I like Alice Springs. Always did."

"Not a fan of Darwin?" I asked.

"Well, it's been my home for twenty years, so I'm almost considered a local," she said with a grin. "But yes, I grew to love it."

"You married again?"

She nodded. "Yes, I married Steve when Sam was six. He's been a great father to him."

"He's lucky," I said, then winced at how that may have come across to her. "I didn't mean that how it sounded."

She smiled, but there was sadness in her eyes. "I know."

The doc released my hand and declared his work done. He put some fancy bandaid on it that covered my entire palm, gave me a prescription for infection and went on to his next patient.

Laura nodded toward the door. "I'll walk up with you," she said, and the three of us headed back to the elevators to go find Ma. "Sam still wants to meet you," she said once the elevator doors closed. "He said he can fly down, but I told him it has to be okay with you. I know it's a shock for him too, but I've asked him to do this on your terms. He said he understood."

Travis was right behind me, and I could feel the tension ease when Laura said that. I knew his concerns with Laura were about how her sudden reappearance in my life affected me, so her saying this all had to be on my terms was obviously a relief to him.

He put his hand on my back. "You feeling better?"

Whether he was asking if I felt better after the whole needle thing or because of what Laura just said, I wasn't sure. But I answered both. "Much."

The elevator doors opened, and as we walked to Ma's room, I asked Laura if she'd talked to Ma much this last week.

"Every day," she said. "She's doing so much better." Then Laura stopped walking. "Before we go in there"—she nodded to Ma's room—"Charlie, you need to know that I understand."

"Understand what?"

"That Ma is your mother," she whispered. She looked sad, but there was a peacefulness in her eyes. "You said she was your mum, and you were right. I get that, and I'm not pretending anything otherwise."

"I'm not pretending either." I shrugged. "She is the only mother I've known. I'm sorry if that's hard to hear, but it's the truth."

"She's a wonderful person," Laura said, getting teary. "And I thank God for her."

I put my hand on her arm. I didn't want to see her cry. "So do I."

She blinked back her tears and smiled. "Let me know when you're ready to meet Sam, and we'll organise it, okay?" She let out a shaky breath, her eyes scanning my face. "You're so much alike."

George walked out of the room, pushing Ma in a wheel-chair. Her doctor came out with them. "There you two are," Ma said. "I was starting to think you got lost. How's your hand?"

I held it up and showed her. "I'll live."

"Good to know. Come on," Ma said, trying to push the wheels on the chair herself. "I've been waiting a week to leave. Even if I have to go out in this stupid chair."

"Wait," I said. "I have a surprise for you." I'd almost forgotten about what Trav and I did this morning. I fished the keys to the new Cruiser out of my pocket and handed it straight to George. "This is for you." Then I corrected, "Well, it's not *yours*, it's *ours*." I waved my hand between all of us. "It belongs to the Station."

George looked at the black key with the Toyota symbol on it, then looked at me. I think I'd shocked him into silence. "Charlie..."

I smiled at him. "Couldn't have Ma goin' home in the old ute. Just wouldn't have it."

Ma, still in the wheelchair, looked up at me. "Charlie, what did you do?"

I smiled at her. "Your new chariot awaits."

Her eyes narrowed, her words short and sharp. "What did you do?"

"Something I should have done a long time ago." I shrugged and leaned down and kissed her cheek. "Now quit your moaning. I thought you wanted to leave."

"Charles Sutton," Ma said, starting to full-name me.

I put my hand up and stopped her. "Trav and I will call into the supermarket and the co-op before we go home. Did you need anything?"

Ma raised one who-the-hell-do-you-think-you-are eyebrow at me. "Don't think you're gonna be fussin' all over me when we get home. I feel just fine."

Her doctor smiled at us. "She needs bed rest. Walking is fine, but she's not to drive or lift anything, and I want to see her again in four weeks."

Ma started grumbling, and George wheeled her off before she started swearing. The doctor sighed. "Well, she's a lot livelier now."

We could still hear her mumblin' at George as they got into the elevator. Travis laughed, and even Laura was smiling. I grinned at the doctor. "That sounds like home to me."

CHAPTER THIRTEEN

WHEN EVERYTHING IS TOO PERFECT, YOU JUST KNOW IT'S GONNA GO TO SHIT.

GROCERY SHOPPING with Travis was uneventful this time. Well, until we got to the car park. There was no little old lady in aisle seven wanting to perform an exorcism on him, thank God. He carried most things because of the stupid cut on my hand, and when we were loading the bags into the back of the ute, I'd put my hand on his shoulder.

That's all. Just a simple touch. Not an intimate touch, not a term of endearment, not an embrace, just a touch.

Jokingly, I'd asked him if he wanted to go take his boots and socks off in the grass again, and he'd laughed and asked if I'd like to get another needle so he could let me face plant off the bed this time, and I'd touched his shoulder.

I'd been so complacent and so caught up in my I-don't-give-a-fuck attitude toward people who had an issue with me being gay that I just didn't even think.

But there were six kids, maybe fourteen or fifteen years old, in the car park who thought it was funny to call out words like 'fag' and 'queer cock-suckers'. My first reaction was to turn around and face them. I wanted to give them a lesson in manners, but then I stopped.

Sure, they were only young, but even teenagers these days were near six foot tall. And we were outnumbered. Would I risk Travis getting hurt? Hell no. And for what? I didn't give a shit what those kids thought.

What I cared about was Travis.

The group of profanity-yellin' kids started to walk over to us.

"Just get in the car," I said quietly, opening my door.

Trav climbed in behind the wheel, and we were gone before they were really anywhere near us. I mean, we weren't threatened in any way, but Trav looked worried. "You okay?" I asked him. "They were just stupid kids."

"Yeah, I'm okay," he said, running his hand through his hair and exhaling through puffed cheeks. He was quiet until we called into the co-op and picked up our order of horse feed and chicken feed, and even then he didn't say much. We filled the ute with fuel and we were headed home on the familiar Plenty Highway before he said what was on his mind.

He had that thinkin' line between his eyebrows and was chewing his bottom lip.

"I'm sorry that happened," he said.

"What? What the hell are you apologising for?" I couldn't believe he said sorry.

Travis shrugged. "You're just getting used to being out, and you've been tellin' people if they don't like it, they can get stuffed, basically."

"Yeah. So?"

"Well, that was different." Travis grimaced like he wasn't getting the words right.

"It *was* different," I agreed.

"*You* were different."

"Me?"

He nodded. "Yeah. With Brian at the co-op, you told him you'd take your business somewhere else, and today buyin' the new SUV, well, that sales guy only had to look at you wrong and you ripped him a new one."

"Exactly."

"And you told his boss you'd fly to Darwin to buy a Cruiser from somewhere else if you had to because of his homophobic piece-of-shit staff."

I snorted. "I really wasn't gonna fly to Darwin."

He rolled his eyes. "I knew that, but he didn't."

"It's different when I'm holding the money, Trav," I explained. "It's different with them because it involves a lot of money. I have it, they want it. That's why I can stand my ground about it and tell 'em gay money is still money, Trav. If they're gonna be homophobic assholes, I will take my business somewhere else. Pure and simple." I sighed. "But those kids in the car park were different."

He didn't have to say he didn't really agree with me. His frown said it all.

"I wasn't about to risk you gettin' hurt," I admitted. "If they wanted a fight, I reckon I probably coulda taken out two or three of them, but if other people joined in, or if they had a knife or something..." I shook my head. "Isn't there some country song about knowin' when to walk away and knowin' when to run?"

He finally smiled. And so God help me, he started to sing. "You gotta know when to hold 'em, know when to fold 'em—"

I held up my injured hand in the universal sign for please-fucking-stop. But of course he didn't. He just laughed and sang the whole damn song. Twice. The only way I could get him to stop was to sing along—louder than him.

Only after he'd laughed himself out of singing, I leaned myself against him with my feet up on the window, lifted his arm over my shoulder so it lay across my chest and I closed my eyes. "Trav?"

"Yeah?"

"You can't sing for shit."

"Neither can you."

"Trav?"

"Yeah?"

"Don't quit your day job."

He snorted. "I can't," he said. "I'm kind of in love with my boss."

I chuckled and kissed the inside of his arm where it hung over my shoulder and alongside my face. "Is he a good sort?"

"I think so. Others might not agree."

I snorted. "I'm sure they wouldn't. But anyway, I hear your boss is taken."

"Is that right?" he played along.

"Yep. Some American guy, or so I hear." I sighed dramatically. "Smart, hot, the sexiest forearms you've ever seen."

Travis laughed. "Sexy forearms, huh?"

"Yep, when he lifts something heavy or pulls the reins on his horse, all the muscles bulge. Or maybe his thighs or his arse, or maybe it's his eyes or his smile, I don't know," I said. "It could be his patience or his sense of humour. Maybe it's the way he listens."

Trav didn't say anything, just gave me a squeeze.

"Anyway, from what I hear, your boss took one look at this American guy and was a goner."

"Goner?"

"Yep. Tripped all over himself and fell head first into love."

Travis snorted out a laugh. "Charlie?"

"Yeah?"

"You're a dickhead sometimes."

I closed my eyes and smiled. "Shut up. I'm trying to sleep."

I spent a few thinkin' minutes in silence. "Trav?"

"Yes?"

"I wanna meet my brother."

———

THE MOOD at the station was happy. There was excitement about the new Land Cruiser—Bacon and Ernie were looking under the bonnet when we pulled up—George was telling funny hospital stories, and everyone was smiling.

But most of all, Ma was home.

If I had to point to the one person who ran this place, regardless who actually owned it or what job they did, it would be her.

This station was like a horse and its rider. I might have owned the horse and kept it fed, but it was Ma who held the reins.

It was such a relief to have her back.

Once we'd unloaded everything and finally got inside, Ma was in the living room, in her favourite chair. I scooped Nugget out of his new playpen and sat down with him on my lap. The little guy was pleased to see me, apparently. He nudged and nuzzled me, scratching the crap out of me, to say hello. When I looked at Ma, she was smiling at me. "How was your trip?" I asked.

"Oh, Charlie," she said. "The new car is just lovely. But I wish you hadn't gone to such expense just for me."

"It wasn't just for you," I said. "It was long overdue."

"Regardless, I do appreciate it," she said. "Though I think George may be in love. He might leave me for a car."

I snorted. "He liked it that much, huh?"

Ma laughed quietly, but then she studied me for a while. "It was lovely, Charlie. You're too kind."

I ignored her compliment. "How do you feel?"

"Okay. Tired, which makes no sense. All I've done this last week is rest."

"You've also just had major surgery."

Ma sighed in a it's-pointless-to-argue kind of way. She looked around the room and nodded toward the wombat-proof crate. "I see Nugget's got himself a bed?"

"Travis made it because he gets into everything, chews on boots, scratches furniture, gets under everyone's feet. You're a pain in the butt, aren't you?" I asked, looking down at Nugget and giving him a scratch behind the ear. He seriously looked like he smiled. I shook my head and chuckled. "He's a character, that's for sure."

"I can see that," Ma said with a fond smile.

I sat back and sighed. "It's real good to have you home, Ma. This place is too damn quiet without you."

"Everything here seems to have gone okay?" she asked. "Hope no one gave Nara a hard time. She seems to have done well."

"She did well," I said. "Handled it perfectly and only told me to get out of the kitchen once."

Ma laughed, but immediately held her stomach. "Oh, don't make me laugh."

"Sorry. You okay?"

"Yeah, I'm fine," she answered. "Just gonna take me a while to get back to good, that's all."

"You take as much time as you need and let us wait on you for a change, huh?"

Ma smiled, but then was serious again. "You talked to Laura?"

I nodded. "Yep. It was better this morning, I think. Easier would probably be a better way to describe it," I said. "I think she understands where I'm coming from."

Ma smiled sadly at me. "I spoke to her too. She popped her head into my room every day. It wasn't easy at first, but she explained what happened. She said she just wanted to make contact and that she knows she went about it all wrong. You know, I think she's genuine, Charlie."

"I do too," I agreed. "Travis doesn't, but his concerns are more about me than her."

Ma smiled. "He's just worried about you, that's all. I'm sure George would be the same about me."

I snorted. "I'm sure he would."

"Where's Travis now?" she asked.

"Checking on the poddy calves. At the rate he's naming them, we're gonna have the battle of the bands."

Ma chuckled. "You two been okay? No more stupid fighting?"

I shook my head. "No stupid fighting," I told her. Then I sighed, long and loud. "He's been my absolute rock, Ma. I'm pretty sure I'd have thrown the towel in a long time ago if it weren't for him."

Ma smiled warmly at me. "You're stronger than you think you are, Charlie. I think he's just helped you see that, that's all."

Just then, the front screen door banged and Travis walked in, falling on to the sofa beside me. He gave Nugget a scratch on the head and said, "Here's the little boot chewer."

"You okay?" I asked. He didn't look too happy.

Trav sighed. "John Lennon died."

I'm sure he saw the confusion on my face. "Um, Trav. That was a long time ago."

"Not *that* John Lennon," he said with a you're-an-idiot kind of eye roll. "The calf. We had The Beatles, well, now they're down to three."

"Oh."

He sighed again. "I know he was kinda sickly when we found him. I shouldn't be surprised. If any of them weren't gonna make it, it was him."

I put my hand on his knee. "Trav, raisin' poddies is a fickle thing. Percentages are never high."

"I know. And I shouldn't be bothered by it, really," he said. "I mean, we're cattle ranchers, after all. They might be cute when they're babies, but they end up being dinner for someone at some point."

I snorted. "Well, yeah. True."

I kind of felt hypocritical about it all. Especially while I was holding a baby wombat that I couldn't even contemplate handin' over to a rescue centre.

I looked down to the content-with-his-nose-buried-under-my-arm little guy on my lap and shifted him onto Travis's lap. Before either of them could protest, I took off my jacket and threw it over Nugget, knowing my scent would placate him and he'd like the burrow-like dark, even if it was on Travis and not me.

I went into the kitchen, made a cup of tea for Ma and a bottle for Nugget, and joined them back in the lounge room. I sat right next to Trav, in a cuddlin'-on-the-couch way while he fed Nugget and Ma sipped her tea.

Everyone else was heading into town in the morning for a much-needed and long-overdue weekend off. It was gonna leave just me, Trav, George, Ma and Nara on hand. Ma was restricted to rest and Nara said she much preferred stayin' here than goin' back to town. It was the only place that truly felt like a home, she'd said. It was a notion I could sympathise with completely.

"You know what?" I said, feeling very content next to Trav. "We should crank up the pizza oven tonight. A bit of a celebration that Ma's home and a thank you to everyone for manning the fort while we've been gone."

Trav kissed the side of my head. "Sounds good."

Despite having a ton of work to do, inside and out, those twenty minutes of blissful everything-is-right-with-the-world peace were almost perfect.

I should have known better than to jinx myself.

THE WEEKEND *WAS* PERFECT. Me and Trav worked together and got a lot done despite my cut hand. George stayed kinda close to the homestead, but was forever busy, whistlin' happily to himself as he worked. Ma was either resting or sitting in the kitchen with Nara most of the time, not physically doing anything, just instructin' her on different recipes and how to best cook ahead. When they weren't in the kitchen, they were at the dining table, and Ma was helping Nara with what looked like schoolwork. I spent Saturday evening getting some office organising things with Greg for the upcoming elections, and when the house was quiet, Trav and I did some movie-watching, couch-cuddling that became take-me-to-bed slow-love-makin'.

It was absolutely never-woulda-thought-it-possible perfect.

But then perfect took a nosedive into reality with Travis's usual Sunday Skype with his mum. She didn't look her cheerful, smilin' self, and when he asked her what was wrong, she burst into tears.

"Oh, Travis," she cried. "It's your grandpa."

"Mom?" he asked quietly.

She spoke through her tears. "It's not good, love. I think you should come home."

CHAPTER FOURTEEN

ANSWER ME THIS. HOW IS IT POSSIBLE THAT
YOUR HEART CAN STILL BEAT IN YOUR
CHEST WHEN IT BOARDS A PLANE TO TEXAS?

NORMALLY I WOULD SAY a quick hello to his mum and any other family that stuck their head in front of their computer during a Skype call. Sometimes I'd stay for a bit and we'd have a laugh, but I'd usually give him some catch-up time with his family.

But not today.

He held my hand to the near bone-breakin' point.

Travis listened as his mum told him about his grandpa, her father, who had a massive stroke, and how the man Travis was named after was in the hospital and not expected to leave. She told Travis the doctors were talkin' in days, not weeks, so if he wanted a chance to say goodbye, then he should come home real quick.

I'd never seen him struggle like that. I'd seen him pissed off, I'd seen him upset and I'd seen him just about ready to walk away.

But I ain't ever seen him so... helpless.

He did this lost-for-words thing where all he could do was bite his lip, shake his head and blink back tears. He took a shaky breath. "Momma, I want to be there," he said. "But I can't just leave."

"Oh, Travis," his mum said.

"What?" I asked him. "Trav, why not?"

Travis looked at me then. His eyes were a haunted kind of sad and the first of his tears started to fall. "I can't leave you. You have so much going on right now and I promised I'd help you."

I cupped his face in my hands, not caring that his mother was witnessing it all via Skype. "I can come with you," I told him.

He shook his head. "But you've got the Beef Farmers elections, your final assessments are due, the supermarket buyer's vet will be here this week, plus everything that's happening with Ma, and Trudy," he said, shaking his head. "Oh God. What about Laura and Sam? Charlie, he's your brother. You said you want to meet him for the very first time." More tears fell as he cried. "You can't just up and leave."

"Travis, they don't matter. You shouldn't go alone—" My words died when something occurred to me. I sighed and closed my eyes, and whispered, "Oh. I can't go." I tried to smile for him and failed miserably. "I don't have a passport."

He was quiet for a long second and he bowed his head. "Oh."

"You have to go, Trav."

He looked at me then. "I don't want you to be alone right now. I pushed you into doing half this stuff. It's my fault you're so swamped."

"I will be just fine. We'll get through it, and you know what? The rest can wait." I wiped his tears with my thumbs. "It can all wait. It doesn't matter if all of those things fall through, Travis. At the end of the day, they're not important."

"Yes, they are," he said. "They're important to you, to this farm."

"Nowhere near as important to me than you," I whispered. "Trav, baby, you have to go."

His eyebrows furrowed and his face fell.

"I know what it's like to not be there," I told him. "I wasn't here when my father passed away, and I don't want you to go through that." I looked back at the computer screen. Travis's mum was still crying, dabbing a tissue to her eyes. "Mrs Craig? He'll be on the next plane."

I GUESS BEIN' busy helped with not-over-thinkin', because I'm pretty sure my head didn't stop spinning until we were a good hour into our trip back to Alice Springs.

That's when my heart started hurtin'.

We'd checked flights from Alice to Sydney and we had to leave in twenty minutes to make the flight. Trav threw God-knows-what into his bag, and neither of us had time to stop and think until we were well on our way.

Then realisation crept in.

I'd have thought it would be more like the scorching summer sun, blistering and unforgiving.

But it wasn't.

Realisation was more like a desert winter. A coldness settled into my bones, making me docile and numb, making my chest heavy and tight. The chill of realisation that crept through me.

Travis was leaving.

We'd only bought a one-way ticket. He'd be gone for as long as he needed to be gone for.

I understood the need for him to go back home, even if he thought I needed him here. And I *did* need him here. I really did. But he needed to say his final goodbye to a man who helped raise him, who taught him how to fish and how to fire a gun. It was his grandpa who taught him how to be in love with one person for almost fifty years and still look at them like they went and hung the moon.

I reckon he did a real good job, and I wished I could go to Texas just so I could thank the man myself.

Travis needed to go home.

I understood it. I just didn't like it.

In fact, it scared me half to death.

But I couldn't show one inkling of doubt. I couldn't tell him I was petrified of doing this on my own. Because I was certain I couldn't. I couldn't do any of this without him.

He was right about one thing: I was swamped. I had a lot going on, a lot to deal with and a lot to get done.

I didn't want to do any of it. I had every intention of crawling into bed and not getting out until Travis came back. That was my plan A. To not deal with life at all.

There was every chance that Plan B involved Ma yelling at me to get my sorry self out of bed each day because this-place-won't-run-on-self-pity-Charlie. But I was gonna work on Plan A for as long they'd let me.

"You okay?" Travis asked.

I gave him the best smile I could fake. *No, I'm not. I'm not okay at all.* "Sure. You?"

"You can't lie, Charlie," he said with a sad smile. "It's not in your genetic coding."

"Huh?"

We'd taken the new Land Cruiser to town. I drove,

despite my injured hand. We were parked at the airport, and he nodded toward the building. "I'm pretty sure I used to have the look on my face just like yours when I had to go the dentist, Charlie."

I laughed at that despite my mood. "I hate the dentist," I told him. "And no, I'm not too fond of airports right now either."

He shook his head. "I don't want to leave," he said with a shrug. "But I know I should. I don't want to say goodbye to you or to my grandpa." He swallowed thickly. "I guess I can't win."

That's when I realised that this wasn't about me. This was about Travis and what he was going through. I could have kicked myself for being so damn selfish. "You need to do this," I told him. "Go home, see your grandpa and spend time with your family. I'll be right here when you get back."

Travis exhaled through puffed-out cheeks. "I changed my mind," he said.

"Trav," I started to reason with him.

"I don't like this car," he added. "I've changed my mind. I prefer the old truck."

I guess he needed a change in conversation. "The ute with no suspension, no air conditioning and busted springs in the seats?" I asked.

He nodded. "I can't lay across the seat in this one. Or you can't lean against me if I drive. It's one of my favourite things, you know," he said quietly.

"Maybe I could have it modified. Instead of the centre console, we could have a bench seat."

He gave me an almost smile. "It'd be much easier to kiss you too, you know. If I could be sitting right next to you instead of all the way over here."

I leaned over the console as far as I could. "We'll learn to improvise."

Trav took my face in his hands and kissed me. And I mean, really kissed me. The intensity took me by surprise, the way he held my face to his, how he tasted me, the passion, the need, the goodbye.

He whispered, all out of breath, "I can't kiss you like that in the airport."

"Well, you could," I said, my head still spinning. "Though we might get arrested for lewd behaviour." I shook my head to clear it and opened the door. "Come on, or you'll miss your flight."

We got him checked in and had to wait fifteen minutes until his plane boarded. Fifteen too-long, nowhere-near-long-enough minutes. We sat in an empty row of seats, away from the other people. Now it seemed as though it was him keeping me distracted, not the other way around. "What are your final two assessment subjects again?" he asked.

"It doesn't matter." I shrugged. "They're not high on my list of priorities right now."

"Charlie, you have to do them. You're almost at the finish line."

I sighed, not wanting to argue with him over something so unimportant. "Analysis of Herbicide resistance and something-or-other, and the other one's about Soil Genetics and whatever." I shrugged. "I'll get to them if I can."

It was a lie. We both knew I had no intention of doing either assessment. But he never said anything else about it. Maybe he didn't want to argue with me either.

Instead, he asked, "When's the Beef Farmers election meeting?"

"Next week."

"Where's the meeting at?"

"Here in Alice Springs. It's a two-day thing, apparently." I shook my head, wishing to God I'd never agreed to signing up for the stupid bloody elections.

"And the vet that Blake was lining up?" he asked. "The supermarket buyer specialist guy?"

"He's this week sometime," I answered. "They were gonna let me know when the schedule is finalised."

"When did Ma need to go back for a check-up?"

I tried to think. "I can't remember. I'm sure she'll tell me."

He nodded. "Oh, don't forget to tell George that Brooks and Dunn are tagged, but the others aren't. Well, I guess he'll see that, won't he?"

"Brooks and Dunn?"

"Two of the new poddy calves we got in yesterday."

I'd gathered that much. "Brooks and Dunn? Really?"

"It was either that or Simon and Garfunkel."

I laughed at him, despite the heavy ache in my chest. "We really need to talk about your taste in music."

Travis's smile slowly morphed into a frown. He stared out the wall of glass, looking at the plane he'd soon be getting on. "I don't know how long I'll be gone," he said quietly. "It could be a week, or two."

"Take as much time as you need," I said mechanically. I didn't mean it. In fact, I meant the exact opposite. It just seemed like the right thing to say.

He nodded, still not looking at me. "You're gonna be so busy you'll hardly have time to miss me."

I snorted at the fucking ridiculousness of that. At least it got him to look at me.

"I remember one of the first things you ever said to me," he said. "We were sitting on your front veranda. It was about my first or second day here, and you said your staff are the best there is."

I nodded. "It's true," I agreed. "I think that is even more true now than it was then."

He looked at me seriously. "Then let them do what you employ them to do, Charlie."

"What?"

He smiled at my what-the-hell-does-that-mean expression. "I know what you're like. You'll go home and try to do everything yourself."

"No I won't."

He laughed, because apparently I really can not lie. "Promise me you'll just worry about what you need to do and let them do the day-to-day stuff, Charlie."

"Well, I won't promise, but I'll try."

"You need to be the best boss you can be," he said.

I nodded. "Yeah, and that means helping and doing what they do. I ain't above them."

"No, you're not," he said with a smile. "But it also means that you need to be the best farmer you can be, who's gonna move this industry forward, Charlie. You need to go to those meetings and talk business, figures and stock rates, and all that stuff you have in your head. Go get elected onto the board of directors and kick some ass, Charlie. Sutton Station is the best run farm out there. It's about time others knew that."

"Is that your motivational speech of the year?" I asked. "Because that was pretty good."

He laughed this time. "Nope. That was me knowing you too well. I know you were thinking of going home and calling Greg to withdraw your nomination."

"No I wasn't." Actually, I really kind of was.

"You can't lie, Charlie," he said with a chuckle and a

shake of his head. Then he was serious. He looked back out the window. "I only encouraged you to do all those things because I want the world to see the Charlie I see." He licked his lips and swallowed. "Because he's really kinda great."

"I can't be that Charlie," I whispered. "Not without you."

His voice cracked. "You have to be."

The PA cracked to life. "Your attention, ladies and gentlemen," a woman announced. "Flight QF790 to Sydney is now boarding."

Slowly, reluctantly, Travis stood up. I did too, and when I finally looked at Travis, he exhaled slowly. "I don't like goodbyes."

"It's not really a goodbye," I told him, trying to smile.

Then why did it feel like one?

If he was only supposed to be going for a week or two, why did it feel like he wasn't coming back?

I wanted to ask him to promise to come back. I wanted to hear him say it, and I wanted to believe it. But I think part of me knew that when he went home, surrounded by family and old friends, that his list of pros and cons for reasons to stay might be a little longer on the side that didn't include me.

I swallowed down my emotions and tried to convince myself that this wasn't about me. This was about him going home to say goodbye to his dying grandpa. "I wish you were going back for something happier," I told him. "Maybe we should have planned a holiday to visit or something."

He was looking at the floor between us. "Bit hard when you don't have a passport, Charlie."

"Well, I've never had a need for one," I said quietly. "I never thought I'd leave my station again, let alone the country."

He looked at me then with teary eyes and a watery smile. "You have no idea how much I'm going to miss you."

"Yeah, I do," I told him. "About half as much as I'm gonna miss you."

He tried to laugh. "Just pretend I'm out fixin' fences or something. I'll be back before you know it."

"Yeah, just a week or two," I said, aiming for conviction. I must have missed my mark.

He cupped my face, and his eyes bore into mine. "I'm coming back. I promise. Have I ever lied to you?"

I nodded, my face still in his hands. "Yep, the other day. You said I couldn't sing. That's clearly a lie."

Travis barked out a laugh, and then like we weren't in a busy airport terminal, like it was just us, he closed his eyes. When I thought he was going to kiss me, he didn't. He nudged his nose to mine.

It took my breath away.

"Believe me now?" he whispered against my cheek.

I shook my head just a little, trying to remember how to breathe.

Trav nudged his nose to mine again and ghosted his lips over mine. I'm pretty sure I swayed, because I could feel him smile against my lips. "How about now?"

I nodded this time and slowly opened my eyes. I felt drunk. "Yeah." Then, trying to keep the mood light because I didn't need to add guilt and my insecurities to his list of worries, I said, "Anyway, you have to come back because I still haven't taken you to Uluru."

"Deal." He smiled at me. "We'll plan it later. Right now I have to go."

"I know. I wish you didn't have to."

He whispered. "I wish I didn't have to either."

"I'm sorry about your grandpa, Trav," I told him. "I really do wish you had a happier reason to go home."

He sighed, and for a second I thought he was gonna cry. He blinked it back. "It'll be just like I'm gone fencing, yeah?"

I nodded, trying to convince myself just as he was. "Yep. Two weeks fencing."

The final boarding call came over the speaker, and Travis looked over at the counter. He straightened up and exhaled slowly. He gave me a quick kiss, and just like he was heading out to the southern paddocks for the day, he said, "See you soon."

I watched him as he handed over his boarding pass and walked through the doors without so much as looking back. I knew other people were staring at me—they'd probably never seen two men kiss before—but I didn't care.

I didn't cry when he left, I didn't cry when I walked out, but I fucking lost it when I got in the car.

I don't remember the trip home. Though it was a three-hour trip, the next thing I knew, I was pulling up at the homestead. It was after nine at night, and Ma and George were waiting. Ma tried to smile, but her face kind of crumpled when she saw me. "Oh, Charlie," she whispered.

"I'm just gonna go to bed," I mumbled, really not wanting to deal with questions and looks of pity.

With sad eyes, Ma said, "Charlie, he won't be gone long, love."

I shook my head. There was a heavy, heavy ache in my chest. The cold, creeping realisation of absence I'd felt earlier was now like lead. I knew. I just knew. I didn't mean to cry, but saying stuff out loud for the first time was so damn hard.

"Travis isn't coming back."

CHAPTER FIFTEEN

LONGING IN THE LONELINESS

I TRIED to do Plan A and wallow in self-pity, but I couldn't sleep. I lay on his side of the bed and smelled his pillow until the sun started to rise and I couldn't stand how pathetic I was anymore.

I had it all mapped out, though. When I was feeding the dogs and horses, Travis was on a plane flying somewhere near Fiji. Then when I was sitting at breakfast, pushin' food around my plate and trying not to look at his empty chair beside me, ignoring the looks of sympathy and not-knowin'-what-to-say kind of silence, Travis was flying over Samoa.

When the others all stopped for lunch and I stayed out on Shelby with her listenin' silence, Travis had crossed from the South Pacific to the North, and when George drove the old ute up to where I was fixin' the fourth bore in the top of the first western paddock and shoved a roast beef sandwich in my hand, Travis would be flyin' over Mexico.

"You need to eat," George said. "Ma wanted to come out here herself, but I had to stop her. Stubborn thing she is." He shook his head at me. "Just about as stubborn as you."

I sat on the ground and took a bite of the sandwich and struggled to swallow it. I had no appetite and no energy. I tried a mouthful of water instead.

George leaned against the old ute and crossed his arms. He had that we're-gonna-have-a-little-talk patience about him, and I knew him finding me wasn't just about making me eat. "Did Travis say he wasn't coming back?"

I wrapped the sandwich up and put it aside. "Not in so many words."

"So he didn't say it?"

"He didn't have to."

"Charlie, you can't go assumin' the worst of people. Give the boy some credit."

I shook my head. He didn't understand. "It was in his eyes. He didn't have to say it, but I could see it," I told him. "He kept sayin' he was coming back, but I think he thought maybe if he kept on sayin' it, it would make it true."

"Well, if he kept on sayin' it, don't that make it true?" he asked. "Travis wouldn't lie, son."

"I'm pretty sure he's gonna get home and realise his family needs him," I said. My voice sounded flat, resigned. "And that maybe he knew once he got back *there*, that *here* wouldn't be special enough to bring him back. I mean, his whole life is over there."

George shook his head. "But he has a life here too."

I shrugged. "But maybe it's not enough. Maybe it's too far from home, maybe he'll realise how much he misses them when he gets there. I can't make him choose between me and his family, George. He shouldn't *have* to choose."

George sighed and bowed his head. "Or maybe it's you."

My eyes shot to his. "What?"

"Maybe it's you," he repeated. "Maybe it's just you bein' absolutely certain you're not worth it. Maybe you're the one who thinks he's better off stayin' over there." He took his hat off and ran his fingers through his short, greying hair. "Did you ever stop to think that maybe you *are* worth coming back for?"

I shook my head without really meaning to.

"Seems that Travis's work here is far from done," George said. His voice was sad and soft. "I thought he was finally getting you to see yourself clearly, but it seems he wasn't even close."

Needing this conversation to be over, I stood up and handed him back the barely eaten sandwich. "Tell Ma I said thanks."

George took it, but he sighed a I'm-sorry sigh. I didn't want to hear it. He followed me into the bore shed and, before he could start sayin' something I most definitely didn't want to hear, I started the generator. The roar of the diesel engine stopped any chance of more conversation, and George sighed again, his shoulders slumped. He started to yell something anyway.

"I can't hear you," I yelled over the engine.

But I never turned it off. In fact, I climbed up on the grounding plate and shoved my still bandaged hand alongside the hydraulic shaft and spread the grease. I ignored the pull on the stitches in my hand and ignored George until he shook his head and walked away. Only when the ute drove off did I shut down the engine, and then I threw the oil rag against the wall. When that wasn't satisfying enough, I kicked the almost empty oil drum as hard as I fucking could.

And because that made me feel a bit better, I kicked it again, sending it clear out of the shed. And then I yelled and cursed a bit, and because I couldn't leave an oil drum where the cattle were, I stomped outside after it.

Shelby was watching me. She lifted her head in an are-you-over-yourself-yet kind of way. I pointed my finger at her. "Don't you fucking start."

Then, because she was a know-it-all pain in my arse, Shelby snorted and shook her head, which was horse speak for "now you need to go home and apologise to George."

Because she was right, I kicked the oil drum back into the shed, not caring where it landed. I locked up the shed, climbed back in to the saddle and headed home.

It was cold and getting on dark by the time I rode in. The hours I spent in the saddle riding home only served for too-much thinking time and not even the cool, ever-changin' colours of the evenin' desert soothed me.

I unsaddled Shelby, fed and watered her, and was brushin' her down when George found me. "Charlie?"

"Sorry about before," I started as soon as I saw him. "I didn't mean it, and you were right. The problem is me," I admitted. "I don't know if I'll ever think I'm good enough, and that's something I'm trying to get right."

He smiled at me. "I know you didn't mean it."

"I just get caught up in my head," I said quietly. I gave Shelby a few hard brushes. "It drives Travis mad."

George chuckled. "I bet it does."

"Is Ma pissed off at me?" I asked.

"She's worried." Then he said, "She shouldn't be stressed out right now, Charlie. She's supposed to be recuperating."

I nodded. "I'm sorry. I'll go check on her."

Before I could leave, he put his hand on my arm. "Charlie, you did the right thing. As hard as it was for you, as hard as it still is now, you did the right thing. Travis did need to go home."

I nodded. "Yeah, I know. He would have regretted not being there."

George nodded, slow and sure. "And in a week or two, when he comes back—and I know he will, Charlie—you'll be better for it."

"You know he'll be back?"

He smiled. "Yep."

"Wish I was that confident."

George looked at me kind, fatherly eyes. "He loves you, Charlie. You need to trust him. If he says he's coming back, then he will."

"I do trust him," I said quickly. "It's not about trust, or fidelity if that's what you're leading to. He wouldn't ever do that." I had no doubt.

"And you believe that he loves you?"

I nodded.

"Then trust his judgement," George said. "If he thinks you're worth givin' his heart to, then maybe you should start believin' it."

I let his words sink in for a while. He had a good argument and a point of view that logically made sense. I sighed, suddenly feelin' every minute of sleep I didn't get last night. "I thought for sure I'd never find anyone, and then he literally walked through my front door. He made me think I could do everything and have it all. I could have everything I was told I couldn't..."

George frowned and put on his tough-love act. "You know what, Charlie? If he doesn't come back, then so be it. Sure, you can bitch and moan for the next fifty years to your broken heart's content, but you still have a business to run, Charlie. You still have seven people that depend on you out here. I know that sounds harsh and cold, given he ain't been gone a day. But I know you, Charlie, and this wallowin' for weeks like you're prone to doin' just won't cut it this time."

"Did Travis write that down for you?" I asked. "Because that sounds like something he'd say."

George laughed and shook his head. "Do you remember when he first got here? He was so full of life and a breath of fresh air, and he was so smug."

I snorted. "Yeah, not much changed."

"What'dya call him? A smug Yank."

I nodded. "Yep. But he's my smug Yank."

George chuckled. "Then show him, Charlie. When he gets back, show him how you can do it all. Show him how you don't need no smug Yank here holding your hand every step of the way."

"But I do."

He smiled like I missed an inside joke. "No you don't. You just think you do. He's like your safety net for tryin'. Before he got here, you were just happy to coast along at mediocre, and there ain't nothing wrong with that, Charlie. It was a good life. A real good life." He shook his head. "But you've got plans, Charlie. To go bigger and better. And that's not Travis's doin'. That's you. He just opened your eyes, that's all. Gave you a little push."

I knew George meant no harm, but I didn't strictly care for his choice of words. "He means more than just a safety net."

George smiled and clapped me on the arm. "Give a man break, son. I'm trying here."

I sighed, long and loud. "When did it all get so complicated?"

He snorted out a laugh. "I remember you bein' fifteen years old complainin' that life out here was boring."

"Well, complicated is overrated," I told him. "Boring sounds pretty good about now."

Just then, Ma called out from the veranda. "Charlie.

Phone call." I looked at my watch, wondering if Travis'd be home by now, but before I could get too excited, she added, "It's Jack Melville."

I groaned, and George laughed. "Just what you need, huh?"

"Not today, no," I said. "If that old bastard says one thing outta line to me, I'll fly to his place tonight so I can punch him in the fucking mouth."

George laughed as we both headed inside. "I'll go with ya. Not to copilot. Just to watch."

I passed Ma at the door, giving her a quick kiss on the cheek as I did. "Dinner's soon," she said. "Ten minutes."

I sat down at my office desk, took a deep breath and picked up the phone. "Jack," I said. "It's Charlie."

"Didn't catch you at bad time, did I?" He sounded like he hoped he did. Even the sound of his voice annoyed me.

"No. Just got in actually. What can I do for you?"

"I heard you scored a buyer's contract through Woolworths."

"You heard correct." I almost smiled, but then wondered where he was going with this conversation. "And how'd you go with them?"

"Yes, yes," he said. "We secured a three-year contract."

I wasn't surprised he'd heard that we'd been contracted to them. I was surprised it took him this long to call and gloat. But he obviously hadn't heard that our deal was for five years, not three. It was very likely part of the reason for his call, so I deliberately didn't tell him.

"That's good news," I replied instead. I didn't exactly have a great deal to say to this man, so I waited for him to speak again.

It didn't take long. "So," he hedged. "This AGM next week..."

"Yes?"

"I see you're nominated for the Board."

"That's right," I said, waiting for the bomb to drop.

"Just wanted to wish you luck," he said.

No he didn't.

"I guess it just surprises me, that's all," he went on to say. "Your father never wanted anything to do with such things."

"I'm not my father."

"No. You're not," he said. His tone was unreadable. I wasn't sure if he meant it in a good or bad way. Either way, this conversation was done.

"Anything else?"

"No, no," he said casually. "Just touching base."

"Right, then I'll see you at the meeting."

"I guess you will."

I hung up the phone and stared at it, wondering what the hell that was actually about. George was at my door. "Everything okay?"

I looked at him, and nodded slowly. "You know what you said before about proving to Travis that I can do this?"

He nodded. "Yeah."

"Well, I'm not sure about that," I told him. "But I'll tell ya what I'm gonna do. And that's show Jack fucking Melville."

George smiled, slow and wide. "Good."

***

IT'S funny how determination and pride can motivate someone. Because if I didn't have enough to do before, I certainly did now. And I had two weeks to do everything.

First things first, I attacked my office. Like a man

possessed, I went through invoices, receipts, accounts and emails until my eyes hurt. I only stopped to feed Nugget and haul my tired arse into bed. I figured if I was tired enough, I wouldn't miss Travis. Which kind of worked, until after the three o'clock fussing-wombat feed and I got back into bed and his side of the bed was cold.

Or until I tripped over his laundry that he'd left on the bathroom floor. That he *always* left on the bathroom floor.

Or until I sat at the table at breakfast time and his chair was too damn empty. There was no smartarse comments, no bursts of laughter. His blue eyes didn't spark with humour and his sandy-blond hair didn't spike out just so.

There was no foot-holding under the table.

Everyone was still kinda quiet around me, not wanting to say the wrong thing. But the truth was, with Travis gone, we were one man down. And what George said was right: we had a business to run, and these guys depended on me.

I had to not think about Travis. I had to not think about how he'd been home already for almost a day and I hadn't heard from him. I had realised if, in the end, Travis didn't come back, then I still had to keep going. As much as it would kill me.

I had to put my head down and get shit done. That was the cold reality of it all. As much as my heart hurt, keeping busy was the very best thing—the only thing—I could do.

I told myself not to stop. Not to think. Not to pay any mind to the ache in my chest that made it hard to breathe.

I told myself Travis was busy, he had horrible family stuff to deal with and he'd call me, email me, Skype me, when he could. I told myself to man up and deal with it, get on with work and not think about him.

But just before lunch when I was with Ernie and Bacon in the holding yard trying to wrangle a day-old Brahman and get a feeding tube down its throat and Nara called out from the veranda that my laptop was making funny pinging noises, I fucking ran.

I yelled for Billy to hold the calf's head while we wrestled with the animal, and I fucking ran inside.

I raced through the house into my office, just as the last Skype ping rang out. I checked the screen. Two missed calls from 'The Craig Household', as Travis had nicknamed his parents Skype account. There was a prompt asking if I wanted to retry. Hell fucking yes, I did. I couldn't hit the yes button quick enough.

My heart was pounding. Not just from the record-breaking hundred metre dash I just did from the holding yard to the house, but in excitement. It was Travis.

Any and all hope of trying to act like I didn't care if he was gone went out the fucking window.

Calling...

Calling...

"Come on, come on," I muttered to the screen. When it changed from calling to connecting, I almost leapt out of my chair.

The screen changed and I almost hugged my fucking laptop. Until I saw his face.

He looked awful. He had dark circles under his sad, sad eyes, and he looked like he'd had the day from hell.

"Hey!" I said. He was sitting in his mother's kitchen. It looked kind of dark.

"Oh my God, Charlie," he said. "It's so good to see you."

"How are you?" I asked. "How was your flight?"

He tried to smile. "Flight was okay. Long, but okay. I went straight from the airport to the hospital to see Grandpa," he said.

"How is he?"

Travis shook his head. "Yeah... he's not good, Charlie." He cleared his throat. "It's real hard to see him like that."

"I wish I was there with you," I told him.

"I wish you were too," he said quietly. He looked so sad, I just wanted to reach through the screen and touch him. "I tried calling a few times. I'm just gonna head upstairs to bed. I haven't really slept since I left you, but I wanted to talk to you first."

"Yeah, I missed your first calls. I was in the holding yard. We got some day-old calves in yesterday that aren't feeding too well, so we're gonna try tube feeding 'em. It's a last resort, but we gotta try, right?"

Trav gave a weak smile. "Yeah. How many?"

"There was three yesterday. We lost one already, so now there's two." Then I told him, "We haven't named 'em yet."

Travis kind of laughed and scrubbed his hands over his face. "When's the buyer's vet getting there?"

"Tomorrow," I told him.

Trav nodded slowly, and even as exhausted as he was, he still looked beautiful to me. "I'm so tired, Charlie. Feel like I could sleep for a week."

"Go to bed, baby," I whispered.

One corner of his lips lifted in a crooked exhausted-cute smile. "I like it when you call me that."

"Call you what?"

He shook his head. "You just called me baby."

"Did I?" I didn't remember saying it.

He stared at me for the longest time. "It's so good to see you."

Just then his mum came into the screen and put her arms around her son. "Hi, Charlie," she said to me. "Travis hasn't stopped talking about you."

"Hi, Mrs Craig," I said. "Look after him for me."

She smiled but looked as tired as Travis. "I will."

"I'll send you an email," Trav said. "When we've worked out what we're doing here and figured out time zones, I'll let you know what times we can chat, okay?"

I nodded. "Call me anytime," I told him. "Even if it's three in the morning, Trav, you can call me. I don't care what time it is." He smiled then, but his blink was slow. "Go to bed, Trav. Get some sleep."

He nodded. "'Kay. Love you, Charlie."

My whole body flushed with warmth at his words, and I grinned. I think I even laughed.

He shook his head at me, then looked off screen. "Mom, what's a famous singing duo?"

I heard Mrs Craig answer. "Um, Sonny and Cher."

"Call them Sonny and Cher."

"What?" I asked.

"The calves. Call them Sonny and Cher," he said.

I sighed, but I hadn't stopped grinning. "Sonny and Cher it is. You know the boys'll give you hell for that."

He snorted out a tired laugh. "Tell 'em I said."

"I will," I told him. "Get some sleep. And Trav?"

"Yeah?"

"I love you too."

We disconnected the call, and the screen froze for a few seconds with a picture of his tired one-sided smile before cutting off. I sat there smilin' and starin' at my computer screen for I don't know how long.

Ma walked slowly to stand at my office door. She had a smug told-you-so smile on her face. "Believe him now?"

I nodded. It was kind of hard not to.

But either way, breathin' got a little easier after that.

CHAPTER SIXTEEN

STRENGTH IN THE SOLITUDE

WE WERE EXPECTING the supermarket's contracted vet around nine, and true to my keeping-myself-busy plan, I did exactly that until not one new Land Rover turned up, but two. It wasn't one vet, but three. There were other people with them, more like a road crew than anything else. Their cars were laden with what looked like enough supplies to get them through the Simpson Desert. As far as I knew, that's exactly what it was for.

After initial handshakes and introductions, the lead vet, who was not a man like I'd presumed but a lady by the name of Jean, clapped her hands together and said, "Right. Where do we start?"

Straight to business, no bullshit. I liked her immediately.

The other two clipboard-holding vets followed her lead, and me, George and Billy showed them the holding yard first. There were thirteen Brahman calves in there, ranging from two days to one week old. Not that these vets were here to inspect veal quality, that's not what they were looking for at all. They wanted to see how we handled our cattle, how they were treated and, basically, if our practices were humane.

They didn't say that exactly. But I knew damn well if these guys saw anything they didn't professionally or ethically agree with, the deal would be off.

I had nothing to hide.

One of the vets, a younger guy called Aaron, nodded to the length of plastic tube that hung over the fence. "What's that for?"

"A few of 'em weren't doin' too well when we got 'em in yesterday," I explained. "So we tried tube feedin' 'em."

Aaron raised his eyebrow. "How'd that go?"

"Alright. They didn't like it, but at least it got milk in their bellies. They're doin' better today."

Jean looked over the calves. "Which two?"

"Um, Sonny and Cher," I said, pointing. "The two at the back."

Her stare was blank. "Sonny and Cher?"

"Oh." I cringed. "Long story." It wasn't long actually. It was just stupid.

"Name all your cattle?" she asked, trying not to smile.

I shook my head and cleared my throat. "Just the poddies."

She climbed through the fence and her two associates followed. They checked Sonny and Cher over, nodding satisfactorily. "They look okay," she said. "Those bigger ones"—she nodded at the first ones we brought in over a week ago—"how long will you keep them here?"

"I'll turn them out as soon as they eat more feed than milk," I answered. "That'll depend on the animal."

The other vet, I think his name was Kevin or Devin, maybe it was Bevan, chuckled. "Suppose they have names too?"

"Well," I hedged, "those three bigger calves are the remaining Beatles. John Lennon didn't make it." The three of them looked at me like I'd lost my freakin' mind. I put my hands up, palm forward. "Wasn't me who named 'em. Just so you know."

Billy, who was standing beside, clapped my shoulder and laughed. "Bet Travis is sorry he missed this."

I smiled at him and spoke through gritted teeth. "If he *was* here right now, I'd kill him."

George and Billy both laughed, and the two younger vets scribbled down notes as Jean spoke quietly amongst them. When she looked up at me, she smiled. Jean was very thorough in her questions, asking me everything I'm pretty sure Blake would have already told her about stock ratios, land size, annual rainfall and feed storage. Then she looked out toward the north. "How far have we gotta go 'til we find some cattle out there?"

"We've got the cows and calves in this first paddock here," I said, nodding to the first western paddock. "There are two bores that service water troughs. How about we start there?"

We spent the rest of the morning doing exactly that. And it wasn't until we were headed back to the homestead at lunch time that Jean pointed to one of the cows and asked "What's that on her neck?"

She was pointing to the solar-powered detection collar around the cow's neck. "That's like a tracking device," I said, explaining how Travis's idea worked. "I only brought the satellite phone with me, not my smartphone. But I can show you how it all works when we get back to the homestead."

Which is what I did. Then, at her request, I showed her the invoices showing what type of grains I fed not only the cattle but the horses as well. I showed her all vet records, vaccinations, worming treatments, insecticides and pesticides—you name it. Jean wanted to see it.

Like I said: thorough.

She loved the tracking device concept, and when I'd shown her a basic tutorial of how it worked, she said something that struck a chord with me.

"Shame you can't monitor your bores from here. You'd save yourself some days in the paddocks, I'm sure."

The convey of vets left, smiling and shaking my hand. Jean said outright she was very happy with what she found out here, and she was happy to sign off on it.

Just like that.

But I couldn't get what she said about the bores out of my head. So I spent a bit of time looking up the Department of Agriculture's website that Travis had found the collars on and started doing some research.

It was a good distraction to say the least, but it was also productive. Travis sent me an email saying he'd hope to catch me on Skype at ten o'clock at night, my time.

I was layin' on the floor in front of the fire watchin' Nugget run himself in circles at nine thirty, waitin' waitin' waitin' for the Skype call to come.

Of course just after I hit answer and Travis's face appeared on the screen, Nugget decided to run across the keyboard and disconnected the call.

I hit redial as quick as I could, holding the little shit under my arm this time, and Trav answered straight away. He laughed. "All I saw was a brown blur and then you yelling at Nugget before it cut off."

I shook my head, but I was smiling. "I couldn't believe it." I held Nugget up to the screen. "Say hello to Dadda," I said.

Travis gave a sad smile. "Aww."

I waved Nugget's little paw at the screen. "Say goodnight. It's bedtime for him. I just wanted you to see him."

Trav looked like smiling—or even talking—was a real hard thing to do.

"Hang on one sec," I said, getting up and putting Nugget in his bed, and quickly going back to my spot in front of the fire. "Okay, he's gone now."

"Thank you," Travis said. "I wish I was there."

"Me too," I said. "How's things over there?" I didn't want to ask outright how his grandpa was, but Trav understood.

He told me he went to the hospital again last night. His grandpa wasn't doin' too good, but was hangin' on. Travis looked like he'd slept some at least, but he still looked tired and sad and just too damn far away.

I told him about the vet appointment and how the lead vet loved his tracking collar setup. "She said, 'Be sure to tell that Travis fellow that I'm impressed,' and I said, 'Good Lord, no. I'm afraid his ego might not let us recover.'"

Travis laughed. "Thanks a lot. Did she really say that?"

"Yep."

"You told her it was my idea?"

"Of course I did. I tell everyone it was your idea," I told him. Trav smiled kinda shyly, so I added, "I also told them you named the poddy calves Sonny and Cher, so any credibility you might have had is gone."

He laughed this time, and it warmed my chest to hear it and to finally see him smile.

Then he said, "You got my email, obviously, about what times we can Skype?"

"Yep."

"But we can't tonight. There's a bit of family dinner on

for me," he said. "Everyone's coming over so I can see them."

"That's okay. That'll be good for you to see everyone," I said, even though I was disappointed.

"But we can talk again the day after," he was quick to add.

"Sure."

"You've been busy, no doubt," he went on to say.

"Always." I was going to tell him about my idea the vet had given me for the pump houses, but didn't want to bore him with work. "Is it good to see everyone? How's your sisters and brother?"

"They're all fine. Paige bought me a tub of Blue Bell. I near ate the whole thing. Felt sick afterward," he said with a laugh. "But I told 'em all about you and everyone there. How's Ma?"

I smiled at him. "She's doin' okay. She's better every day."

"Tell her I'm thinking of her."

"I will."

"I miss you," he said again, back to frowning.

"I miss you too."

"I'll call you in two days."

"I'll be here."

"I love you, Charlie."

"Love you too."

We disconnected the call, and I lay there on the floor in front of the fire, wishin' with all my might I could just touch him. Just hold his hand or smell his just-showered skin. Just any one little thing.

But I couldn't.

I packed up my laptop and went to bed, then spent the

next two time-crawlin' days with my head down and my heart achin' in my chest.

Keepin' busy for those next two days outside checkin' on calving cows suited me better than sittin' inside wishin' my laptop would ping with a Skype call. But on the second day after dinner, when I finally got around to some office work, there were emails from Sydney University thankin' me for submitting two assessments.

My two final assessments, which I most definitely did not submit. Hell, I hadn't even thought about them.

I was still sitting at my desk when my laptop told me Travis was calling, right when he said he would. Just seein' his face was like a full breath of air to starvin' lungs.

"Hey you," he said.

"Hey you too," I replied. "Um, Trav?"

"Yeah?"

"Care to tell me why Sydney Uni thinks I've done two assessments that I really haven't done?" I asked. "Actually, care to tell me *how* you did that?"

He laughed. "I tried getting the subject out of you at the airport, but you wouldn't tell me. So I logged in to your email and read what they sent you," he said simply. "And then I logged in to your college website and uploaded them. It really wasn't hard." Then he added, "You really should change your passwords, Charlie."

"Yeah, God forbid someone hacks into my email and finishes my degree for me." I couldn't believe he did that. "Isn't there some law that says you can't do that?"

"Probably is. There's also probably a law that says I shouldn't have used my old school assignments and passed them off as yours, but I did that too."

"Travis!"

He laughed. "I changed them a bit. I'm sure I read

somewhere that there needed to be fifteen percent difference or something," he said with a shrug. "So I changed them up a little."

All I could do was shake my head. "I can't believe you did that."

His smile faltered and he sighed. "I didn't want you to fail because of me."

"Oh, Trav."

"Like you said, I threw you head first into finishing your degree, without asking, and when you didn't have time. Then when it came to the final assessments, when you were so busy with everything else, instead of helping, I had to leave," he said. "I wanted to do something to help, Charlie. So, from the other side of the world, I helped out the only way I could. Please don't be mad."

He looked so worried and tired, and I wished I could run my hand through his hair and pull him against me. I wished, so much. "How the hell can I be mad at you?"

"It's one less thing you have to worry about," he said.

"And what about you?" I asked. "You look so tired. How's your grandpa?"

Trav tried to smile and failed. "He's holding on. He just kind of lies there asleep or something. He doesn't talk or even open his eyes really. It's not how I want to remember him..."

"Then don't," I said. "Remember the man you told me about. The one who took you fishing and helped you build stuff. Remember him like that, Trav."

Travis stared at me for a long while, like he wasn't quite sure what to say. "You have no idea how much I miss you right now."

"You have no idea how much I wish I was with you right now."

He sighed. "We're heading back into the hospital after breakfast. It's so draining."

"I wish I could do something to help you."

"Just seeing your face helps me."

I could hear a voice in the background, and he sighed again. "That's Mom calling me down for breakfast," he said. "I'll talk to you soon."

"It's real good to see your face too, Trav."

THE NEW TRACKING beacons I'd ordered arrived, and workin' out how to calibrate them to do what I wanted was a welcome, welcome distraction. I spent four days installing 'em, getting 'em right.

I spent my nights talking to Trav via Skype, and I told him what I was doin' with the beacons, askin' him if what I was doin' was right. So, from opposite ends of the planet, we worked on it together.

I think it was a welcome distraction for him too. When I'd told him what I was tryin' to do but couldn't get it to work, he was all over it. The next day he showed me notes he'd written on how to make the bore-tracking beacons work like the cattle-tracking ones.

And by day four, almost two weeks after he'd left, I could sit in my office, and through my tracking app, I could see which bores were pumping, and how many litres per hour.

It was all part of my plan to show the likes of Melville at the upcoming Beef Farmers meeting that I'd drag the beef industry into the twenty-first century if it killed me.

When I said goodbye to Trav the night before I left for

Alice Springs, he'd put his hand on the screen, told me he loved me and wished me luck.

It was with those words—and George's speech about bein' a better farmer for the right reasons—I packed my bags into the new Cruiser and drove to the annual meeting of the Beef Farmers Association.

I MET Greg out the front of the clubhouse where the meeting was taking place. He grinned when he saw me, like a kid at Christmas. "Ready to show these old guys or what?"

I shook his proffered hand. "I think so."

Greg looked over at the Land Cruiser. "New wheels?"

"Yeah. I've done more trips to the Alice this last six months than I've done in my life," I told him. "It was about time I bought something a little more comfortable."

He was still smiling. "Next meeting is in Darwin. Ready for that?"

I sighed. "Man, I have so much on right now. I almost didn't turn up."

"What?"

I nodded. "Yeah. It was just a phone call from the ever-charming Jack Melville that made me show up. I'm really only here to see him lose."

Greg barked out a laugh. He looked around, obviously searching for someone. "Where's Travis?"

"Oh," I said. "He's gone home."

"Have you got staff sick or something?"

"No, no. He's gone *home* home. As in Texas."

Greg's eyes near popped out of his head. "What? For good?"

I shrugged. "I don't know. I hope not." I gave him what I hoped was a smile. "His grandfather isn't well."

"Oh," Greg said, sighing with relief. "Man, don't give me a heart attack like that. I thought you two were, you know, the real deal."

I snorted. "So did I."

He tilted his head and studied me for a minute. "You don't think he's coming back." It wasn't a question.

"Well, he says he is," I admitted. "But it's always different when you go home. All his family's there and old friends..."

Greg clapped his hand on my shoulder. "If he says he is, then he is."

"You sound like George and Ma."

He laughed at that. "Oh, how is Ma?"

I told him how she was getting better one day at a time, then we talked about the sleep-stealing joy of spring and calving season. It wasn't long before Allan joined us and our talk turned to the meeting.

There were formalities to go through first, then nominations would be read and each of the nominees would get up and do a spiel on themselves and why they wanted a place on the board.

"Excellent," I mumbled, rolling my eyes. "Can't wait."

"You hardly need to say anything," Greg said with a smile. "You're Charlie Sutton, for God's sake."

"Fat lot of good that will do me if I stand up there and they all think I'm a dickhead."

Allan laughed. "Oh please. Everyone thinks half the current board are dickheads and they manage just fine."

Greg looked at his watch, then at the doors to the auditorium. "You guys ready?"

"No," I said. "But do I have a choice?"

Greg and Allan both smiled and answered together. "Nope."

And with that, we walked inside.

THE FORMALITIES WERE all business details, finance reports and minutes of the last meeting, boring, but necessary. We broke for lunch and there were whispered conversations with the occasional glance at me from other attendees. When I sighed, Greg asked, "What's up?"

"Do you reckon Jack Melville sent out a memo to everyone to be wary of the fairy farmer?"

He looked around the room. People were trying not to openly stare, but weren't real good at hiding it. "Ignore 'em, Charlie."

"I hope it doesn't ruin our chances," I said, realising that it probably already had. No wonder Jack Melville was looking so smug.

"It's wrong, you know," Allan said. He'd never said much about me being gay. I knew that he knew, but he'd never spoken about it. "It don't make no difference. What people do behind closed doors don't make 'em any less a farmer than the next bloke." He shook his head. "I've got three boys. They're only kinda young and it's too early to be guessin' which teams they're on, if you know what I mean," he said, embarrassed. "But my middle boy... well, I dunno. But I tell ya, Charlie, it don't make no difference to me. And I'll be damned if I'll let the likes of Jack fucking Melville tell me that one of my boys isn't good enough. So you stand up there and do your speech, Charlie, and look that arsehole in the eye with your head held high. Because fuck him."

Greg threw his head back and laughed. "Shit, Allan. Tell us what you really think."

I was stunned. And humbled.

Allan wasn't finished. "It's hard enough out there," he said, shaking his head. "It's hard enough to get kids to carry on the family business as it is. I mean, makin' money outta red dirt is the cruellest job on earth, yet some kids are brave enough to take it on. And if one gay kid in this whole territory can see that Charlie Sutton can make it, then it just might stop them from walkin' away. It might stop one parent from losing a kid. Know what I mean?"

Greg wasn't laughing now, and I had to swallow the lump in my throat.

I think he was calling me some kind of role model for his could-be, might-be gay kid.

It was one of those profound life moments, and I was standing there with a sandwich halfway to my hangin'-open mouth. I slowly put my hand down and swallowed hard. "Uh..."

Greg laughed beside me, and Allan smiled. "It's the truth."

"I could kiss you right now," I said to him, without really thinking how that might sound to a straight guy. "Well... you know... if you were half a foot taller, twenty pounds lighter, and blond with a Texan accent."

Greg laughed some more, and Allan looked a mix of embarrassed and offended. He patted his midsection. "Twenty pounds lighter?"

"Yeah, I didn't mean that how it sounded... I just meant that you weren't Travis..." I cringed. God I was making it worse. I looked around at the bar. "Is it too early for bourbon?"

Allan threw his head back and laughed, just as the auditorium doors opened and some guy called the meeting back on.

"Righteo," Greg said with a deep breath. "It's game on."

Greg went first. Considering he'd been to every meeting in the last few years, it only seemed right. He knew everyone by name and told the room of some fifty people that he'd spare them a long and boring speech. They knew who he was, and if they wanted this industry and this Association to have a future, then it was time for a change. Short, to the point, and no-nonsense.

A few other guys spoke, telling more of their company and not saying a great deal about what they represented. I got that, I really did. If I had to describe myself, I'd probably describe Sutton Station instead, and people would see who I was.

But I wanted to show them more than that.

When it was Allan's turn, he spoke of family and future, but then he went into how he thought we needed to be aware of health issues and depression in particular.

I wasn't expecting that at all.

He gave figures on the rates of depression and suicides in the farming community across the country, and he said as an Association, we should be doing more. There should be some kind of system, he said, because there's pressure, familial and financial, that can bury a man out in that desert.

It was sobering.

And maybe it hit just a little too close to home. Because I wondered, for just a moment, how different my life might have been if my father had someone to talk to when life got him down.

Allan said it was the twenty-first century, for God's sake. We're not living in the fifties anymore. We know these things exist, and we know it's okay to get help. There were means to get help, and hell, it didn't have to be formal. If monthly meetings were a BBQ and a few beers or a fishing trip up north—if it was just a bloody game of cricket—that once-a-month weekend just might be someone's light in the dark.

He thanked everyone and took his seat between me and Greg, and the room was stock-still and silent. Until someone started clapping, and then everyone did. I nudged his knee with mine. "You did real good," I told him.

Allan exhaled loudly. "Still too early for that bourbon?"

I chuckled at him. "How about we make them doubles."

He smiled. "Sounds like a plan."

Then the speaker announced, "Next speaker is Charles Sutton."

Great.

I hated speaking in front of a group of people. But I was doing this, not just for Travis or for Sutton Station. I wasn't even really doing this to show Jack Melville that he was a fossil stuck in 1982.

I was doing this for me.

I took my laptop case with me and took a minute to get it all connected up to the Smart Board, thankin' God I remembered how to do it since my uni days. I ignored the chatter behind me and tried not to wonder if any of them had turned up just to see what a gay man looked like or to see if my handbag matched my dress.

I laughed to myself and covered it with a cough. I made a mental note to tell that joke to Travis because he'd think it was funny too, and with a smile still on my face, I faced my audience.

"My name is Charlie Sutton." I didn't have to tell them any more than that. They knew the name, most of them knew my father, and I didn't need to spiel off my credentials or rave about the reputation of Sutton Station.

"You've seen the emails we've sent out that talked of technology and the future of farming," I said. "Well, I'm gonna show you what we mean.

"I know what it's like, you hear someone talking about technology and you tune out because you don't have the time, the resources, or you think it just doesn't apply to us out here. But I'm going to show you how it does."

I pulled out one of Travis's cattle tracking collars and held it up. "This is a tracking collar. A somewhat crude but effective alert device that is simply worn by your cattle, and it works like this," I said, pressing the button on my laptop. The Smart Board behind me lit up, and on it was a satellite map with the boundary of Sutton Station outlined.

"This is my place," I told them. "It's... kinda big."

There were a few chuckles around the room, but suddenly they were interested. All eyes were on the board.

"Two point five eight million acres, give or take a few," I said. "That's two-thousand, six-hundred kilometres of fencing, three thousand head of cattle, twelve bores and a helluva lot of man hours to cover."

There were nods of agreement. "Now, what if I told you that I didn't have to leave my office to see it?"

I pressed another button, and an array of dots covered my property on the screen. "Twelve blue dots, twelve bores. The ten red dots?" I held up the collar again. "Are these."

"I have ten animals tagged. Five cows, five steers. Each in segregated mobs, as you can see"—I waved my hand at the screen—"in different paddocks over the entire property, hundreds of kilometres apart. Every bore on my property is solar powered, as most of them are these days. These collars are networked into those battery cells."

"Just the other day, a vet wanted to check some grazing cattle," I told them. "Which isn't such a big deal, but instead of looking for one needle in a haystack that's a few hundred square kilometres wide, I could pinpoint the herd to within a few metres."

I pressed another button, and the GPS coordinates came up on the screen. "Every collar has a code, every code has a GPS location."

I went back to the mapping screen and asked a guy at the closest table to pick one of the red dots on the screen. He chose a random dot and I clicked on it, bringing up another screen of numbers. "This collar is on a steer. Two years old, with a data-recorded complete insecticide drenching history, and there's even a migration history since he was fitted with the collar. You can see on average what percentage the animal spends grazing, and if that spikes or declines, I want to know why."

There were some blinks in surprise, a few head tilts and a few smiles. "You might think it's just one animal, what good is that?" I asked rhetorically. "Well, I know if he's there in the top western paddock, so are about another two hundred two-year old steers and heifers. Now before these collars, I could have guessed that's where they were, roughly. But with these collars, I don't need to send two of my team up there to check. I don't need to waste days and dollars. I can see it all from here."

"The blue dots—" I clicked on one of them, and again, a screen of numbers filled the Smart Board. "This is bore number seven. And you can see right now, in real time, the numbers clicking over?" Most people nodded. "That's how many kilolitres an hour that bore is pumping. And when a blue dot flashes, it means it's not pumping, which means I can fix it before I blow a piston or a drilling rig that would cost me ten grand to replace."

I held up my phone. "I can also see everything on this. It has, as part of the app, current stock rates, interest rates, weather forecasts and prices on feed and fuel. I can check almost anything to do with farming, right here, right now. I can make informed decisions on making the market work for me."

I smiled at them. "And the question you're all dying to ask? How much this costs me?" Nearly everyone nodded. "The collars cost three hundred dollars each. I have eleven collars, so thirty-three hundred bucks all up for the cattle collars, and they've saved me that much in man-hours in two months alone." I let them think about that for a moment. "The bore beacons weren't really designed to do what I use 'em for, but with the help of an American agronomy guy currently in the States—" I smiled to myself. "—we calibrated 'em via video chats on my laptop."

I pointed back to the Smart Board. "This is what farming in the future looks like. It doesn't take anything away from tradition or a lifetime of knowledge on your land. Nothing ever will. That's not what this is about. This is working smarter. This is using technology to make our lives a little easier, because we're spending more time in our offices now than we ever have. Paperwork, taxes, it doesn't seem to end." Everyone nodded like they knew all too well.

"So when we talk about driving this industry forward and taking it to the twenty-first century, this is what we're talking about. And this information, or ideas just like it, needs to be discussed and trialled. *That's* what this Association needs. We should be putting information out there for everyone to use, just like this collar system, not just to make us better farmers or to make one station better than another one, but to make us a better industry."

I finished by telling them if any of them were interested to come see me afterward. I'd be real happy to help. My speech, if that's what you'd call it, concluded the meeting and the chairman called it a day. We, of course, headed straight for the bar.

Greg handed me a beer and smiled. "You consider running for politics?"

I took a mouthful. "Shut the fuck up. That whole thing was painful."

"That was brilliant," he said.

I ignored his compliment and tapped my bottle to Allan's. "As was yours, mate. There is shit we should talk about, like asking for help, and not treat it like it's shameful or a weakness." I took another mouthful of beer and swallowed it down. "And you know what? If we don't get elected, we should still do this shit anyway. We don't need the Association to accomplish things. I mean, the corporate umbrella is useful, but it's not necessary."

Greg shook his head at me. "Jesus, Sutton, you're really into this, aren't you?"

"It's your fault I'm even here," I said, pointing my beer bottle at him. "You and Travis. He push, push, pushes me to do the best, to be the best. He gets right up my arse about it."

Greg grinned behind his beer bottle. "I bet he does."

Allan spat beer across the table, and Greg busted up laughing so hard, I think he almost did himself some internal damage.

I thought about what I'd said... *Travis gets right up my arse...*

Oh. My. God.

I must have turned every shade of mortified, which just made them laugh some more. I held up my wallet to the barman. "Bourbon, please."

"How many?"

I looked at Greg and Allan, who were both still doubled over laughing, then back to the barman. "All of it."

I hadn't even got one bourbon when a guy from the meeting came up to me. "Charles?"

"Charlie." I waved my hand at Greg and Allan, who were trying to compose themselves, and said, "Ignore these idiots."

He smiled. "You said if we had any questions, just to ask."

"Fire away."

It turns out he had a couple thousand acres up near Tennant Creek, and was real interested in the tracking collars because he'd had some cattle stolen from his property. The next guy was interested in the bore metres and the one after that thought the whole thing was an ingenious idea and wanted to know where I got them from.

It was a funny night. Our circle of friends got bigger and bigger, and we talked of ideas and how traditional farming was morphing into the future and how we were excited to see where it goes. I wished and *wished* that Travis was there. He would have loved it. He would have been in his element.

When we'd called it a night, I went back to my motel room and tried calling Travis. I wanted to share my night with him, but my Skype calls went unanswered. Cursing time zones, distance and the deep pang of missing him, I went to bed.

I was just about asleep when it occurred to me that I

didn't see Jack Melville for the rest of the night. In the morning we found out why.

He'd withdrawn from the election.

With no explanation and barely even an apology, the man simply stood down.

"Maybe he wanted to lose with dignity," Greg said. "That, or he didn't want to give any of us the satisfaction of beating him."

And when Greg, Allan and myself were announced as new directors of the Northern Territory Beef Farmers Association, the pill that old Jack Melville seemed to swallow looked particularly bitter.

I watched as the man walked away and wasn't sure how I felt about that. I didn't want the man to think he wasn't good enough. I just wanted to show him that the industry needed to move forward.

Allan patted my shoulder. "Let him go lick his wounds. He'll be back, in some way or another."

I grabbed his arm. "Come with me," I said, walking toward the door Jack just walked out of.

We got to the door, and I could see him and his wife hadn't got too far. I called out to him. "Jack! Wait."

The look on his face pretty much said I was the last person on the planet he wanted to see right now, and the smile his wife gave us wasn't too kindly either.

"If you've come to gloat, Sutton, or for me to offer my congratulations, you're out of luck," he sniffed.

Jesus, this man was a piece of work.

"Actually, no," I said. "I wanted to tell you thank you, and that you're right."

He looked between me and Allan, I guessed looking for some hint of sincerity. Allan was lookin' at me like I'd lost my mind in offering this man any kind of olive branch.

"You want to thank me?" Melville asked.

"Yes. You've done this Association a great many years' service, and that deserves thanks."

I don't know who was more stunned at my words: Jack, Allan or me.

I took a deep breath. "And you were right. I am *not* my father. I am a better farmer than him, because that's what he taught me to be, whether that was his intention or not. I'm sorry you didn't run for your old seat, and your reasons for withdrawing are yours alone and I respect that. It's a shame, though, because we could have used your experience."

Jack eyed me cautiously, like he was waiting for a punchline.

There wasn't one.

I tipped my hat at his wife and bid them a good day, leaving them kind of speechless. When we got back inside, Allan looked at me. "What the hell was that about?"

"Yesterday, you talked of speaking up to people who need it, right?" I said. "So that's what I did. I didn't want him to leave here bein' all depressed and shit. He's been farmin' out here for sixty years. That deserves some respect."

Allan shook his head at me. "After everything he said about you?"

I shrugged it off. "Him spruiking off about hate and discrimination said more about him than it ever did about me."

It seemed all Allan could do was shake his head. "Jesus. You're a bigger man than him, that's for sure."

I snorted. "Yep, and now he knows it. And the fact I'm gay and have more spine and bigger balls than him must just be eating him alive."

Allan laughed. "There's the Charlie I know."

NOT WASTING A MINUTE, we sat for our very first meeting, which was more preliminary than productive: we confirmed the date for the next meeting in Darwin, shook hands and went our separate ways.

I couldn't wait to get home.

I was excited, almost bouncing in my seat the whole way, and quite often found myself smiling for no good reason.

I just couldn't wait to tell Travis. He was gonna be stoked, and out of all the things we did and felt, Travis being proud of me was the best feeling ever.

Of course I had to relay the events of the last two days to everyone at home first, which only helped to feed my buzz. And by the time I finally got through to Travis on Skype, I was almost laughing as I talked.

As soon as I saw his face on my screen, I just started talking. A hundred mile a minute, I started telling him everything that happened, how my speech went, what I said and I laughed when I told him how I showed them all the genius ideas he'd come up with and I totally took credit for. I told him I got elected and how I owed it all to him...

But his face just looked all wrong. He looked distracted and like he'd barely survived an emotional cyclone.

"Trav, baby, what's wrong?"

His eyes filled with tears and they spilled down his cheeks. "Charlie, my grandpa died today."

OF ALL THE THINGS

OF ALL THE things that distance put me through, helplessness was by far the worst.

He was hurting so much, and I couldn't do one single thing.

I wanted to wipe his tears and hold him. I wanted to be there, to listen to him rant and rave or to sit in silence—like all the times he did that for me.

But I couldn't.

"Tell me what to do, Travis," I begged him. "Please. I'll do it."

"I need you," he said, scrubbing his face.

The one thing. He needed me to do the one thing I couldn't do.

"I wish you were here," he said.

"Can I apply for something?" I asked. "Does the government have some special visa or lenience thing for people without passports? I can fly to Sydney tonight." I looked at my watch. Shit. "Tomorrow. I can fly there tomorrow, and I don't know, Trav, but there has to be something I can do. I need to be there."

"There isn't." He shook his head and took a deep breath. "It's okay, Charlie. I know you can't. I just wish…"

"Me too. Trav, I wish so much."

He nodded and looked down from the screen for a long second. "Maybe I should go. You had such a good day and I ruined it," he whispered, putting his hand out as though to shut his laptop.

"No, no, Trav, wait," I cried. "Don't go. Please stay. Talk to me. Don't go."

"It's late, and it's been a horrible day," he whispered. "I'm so tired."

He looked it. "Climb into bed, baby," I told him. I carried my laptop into our room and sat on our bed with my back against the headboard. When he appeared again on the screen, he was lying on his side, with a pillow and one arm folded under his head. The room was dark—the only light was the screen of the laptop he was using—and he was looking at me, much like he did when he was lying right next to me.

His hair was kinda flopping up, and I stupidly tried to touch it. And it shot an ache straight to my heart that all I could feel was my laptop screen and not the fine strands of his getting-too-long hair, or that I couldn't swipe my thumbs over his cheekbones or down his jaw.

So I did what I could do.

I talked to him.

I told him of all the little things, the stupid, inconsequential things, the everyday things, and watched as his blinks got longer and longer. I told him how the other day I took Texas for a ride and how Shelby threw a too-damn-spoiled tantrum because I took him and not her, and how she refused to even look at me for a whole day, how it took me bribing her with an apple before she came around.

I told him how Nugget was eating more and drinkin' less and how I was hoping he'd be quitting those night feeds soon. I told him the little guy was still funny as hell, and how I'm pretty sure the wombat knew damn well he had us all wrapped around his little finger. Or paw. Or whatever.

Trav closed his eyes and smiled. "I'm listening."

So I told him about the poddy calves and how the little buggers had finally learned there was an art to the production-line feeding and it really worked better for everyone involved when it wasn't a free-for-all. I told him the three surviving Beatles were doing just fine and that Sonny and Cher were growing bigger every day.

I'm pretty sure it wasn't what I was saying, it was just the sound of my voice, but his eyes stayed closed. And if my words were a soothing blanket for him, then I would talk all night if that's what it took.

So then I told him all about the holiday we'd take when he got back and this time I'd take him to Uluru, and how we had a Beef Farmers meeting scheduled for later in the year in Darwin, so we could take some time then and do whatever he wanted.

And I would. I'd do whatever he wanted.

His lips parted slightly, his eyes were closed. It was a sight I'd seen countless times. A sight I'd long ago burned into memory, a sight I swore I'd never take for granted, and yet, I felt I somehow had.

He was asleep.

I traced my finger on the screen along his eyebrow, across his lips. I told him I was sorry I wasn't there when he needed me. I told him I loved him.

And I disconnected the call.

I GUESS I didn't have to tell anyone that my mood had gone from happy to helpless. I'm pretty sure it was written clear on my face. I told them in the morning that Trav's grandpa died and how wishin' wasn't a strong enough word for how much I wanted to be there.

That night after dinner, Ma sat with me. She looked better, healthier, but her eyes were sad for me. "Oh, love. What a day, huh?"

"I feel so bad," I told her. "There I was bein' all excited and laughing, and he'd had one of the worst days of his life."

"You weren't to know."

"I should have asked him first instead of just jumpin' right in and rattlin' off everything I'd done."

"He won't think bad of you, love."

"Maybe." I shook my head. "I shouldn't be surprised that he doesn't want to talk to me, really. Because I keep thinkin', Ma, that if it was reversed, if it was him having a great time and me suffering like that, well, I'm pretty sure I wouldn't want to be talking to him either. Actually, I'd be a whole lotta hurt and pissed off."

She smiled at me. "Yes, but we all know how you carry on, love."

Her attempt at making me smile worked, even if just for a second. "Gee, thanks."

"Was he okay when you said goodbye?"

I shrugged, a bit embarrassed. "Well, I dunno. He was really tired, so I just talked to him 'til he fell asleep."

"Aww," she said with a that's-so-sweet look on her face. "I'm sure he appreciated that, love."

"I dunno," I said, shrugging again. "It's not like I could do anything else."

I guess he did appreciate it, because when I woke up the next day, there was an email from him.

Thank you for last night. Sorry I fell asleep. I needed you and you were there for me, even on the other side of the world. Hearing your voice was everything.

Don't worry if you don't hear from me for a few days. We're busy with funeral arrangements. Will talk when I can. You're never far from my thoughts.

I didn't hear from him for a few days, just like he said, but then I didn't hear from him for a few days more after that.

Then it was a week.

I kept refreshing my inbox, thinking maybe something was wrong with it, and then I checked my Skype settings a few times to see if something wasn't wrong with that too.

There was nothing wrong with them at all.

I still had work to do, a station to run, a business. I still had other people who depended on me, and I had to put one foot in front of the other, not for me, but for them.

It didn't stop the hollow ache in my chest; it didn't stop the God-awful-missing-him that kept me awake at night. When I did sleep, my dreams were filled with snippets of blue eyes and bright, blinding smiles, slow Texan drawls that whispered words of sex and promise.

And every morning I woke up alone, and the emptiness that somehow felt like lead sat heavy in my chest.

It was simply a case of inhale, exhale, repeat. As much as it hurt to breathe, the numbing daily routine that I once cursed was my saving grace. It had been three weeks since he'd left. Three long-as-hell, heart-aching weeks.

Everyone kinda kept their distance, giving me what they thought I wanted. How wrong they were. The old version of me would have wanted solitude, but this version of me—the Travis'ed version of me—wanted company.

I actually think bein' alone would just about kill me.

On the Friday, I woke to an email in my inbox and I just about had a heart attack trying to open it, followed by a weight of disappointment.

Funeral was yesterday. Miss you more than words can say.

That was it. One line, two sentences. I'd waited all these heartbreakin' days for that. It was everything, and it was nowhere near enough. I wasn't sure what was worse: getting no email or getting an email that didn't mention coming home.

I didn't reply. Not yet, anyway.

He was going through a family crisis, and he certainly didn't need my hurt feelings to contend with. I guessed a spiteful is-that-all-I'm-worth-to-you ranty email wouldn't have helped either.

So I closed my laptop and stared at the wall for a while instead. And that's when the two boxes on top of the filing cabinet caught my eye. I hadn't thought about them in a while and I found myself emptying both boxes of my child-hood mementos onto my desk. I went through the news-paper cut outs from the scrapbook of Samuel's things—my brother's things—and read them one more time.

Maybe I wasn't in the best frame of mind, maybe I was missing Travis too much, maybe I was hurting. Or maybe it *was* time and the right thing to do, but I riffled through the desk drawer until I found the scrap piece of paper I was looking for. Before I could change my mind, I picked up the phone and dialled the number written down. "Laura? It's me, Charlie. I want to meet Sam."

MA FOUND me in the lounge room where I was folding laundry and telling Nugget not to undo my good work as he barrelled over every damn thing I'd just folded.

It had been two days since Travis's two-sentence email. There'd been nothing else from him, and I hadn't replied yet.

Ma sat down and eyed me cautiously. "You okay, hun?"

"Sure, why wouldn't I be?"

She looked at the clothes I was folding. "You washed his shirts."

"Had to do it sometime," I said. "Anyways, they didn't smell like him anymore. I wore 'em too much."

Ma nodded sadly. "I wish I knew how to help you."

I sighed and the shirt I was folding was now crumpled in my lap. "I guess it had to happen sometime, right?"

"You don't know he's not coming back."

"I don't know he is, either," I said. Nugget tackled the laundry basket, and I almost even smiled.

"Have you checked your emails this afternoon?" she asked.

I shook my head. "I'm not up for the disappointment, to be honest."

Ma frowned. "Oh, Charlie."

"It's okay, Ma," I told her, starting to refold the shirt I was still holding. Although it wasn't okay. *I* wasn't okay. There was a gaping hole in my life. "Life goes on, right?" I said. "I mean, the world hasn't stopped turning, people are still carryin' on like nothing's changed."

"I guess so," she said. I could tell she didn't agree with me, that she just didn't want to argue.

We both watched Nugget in silence as he managed to flip the washing basket on its side and then ran in and out of it half a dozen times.

"Can I tell you something?" Ma said. It wasn't really a question, because I knew she was telling me whether I wanted to hear it or not. "Do you remember, not too long ago, when you said you couldn't do any of this without Travis?"

I didn't have to answer that. We both knew it was true.

"You were so sure you couldn't do anything without him," she went on to say. "You thought you could only get through your list of things to do if he was here. But you know what, Charlie? Despite how much your heart is hurting right now, you've more than proved you can do it all. You're on the Board of Directors, you've got a contract with the supermarket buyer, you've finished your assessments for your degree—"

"Well, Travis finished those."

"You're meeting your brother," she said.

"I really wanted Travis here for that," I admitted quietly. "If there's one thing I can't get through without him, it might be that. I don't know why I agreed to meet him this weekend..." Well, I did know why. Laura was heading back to Darwin next week, so it made sense that Sam come down to the Alice while she was still here. But still, I was gonna need Travis here for that.

And, well, that wasn't going to happen.

"You'll do just fine, Charlie."

I didn't speak for a little while. I didn't trust my voice not to crack, and I didn't want to cry. Because I wasn't fine. I was alone. I should have never dared to hope that he would come back. When he was at the airport, I knew then he wasn't coming home. I was foolish to hope. Finally, I took a breath and said, "I miss him, Ma. I can run this station, I can have bigger dreams and hopes for this farm, but I miss him."

"I know you do, love."

I shook my head. "It's like having one lung removed. I can still live and breathe, but God, it's not the same. My chest hurts and I have this hollow emptiness that weighs me down. And sometimes I think of him out of the blue and it stops me right where I stand, and I have to catch my breath."

Ma's eyes got watery. "I wish I knew what to say, Charlie."

I went back to foldin' laundry, and then the upturned washing basket ran into the door. The basket hit with such force, it kind of toppled to the side, leaving a very stunned, very sad-looking Nugget wondering what the hell just happened.

I barked out a laugh, then went over and picked him up. "You're such a little dufus. What did you think was gonna happen if you ran into the door?"

"Underneath a washing basket?" Ma added. She was smiling now. "Is he okay?"

I ruffled Nugget's forehead with my finger and tucked him into the crook of my arm. "He's fine. Just needs a bit of a cuddle, don't ya, mate?"

I could tell from the way Ma looked at me, she thought he wasn't the only one. Before she left, she said, "Don't leave his email unanswered, Charlie. If he taught you anything, it was to tell him how you were feeling. It don't matter if you think he's not doing the same. You keep up your end of the bargain—do everything you can do—and let the chips fall where they may."

Later that night, with Ma's words in my head, I did exactly that. I tried several times, typing out long-winded lines about time and distance, about feeling lost and how the pain of his absence kept me awake at night. But nothing I said seemed right. So in the end, I kept it short and simple and hit Send before I could change my mind.

Travis,

If this is your goodbye, please know that I am, and will always be, grateful for you.

This desert has not changed in ten thousand years, yet now it is not the same. Like me, I guess.

I washed your shirts today. They didn't smell like you anymore.

I will wait for you.

I love you.

If this is your goodbye, don't tell me.

I don't want to know.

CHAPTER EIGHTEEN

IF THIS IS YOUR GOODBYE

NUMB IS how I would describe the next three days. Travis didn't reply in the first twenty-four hours after I sent my email, and I stopped checking after that.

And in all fairness, if he wasn't coming back, I asked him not to tell me.

So I guessed that this was him not telling me.

Everyone was kinda good about it. I never said a word, but they weren't blind or stupid. They gave me not-knowing-what-to-say looks and made a point of not saying his name. Billy stuck close to me, making sure I was busy and distracted, and when Billy wasn't there, Ernie was, or Bacon or Trudy, and I realised they were taking shifts to babysit me.

I'm pretty sure just a year ago that would have pissed me off, but now it was kind of... nice.

Reassuring.

I wasn't alone.

But there's a mile-wide difference between bein' alone and bein' lonely.

Those three days were okay, but the nights damn near

killed me. That was when bein' lonely and bein' alone seemed one and the same. That was when the missing-him was at its worst.

And I probably wasn't in the right frame of mind to be meeting Sam, the guy who might or might not be my brother. I had no idea what to expect and no one to lean on.

Well, correction. I had no Travis to lean on.

And maybe the numbness in missing him helped tamp down any nerves I might have had in meeting Sam. Because when the car pulled up at the homestead and I was meeting him for the very first time, I wasn't nervous at all.

If I had ever doubted that this guy who was raised in the city was any relation of mine, it was gone the second I saw him.

Because the guy who got out of the car along with Laura and another blonde woman was a mirror image of me.

Well, he was all clean-clothes and fancy-shoes and I was all worn-boots and red-dirt, but we looked the same.

I walked down the veranda steps toward them. I said hello to Laura first and held out my hand to Sam. "I'm Charlie."

He shook my hand and smiled. "Sam." He introduced the woman with him. "And this is my girlfriend, Ainsley."

"Nice to meet you," I said, shaking her hand as well.

Ainsley was thin, tall, blonde and pretty. She smiled warmly and looked at Laura. "You weren't joking when you said they looked alike."

Laura laughed, a mix of nervous and relieved, but she looked at me fondly. "Thanks for inviting us, Charlie."

"You're welcome," I said just as George came over.

He looked at Sam, then at me, then back to Sam. "Well, holy shit."

I laughed again and nodded toward the house. "Come

on, let's go inside. You guys might want to freshen up, since it's a bit of a drive from town to here. Nara has morning tea ready if you're hungry."

We grabbed their bags from the car and took them inside. The plan was they'd stay a night or two if they wanted. This was new to all of us, but there would be no pressure. If it was awkward or uncomfortable or too much too soon, then they could leave at any time.

I gave a quick tour of the house, not that there was a great deal to see, and we sat at the dining table. Nara had served scones with some jams and cream, and pots of tea and coffee. She was pleased with herself, and I smiled at her. "Thanks. It looks great."

Ma came in, still walking a little gingerly. "She did it all by herself too," Ma said, patting Nara's arm. Nara blushed and darted out of the room, just as Laura stood up to help Ma sit down.

Laura kissed her cheek. "Wow, you look so much better!" she said.

"She's still supposed to be taking it easy," I told her. "But she doesn't listen."

Ma got comfortable in the seat next to me—Travis's seat—and smiled warmly at me. "Learned it from you, love."

I introduced Ma around the table and then George, who came in just after. I had asked them both to be with me today, not knowin' how it would go, and they both said they wouldn't miss it.

This whole meeting was for me and Sam to meet and get to know each other, so I figured I'd better start the conversation. I was just about to ask Sam and Ainsley how their flight was when Laura asked, "Where's Travis?"

"Oh," I started. I wasn't ready for that question, and

hearing his name made my heart clench. "He's, um, he's gone home."

Maybe it was the beat of silence, maybe it was how my eyes flicked to Ma just a fraction, but I think Laura got the gist of it. Or maybe not. "Oh. For how long?"

"I don't know," I told her.

"Oh." Now she got it.

Ignoring the lump in my throat and the ache in my chest, I smiled at Sam. "So, how was your flight?"

"Good," he said. "It's been years since I've been to the Alice. Ainsley's never been, so it was good for her to see it too."

"And the drive out here wasn't too boring, I hope," I said, looking at them both.

He smiled. "It sure is different."

"And flat," Ainsley said. "And red."

I laughed at that. "That pretty much sums it up."

It turned out Sam was in corporate finance insurance with one of the big banks, which is where he met Ainsley. He went to school and uni in Darwin, and he loves it. "Stinking hot and humid are my two favourite seasons," he said with a bit of a laugh.

He could ride a horse, but he hadn't in years. He rode a motorbike to work, loved kayaking and played footy on weekends. "That's what's so good about Darwin," he said. "The city's there if you want, but it's more like a big-country coastal town."

"I was only in Darwin a month or two ago," I told him. "Well, we flew up and went out to Kakadu. So it wasn't a long trip. But the city's not really my scene. I spent three years in Sydney—that was enough for me."

"Three years?" he asked.

"Yep. I went to uni there," I said, omitting the whole

my-father-made-me-go-because-I'm-gay part of the conversation. "Loved it when I was there, but not sure I could go back now."

We'd long finished the scones and tea, and I knew Nara would want the table for lunch soon. I made a point of looking at my watch. "We're about to be trampled by the lunchtime crowd," I said and then suggested I show them around outside.

So before the station hands came in, we headed outside. We walked around the homestead, just strolling and talking, and we ended up at the stables and I introduced them to Shelby. Then it was Laura who suggested that maybe me and Sam might like to go for a ride. Just us, no interruptions, no one listening, no one watching and judging. We had some years to catch up on, she'd said.

I thought it sounded like a pretty good idea.

I considered giving him Shelby, because she was quiet as a lamb most of the time, but she could also be a bad-tempered thing if she wanted. And considering how, after the last time I got on Texas, Shelby almost put me through the fence, I figured Sam would be safer on Travis's horse.

I told George where we'd be going, saddled the horses, and headed east. Sam relaxed a bit, and maybe I did too. "So, your mum dropped a bombshell by telling you about me, huh?" I asked.

He snorted. "Ah, yeah. I was shocked and a bit pissed off, to be honest, but I guess she had her reasons for only telling me now."

"Yeah, it was a bit of a shock to me too," I told him. "I'd had no clue, about her or you. She just turned up one day."

"I think she feels bad about that," he said. "She said she doesn't really even remember driving out here. She found that magazine with you on the cover and the next thing she knew she pulled up out the front of your house."

I laughed at that. "Yeah, it was a surprise. Well, not her so much, but the news of you was, that's for sure."

"Me?"

"Yeah, a brother," I said, embarrassed. Maybe I shouldn't have used that word just yet. "I spent a whole lotta years out here wonderin' what it'd be like to have someone else my age around."

Sam looked out across the red and barren landscape, and shook his head, almost in wonder. "I can't imagine what it was like to grow up out here."

"It was pretty good," I told him. "It was fun, when I was a kid anyway. I got into enough mischief to drive Ma crazy."

Sam laughed. "She seems real nice."

"Who, Ma? She's the best." Then I thought since we were on the subject of mothers... "You know, I don't blame your mum for leavin'. I just wanted you to know that."

Sam shifted in the saddle and seemed to think about my words for a while. "I don't either," he said. "I didn't get it at first, to be honest. But the more I thought about it, the more I think she made the only decision she felt she could at that time, you know? It must have been hard."

"Yeah," I agreed. "I don't remember her. I remember brown hair, that's all. I think I was four when she left. But Ma's been my real mum every day since. And you know what? That's how I like it."

"And your dad?" he asked. "Well, technically my dad too, I guess."

I chuckled. "It's a bit to get your head around, isn't it?" Then I sighed and told him the truth. "My dad was okay. Growin' up, when I was still a kid, he was okay. He worked a lot, always busy runnin' this place, and that was fine. I had

Ma and George too. But when I got older, he... well, he wasn't so nice."

Sam frowned. "I'm sorry to hear that."

"You know," I said, "I think I've learned more about my father since he died than I did when he was still here."

"And what's that?"

"That I didn't know him at all," I said. "But your mum remarried, yeah?"

Sam smiled. "Yeah. He's great. I call him my dad. Always have."

"And Ainsley?" I asked. "How long have you been together?"

"Two years," he answered. "I hope you didn't mind her coming here. I asked her to come with me to meet you, you know, for moral support."

"It's fine. I'm glad she's here." It was something I understood. Something I wished I had. "Um, Travis... he's my boyfriend... well, he *was*... he went home, back to the States. His grandpa died, so it's not like he wanted to go," I said, trying not to sound too pathetic. "But he's been gone almost four weeks and I haven't heard from him in almost two weeks..."

"You miss him."

"Very much."

Then I thought about it. "I assume Laura told you that I was gay."

Sam snorted. "Yeah."

"Something funny?"

He smiled. "Mum was kind of excited actually. She said this way she gets a daughter-in-law and a son-in-law." He shook his head. "But she thinks Travis—is that his name?"

I nodded.

"She thinks Travis doesn't like her very much." Then he

corrected, "Well, not that he doesn't like her, more that he's very protective of you."

I nodded and couldn't help but smile. "I dunno," I said. "He was only supposed to be gone for a little while, but now he won't answer my emails or Skype calls, so I can just assume the worst, yeah?"

"Maybe he's just busy or something," he offered.

"Yeah, maybe."

"I don't have a problem with it," he said quickly. "I mean, it's fine with me. I don't care either way."

"Well, good," I said flatly. "Because if you did, you'd be gettin' off my boyfriend's horse and walkin' home."

I didn't care if I offended him. I was finally—*finally*—comfortable in my own skin, and I wasn't having some stranger turn up at my house and have a problem with who I was. But I needn't have worried, because Sam threw his head back and laughed.

"You can laugh all you want," I told him, smiling. Then after a pause, I said, "Your mum seemed okay with it. With me and Trav. She didn't even bat an eyelid."

Sam smiled at that. "Nah, not much fazes her. Dunno if it's 'cause she's a nurse or what, but she's pretty cool with most things. And she said you and I have the same taste in partners," he said with a grin. "Blond hair, blue eyes?"

I considered that. "I guess we do."

Sam looked out over the saltbush to the flat, flat horizon. "Tell me about this place. What do you actually do?"

So I told him. We rode and talked for hours, but it went by so fast. He was easy to talk to: we found the same things funny, we even laughed alike. It was uncanny and disconcerting, in a good way, that we could have nothing but DNA in common—we'd never spent a minute together before now—yet we were so similar.

It was like something out of the *Twilight Zone*.

We weren't the same in every aspect. He was city raised and had an office job, his office was a cubicle, and my office was 2.58 million acres. He liked the convenience of takeout food and going to bars on weekends, whereas that was all so foreign to me. He liked bands I'd never heard of, and he talked of his friends like he had a hundred of them. He loved the ocean and open water, and I was a desert-dweller.

There were fundamental differences between us.

But there was also something very fundamentally the same. We were woven from the same cloth. And there was something unexpected but oddly comforting about that.

By the time we rode back home, I had no doubt that me and Sam would be okay. I had no idea what the future might bring, but I was pretty certain we'd stay in touch at least. We unsaddled the horses, brushed them down and fed them, and he was still smiling when we walked inside.

"We're in here," Ma called out from the lounge room. They were having a cup of tea, and Ma smiled when she saw that Sam and I had gotten along. "Nugget's keeping us entertained."

"Where is the little guy?" I asked just as the tiny wombat did his little jumpy-run out from behind one lounge and tackled his Rumble Bear. I scooped him up and ruffled his forehead. "Are you being a show off?"

Sam took a seat next to Ainsley. "Isn't he just the cutest thing you've ever seen?" she cried.

"Cute?" I asked. "He's a monster. A sleep-stealin', boot-chewin' monster." I looked at Ma. "Has he been fed?"

"About an hour ago," she said. "I thought we might get the pizza oven fired up tonight. How does that sound?"

"Perfect."

And it was. Everyone had met Laura and Ainsley in the

hours that Sam and I were riding, so when they all came in for dinner, I introduced him. There were a few stares and comments about the likeness between us, but as the night went on, he talked and chatted with everyone, laughing and taking the piss about football.

Ma sat down beside me. "He's a nice kid," she said. "For what it's worth, I'm glad you decided to meet him."

"Me too," I said. I took a deep breath. "I wish Trav could have met him, Ma. He'd like him."

Ma's face fell. "I wish he could have too, love."

Then Trudy stood up. "If I could have a minute," she said loudly. "Um, while everyone's here, I guess now is a good time to tell you all that I'm pregnant." She looked right at me and nodded. "Me and Bacon are having a baby."

I had to blink back instant tears, but I stood up and hugged her so damn hard. "Thank you, thank you," I whispered. "You're gonna do great."

I got shunted out of the way by everyone else congratulating them, and it was such, such good news. Ma was crying and just kept repeatin' "A baby. We're having a baby" until George hugged her to shut her up. I was so happy for them, yet all I kept thinking was I wished Travis was here. I wished so damn much it hurt.

Later that night when I was lyin' in bed with nothing but silence and heartache, I reached out and touched his pillow. "I wish you were here," I told him. "I wish you didn't leave me."

Nobody answered.

THE NEXT MORNING WAS BUSY. I was up early to get the dogs and horses fed before helping Nara in the kitchen. Breakfast was a loud affair, with much laughing and chatter. I don't think Sam and Ainsley were strictly morning people, but they sure were grateful for Travis's coffee machine and were soon smiling.

George took a phone call after breakfast and said the delivery I'd ordered at the co-op had arrived. He said Ma needed something in town as well, and considering I had company, he took the new Cruiser and drove out. By the way he was smiling, I think Ma might have been right about his love affair with the new car.

We spent the morning checking poddy calves. It was interesting to see Laura get right in and help, but Sam and Ainsley kind of stood back. Like I said, we were similar, but we weren't the same.

It was great for them to visit, but this was still a working farm. As much as I would have liked to talk to them all day, things still needed to get done.

Bacon, Ernie and Billy headed out in the first western paddock to do a check for sick and abandoned calves and would be gone for most of the day. And just before lunch, Ma stood on the veranda waving. "It's Ernie. He's on the two-way radio."

Not knowing what was wrong, I ran into my office and lifted the receiver of the two-way. "What's up?"

Ernie's voice crackled through. "Charlie, we got a birthing cow down. Her back legs don't work. She's not looking too good."

"Goddammit."

Great. Just what I didn't need. Pregnancy paraplegia wasn't too uncommon. It was where the unborn calf would press against the nerve to the back legs. The cow would regain full use of the legs once the pressure was eased once the calf was born. But it meant the cow couldn't birth properly and usually the calf would die and, more often than not, the mother as well.

"Where abouts are you?" I asked. "First western paddock, yes?" Which was only about a thousand square kilometres of desert. "How far in? Are you near one of the bores?"

"Charlie," Ernie's voice cracked again. "This cow, it's wearing one of those tracking device collars."

I flipped open my laptop and brought up the tracking screen and checked the location feature. "There are three cows in that paddock wearing them," I told him.

"We went northeast of the third bore," Ernie said. "Dunno how long for. Maybe fifteen, twenty kays."

I looked on the screen, and right about where Ernie said, there was a little red flashing circle along with the GPS coordinates. "I can see you. I know exactly where you are. I'm on my way."

I picked my backpack, the one I always had ready with a phone and some bottled water, just as Laura came inside followed by Sam and Ainsley. "Everything okay?" Laura asked.

"We've got a birthing cow in trouble," I told her. "Wanna come?"

She nodded quickly and looked at Sam and Ainsley. "You two can come too."

Ma looked at the clock. She looked anxious, like she had something to say but didn't want to. Or couldn't. "You okay, Ma?"

She made a face. "George will be back any minute. Maybe you should wait—"

"No time. But when he gets in, tell him where we are." I turned my laptop around so she could see the screen and pointed to the red dot in particular. "Show him this. He'll know exactly where to find us."

I jumped into the old ute, and Laura climbed in beside me. Sam climbed up onto the tray back and helped pull Ainsley up. I smiled at the horrified look on her face as she sat down on the dirty, rusted, cowshit-covered tray, and I drove out into the desert.

There wasn't a track to follow, but Laura navigated using the tracking app on my phone, and it wasn't long until we found them.

The cow, lying down and mewling, was weak, and the calf was not yet presented. At this rate, it wasn't looking good for either one of them to survive.

I knelt at the business end of the cow. Laura surprised me, but I guessed with nurse training, it shouldn't have. She knelt beside me. "Tell me what to do."

"I need to check the calf," I told her. "We need two front hooves and a nose first. If it's breech... well, if it's breech, they'll both die."

So, like I'd done about twenty times before, I gently slid my hand into the birth canal of the cow. Fully dilated, but unable to push, the unborn calf was literally stuck.

And I could feel it. Slimy, wet and hot, right where they should be, were two front hooves.

"Right. It's in the right position," I said, gently pulling my hand back out. Laura was still beside me. "Wanna feel?"

She nodded. "Can I?"

"Just be careful," I told her. "Nice and slow. The cow can't move her back legs, but if you've got your arm in there and she tries to roll, you'll snap your shoulder."

With what I presumed was a nurse's inquisitive precision, Laura did just as I had done, and she looked up at me and smiled. "Two front feet."

I looked over to Sam and Ainsley. Sam looked a little grossed out, whereas Ainsley had a look on her face that told me she hadn't looked horrified before at the dirty ute. She looked horrified now. "Sam, there's some rope coiled on the back of the ute. Can you bring it over, please?"

He ran over, grabbed the rope and brought it to me, but then took a quick few steps back. Obviously not his thing. I smiled. Sam and I might be full brothers and yes, we looked alike, but he was city through and through, and I... well, I was made of red desert sand.

I tied a double slipknot in the end of the rope and, holding onto it, went back inside the cow and secured the knot around the front two hooves of the unborn calf. "Ernie," I said. "I'm gonna need your help down this end. Laura, I need you to hold the cow's head. Try to keep her still."

I dug myself a bit of traction in the sand near the cow's leg, wrapped the rope around my hands a few times, and waited for Ernie to do the same. But as soon as we started to pull, the cow bellowed and started to roll, knocking Laura backward. She was quick to get back up. "I'm all right, I'm all right," she said and went straight back to holding the cow.

I liked that she was so hands-on, but it wasn't enough. I was just about to tell Sam he had to get his city-boy hands dirty when the new Cruiser arrived in a cloud of dust. Like some saving grace, and not a moment too soon, George was here. He'd done this more times than I could count—hell, he was the one who showed me how to do it—and I wanted him pulling with me.

"Ernie, get up and put your knee on the shoulder," I instructed. "Put your weight on her. Hold her down."

"She's not looking too good, Charlie," Laura said. "Her breathing's laboured. Her eyes are rolling."

Shit.

"George!" I yelled. "We're out of time!"

And the knot slipped off. Goddammit. I went back into the cow up to my elbow to refix the rope around the calf's legs when two knees dropped down beside me. I tightened the rope the best I could and slid my hand back out, holding the rope up to George.

Only it wasn't George at all.

It was blue eyes and a Texas smile.

CHAPTER NINETEEN

HOME

THE WORLD STOPPED SPINNING and there was no one else, nothing else but him. In that instant, I could finally breathe, and I wanted to laugh and cry and he was smiling at me like he'd never left. My brain kept telling me to say something, *say something, Charlie.* So I did.

"You're late."

He laughed, and I swear, everything—*everything*—was right with my world. "Missed you too," he said.

"Ah," Ernie said. "Trav, mate, it's real good to have you home, but, Charlie, she's losing it."

Oh. That's right. The cow. The calf.

I forgot what I was doing.

"Help me pull it out," I said to Travis. "Grab the rope." He did. "We're gonna pull on three," I said. "One. Two." I wrapped the rope around my hand another time. "Three."

And pull we did. Every muscle straining, using every ounce of strength we had, we leaned back and pulled. Two hooves first, then a bloodied, purplish nose, and we kept on pulling, until the baby Brahman calf was born.

It wasn't pretty. We were covered in afterbirth, and the

smell was even worse. We'd kind of ended up leaning right back, pulling the rope through our feet, and when it was done, Travis looked at me and laughed. "Is this your idea of a welcome?"

"It's not over yet," I said, scrambling to my feet. "Come on, help me lift him."

Lifting forty kilos of slippery Brahman calf isn't exactly easy, but we carried it over to the ute and lifted his back legs over the bullbar so his head hung down toward the ground.

"What are we doing?" Travis asked.

"Rub him down, hard, like this." I ran my hands down the calf, from his hind legs to his shoulders, in hard, fast movements.

Travis started to do as I showed him. The calf was slimy, covered in blood and gunk, and not breathing. "How long have I gotta do this for?" he asked, suddenly more serious.

And then the calf made a half-cry, half-bleat sound.

"Until you hear that," I said.

We carried the calf back to the mother, and everyone stood back and took in what we'd just been part of. It was a pretty remarkable thing.

"That was incredible," Laura said. She was grinning from ear to ear. Even Sam was smiling. I'm pretty sure from the look on Ainsley's face, that we'd just converted her into a lifelong vegetarian.

I finally looked at Travis. He was already staring at me. He took three long strides and damn near knocked me off my feet, he hugged me so hard. "You wanna tell me what *if this is your goodbye* was all about?" he whispered into my neck. "It fucking nearly killed me."

"I thought you'd gone home for good," I whispered.

He shook his head. "I *am* home," he said. "Here, with you. I'm home."

"You're really here."

"I really am."

He pulled back, grabbed hold of my face and kissed me before hugging me again.

God, he felt so right. Like I hadn't missed him, like I hadn't felt alone and abandoned, he was here and when he held me like that, it made everything right.

I pulled back and pushed his shoulder. Hard. "I thought you left me, you arsehole."

He half laughed, half cried and shook his head. "Never."

I fisted his shirt and pulled him against me again, but George, who I hadn't seen until just now, clapped his hand on my shoulder. "Um, there's company, boys."

I let go of Trav and looked at George. "A delivery from the co-op?"

He grinned at me. "Surprise!"

I shook my head at him. "You knew? You knew he was here and you didn't say!"

George looked as happy now as he did when we brought Ma home from hospital. "It's a long story, apparently. I'm sure he'll tell you all about it."

I shot Travis a look. "He better."

Travis pulled me by the neck and he kissed the side of my head. "I will." But then he looked around at the expectant faces. He nodded to Laura. "Hello again."

"Hi, Travis," she answered with a smile.

"Um, Trav," I said. "I'd like to introduce you to Sam, Laura's son, my... brother." It felt weird to say that. "And this is Ainsley, Sam's girlfriend."

Travis was stuck staring at Sam, then back at me, then back to Sam. "Holy shit."

I laughed. "You're not the first to say that."

Travis wiped his hand on his jeans and extended it to Sam. "It's real good to meet you."

Sam smiled. "I've heard a bit about you. Nice to meet you too. Despite the cow-afterbirth handshake."

Travis laughed and wiped his hands again, this time on his shirt. "Yeah, sorry about that."

"Ah, Charlie," Ernie called out. "The cow. She didn't make it."

Shit.

George and I checked her over, but there was no sign of life. It was always a shame to lose breeding stock. The barely standing wobbly kneed baby Brahman was indeed an orphan. I pulled back the hind leg of the dead cow, and George tried to get the calf to feed.

"It needs the colostrum," I explained to the others. "Or chances are it won't survive either."

"Come on, little one," George urged, milking a teat into its mouth. It latched on for only half a minute, but hopefully it would be enough.

I looked over at Travis to see him shake hands with Ernie and give him a bit of a side-on hug. "It's good to have you back," Ernie said to him. "Maybe someone won't be lookin' so lost now that you're home."

I opened my mouth to say something, but George beat me to it. "Come on," he declared. "Let's get this little one back home." He looked at Laura, Sam and Ainsley. "You three can come with me. Charlie, you take the calf. It's not going in the new car." Then he told Ernie to come back and take care of the dead cow, and that effectively left me alone with Trav.

They'd barely driven away before Trav was in front of me. He put his hand to my face and looked into my eyes for the longest minute. "I have missed you so much," he whispered.

"Why didn't you email me?" I asked. "Or answer my calls, Travis. I know you went back for your grandpa's funeral, and I tried not to make it about me, but it was a bit hard when you just ignored me. I thought you weren't coming back." I couldn't stop the tears. It was so overwhelming. To be so sure he was gone, only to have him back again. "If you had just answered my email..."

"I'll tell you everything," he said, wiping my cheeks with his thumbs. "In fact, I can show you. When we get back home, I can show you. I didn't ignore you, Charlie. I was always coming back. Always." He put his forehead to mine. "You keep calling Texas my home, but I can tell you right now, going back to Texas made me realise something, Charlie. My home is here. With you. You keep saying I want to go home, well, I *am* home. Now. Here. With you."

Then he pressed his lips to mine, softly, reverently, like he couldn't believe it. When I opened my lips for him, he made a groany-whimper sound that made my knees go weak. He kissed me deeply, thoroughly, and held me so perfectly. Standing right there in the middle of the desert, surrounded by vast open plains of red, red dirt, with his touch, his kiss, his smell, he was right about one thing.

He was home.

Then the little hour-old calf near us bleated and scared the shit outta me.

Trav and I broke apart, half laughing, half trying to catch our breath. It was then I noticed the dark circles under his eyes. "You look tired," I told him.

"I've only slept about six hours in the last thirty-something," he explained. "It was a helluva trip to get back here. Five layovers, from Dallas to Vegas, to Sydney, to Darwin, then to Alice. I've been flying non-stop just to get here, Charlie. I don't even know what day it is."

I put my hand to his face. "It's quite possibly the best day of my life." He smiled and slow-blinked as though exhaustion had just caught up with him, so I kissed him softly. "Let's get you home."

Travis picked up the bleating calf, all forty kilos of it, and somehow managed to fit inside the ute. I climbed in behind the wheel. Seeing him smile at me made me almost giddy. It was ridiculous.

He leaned his head back, holdin' the calf and lookin' at me. He had a tired smile on his face and his blinks were peaceful and slow as he listened to me talk.

I told him everything that had happened these last weeks. From my bein' elected onto the Board, to Trudy's keeping-the-baby announcement last night, to meeting Sam and Ainsley, and to seein' Laura in a different light today when she helped me birth the cow. I told him if missin' him were miles, I'd have gone as far as the moon and back, and how I realised that I *could* be me without him, I just didn't want to be. Not ever again.

He shuffled the calf a bit so he could hold out his hand. I took it without thinking, and he squeezed my fingers and sighed. He was just staring at me, not saying a whole lot of anything.

"You okay, Trav?" I asked.

He nodded. "Just wanna look at you."

So he did just that, all the way home.

WE ONLY GOT AS FAR the holding yard, where everyone was waiting. They'd obviously heard Travis was back, and he was met with warm hugs and wide smiles. Hearing his voice and his laughter made my chest all tight.

He had a long hug from Ma, and I'm pretty sure I heard her whisperin' warnings in his ear about breaking my heart, but he had yet to stop smiling. He wasted no time in trying to get the newborn calf to feed, which as it turns out was a female cow. "I think I'll call her Delilah," he declared.

"Delilah?" I questioned. "Is that the name of a singer?"

"Dunno," he said. "She's not like the rest. And I don't think she'll be ever getting on a truck, Charlie," he stated, shaking his head. "Not her. She's special."

I was almost afraid to ask. "Special?"

He ignored the way everyone stared at him like he was crazy. He knelt beside the knobby-kneed baby Brahman. "We helped her be born, Charlie. She's special. And she's too pretty. Look at these eyelashes."

I sighed, and instead of telling him no, instead of telling him that cow would be used for breeding stock or meat production, all I could do was smile. I was pretty sure right then, I'd have said yes to anything.

George barked out a laugh beside me and clapped his big hand on my shoulder. "Nothin's changed, huh."

When Travis was sure Delilah had fed, he climbed through the railings of the holding yard fence. Obviously not caring one bit about the ten other people still standing around, he put his arms around me. "God, you stink," he said.

I ignored how everyone laughed. "I'm covered in cow shit and afterbirth," I said. "Same as you."

As much as he wanted to stay and talk with everyone, Travis was just about dead on his feet. "I hope y'all don't think I'm rude, but I need a hot shower and a few hours' sleep. I haven't slept in—" He looked at his watch. "—well, shit. What day is it?"

"Mmm, shower," I said, not really meaning to say it out loud, but Travis mentioned it and my mind went straight to very-naked very-wet Travis. He still had his arm around me, so I pushed us toward the house.

"Charlie," Ma hissed. She shot me a glare that said "we have guests, Charlie, where are your manners?"

I replied with a shameless but-I-haven't-seen-him-in-so-long look. She trumped me with her don't-make-me-come-over-there eyebrow.

Travis laughed and took his arm from around me. "I'll go first, then, shall I?"

He went and showered—without me—and I brought his bag inside. All the staff went back about their jobs, but me, Ma, Sam, Ainsley and Laura went into the lounge room.

"Well, you look a lot happier," Laura said with a smile.

"Oh, man, I had no idea," I said, shaking my head. I hadn't stopped smiling yet.

Ma made an odd meep sound. "George told me this morning," she said. "I wanted to tell you so bad, but George made me promise."

"You knew?"

"Well, Travis called from Darwin this morning, said his flight was getting in to Alice..." Her words ran out of steam. "Oh, don't look at me like that, Charlie. You knew about Trudy and Bacon having a baby and didn't say anything."

"But that was different."

"Not really."

"Yes, really."

"What are you two fighting about now?" Travis said, walking out all clean smelling with still wet hair. He collected Nugget from the bed box he'd made and gave the little guy a hug. "Boy, you've gotten heavier." He looked even more tired now.

"You need some sleep," I told him.

He nodded and apologised again for seeming rude, but he could barely keep his eyes open.

"Charlie, can I show you something first?" he said.

"Boys," Ma admonished us again.

"In the office," Travis said with a smile. "Not the bedroom."

The others laughed, and I followed him into my office, wondering what it was he wanted to show me.

"I didn't want to go to sleep yet," he'd said. "Not until you'd seen this." He asked for my laptop and said he hoped I'd understand.

I sat in the desk seat, and he knelt beside me. Holding Nugget under one arm, he logged out of my email, logged in to his own and turned the screen to me. All I could see was emails from me and some airplane flight confirmations. I shook my head. "I don't know what I'm looking for."

"Look at the draft folder," he said. "Open it."

There was one email in the draft folder. It was an unsent email to me.

Charlie,

Sorry I've been so absent. There's been a lot of family here for the funeral and the house has been so busy. Please know that I've read every email and each one has been the highlight of my day.

I miss you like crazy.

We're heading out to the lake tomorrow. My mom wants the whole family to go because it'll be the last time we're all in the one place for a while. There's no internet. I'll be gone a whole week, but when I get back, I'm coming straight home.

I need you to promise me, Charlie, that you believe I'm

coming home. I know you, and I know you'll be thinking the worst, but I promise you, I'm coming home.

You're my home, Charlie. Not here, not Texas, not even Sutton Station. You.

Just one more week, and I'll be with you.

I love you. I even miss Nugget, can you believe that?

See you soon,

T

I read it. Then I read it again.

"Look at the date," he whispered. It was the day after he sent me that one-line, two-sentence email. "I thought I hit Send. I could have sworn I did. But when I got back, I read your emails, and the last one... the 'if this is your goodbye' email... then I realised this was still in the draft folder. You hadn't read it. You didn't know I was away and had no internet, and you must have thought I was ignoring you." He shook his head. "Jesus, Charlie. Your email broke my heart."

"I thought you went home and realised that's where you were supposed to be."

He held my face and searched my eyes. "You have to stop thinking I'm gonna leave you. You're it for me, Charlie. Forever."

"I just thought—"

"I know what you thought," he said softly. He spun my office chair so he was kneeling in front of me and took my hands. "Charlie, I won't lie to you. My mom wanted me to stay. She thought that maybe since I was back, she could convince me to stay. I told her where my heart was, and... She didn't mean anything by it, Charlie. She just wanted her son home, ya know?

"But then when we got back from the lake house and I found your email..." He shook his head. "It wrecked me, Charlie. You have no idea. She started packing my things, and she drove me to the airport herself. I could have waited half a day to get a more direct flight, but she said I couldn't wait. I had to get back to you. So I've been on a plane for thirty-something hours, Charlie." He squeezed my hands and looked up at me with tears in his tired, tired eyes. "Please tell me you don't think I was leaving you."

I shook my head. "I believe you."

"Do you? Do you finally believe me? Are you gonna stop wondering when I'm gonna get sick of you and walk away? Because I'm telling you, Charlie, it ain't ever gonna happen."

I leaned forward and kissed him. "I believe you."

He sighed like a weight was finally, *finally* lifted. "You said you realised you could survive without me," he said with a teary frown. "Well, guess what I realised? I'm not as strong as that, because I can't live without you."

I pulled him up to his feet then and pulled him hard against me, kinda squishing Nugget between us. "I said I *could* do this without you. I didn't say I did it well," I told him, and he chuckled into my neck. "I don't want to do this without you."

I held him just like that until he swayed in my arms, so I took Nugget from him and led him to bed. I pulled back the covers and tucked him in. He was already half-asleep when I kissed him softly.

"Just need to sleep a minute," he mumbled.

"I won't be far away," I told him, but I think he was already asleep.

I checked on him a few times over the afternoon, and he'd barely even moved. He'd wrapped himself around my pillow, which was kinda sweet until I realised he was also drooling on my pillow, and then I decided to make that one *his* pillow.

Laura, Sam and Ainsley had decided not to go home until the morning. They wanted to stay a little while longer, and the truth was, I wanted them to meet Travis properly. I wanted them to know him, and I wanted Travis to get to know Sam. I wanted Travis to see that Laura wasn't such a bad person.

They spent the afternoon riding the dirt bikes, Ainsley learned how to ride the quad runner, and George took them each up for a scenic chopper tour. They helped feed the poddy calves, and we had a BBQ dinner.

And Travis never stirred.

"If he'd been awake for almost thirty hours," Laura said, "then he probably won't wake 'til the morning."

I might have pouted.

They all might have tried not to smile.

I left it as late as what was polite—at least the sun had gone down—and I told them goodnight. "I, um, I'm really tired," I said. Travis was right: I really sucked at lying. "I, ah... yeah, it's late."

Bacon looked at his watch. "It's seven thirty."

I cleared my throat and shot him a shut-the-hell-up look. "Nugget's been fed," I told anyone who cared and took the back stairs two at a time.

"Don't you wake him," Ma called out, but I was already inside.

I heard Trudy's voice next. "He's so gonna wake him." Then everyone laughed.

But I didn't have to wake him. I simply stripped off and slid into bed next to him. Like a magnet, he snuggled in to me, then draped himself over me, then mumbled my name and kinda woke himself up. "Tell me I'm not dreaming," he murmured.

"You're not dreaming," I whispered.

And that was all it took.

Almost four weeks of no touching, no kissing, no anything was just too damn long. I got him out of his slept-in clothes, and he got me on my back. His hands were all over me, urgent and wanton, his mouth, his tongue. He kissed me like he'd never kissed me, rough and pleading. He slid his arms underneath me and held me so *so* tight, and he rolled his hips into mine, our hard cocks rubbing together, and he bucked once, twice, and groaned low and convulsed as he came.

I followed just moments after him, and he never moved despite the mess between us.

He simply leaned his forehead against mine with his eyes closed for a breath-catchin' minute. His eyes were still closed, and he whispered, "Promise me forever, Charlie. Tell me we're in this forever."

My heart near burst out of my chest. "Forever."

Then he did my most favourite thing in the world. He nudged his nose to mine. "Make love to me, Charlie," he murmured. "Show me how much you love me." He kissed me then and trailed his lips down my jaw so he could whisper warm and husky in my ear. "I need you inside me."

I rolled us over and pinned his hands above his head. I gave him everything he wanted, needed, begged for. I spent every lovemakin' minute of the next few hours goin' over every inch of his skin. By the time we were done, he was so spent and pliable, well-loved and certain—he'd never been more certain—of just how much I loved him.

WHEN I WOKE UP, Travis was gone. I wondered for just

a second if I'd dreamed him coming home, but the ache in my muscles told me otherwise.

His clothes and shit all over the floor told me otherwise too. It was early. The sun hadn't even thought about gettin' up, but there was enough light for me to see his half-unpacked bag strewn across the room.

It made me smile.

I never once, not ever, thought I'd be happy to see his mess on the floor.

I pulled on some pants and went looking for him. I only got to the hall when I heard him talking. He and Laura were deep in conversation, and I briefly considered turning around when I heard my name.

"Charlie's happy you're here," Travis said quietly. "And Sam."

"He's been really good about everything," Laura said. "He could have said no to us and no one would have blamed him. He could have told me to turn around and leave that first day, but he didn't. I'm so grateful."

"I was probably a bit rude," Trav said. "Sorry about that."

Laura laughed quietly. "Oh, please don't apologise. You're protective of him, and I'm glad he has someone on his side."

"He has a lot of people on his side. The folks here are a wild and crazy bunch of people, but they're his family."

"And you. He has you."

"He certainly does."

"I don't think he coped too well with you gone," Laura said. "Ma said he's been miserable."

Trav snorted. "Well, I don't think he'll have to worry about me leaving him again anytime soon."

I smiled at that.

"Not going home again?" Laura asked.

Travis's answer was so immediate and definitive, it caught my breath. "I am home."

I moved then, walking out through the foyer and into the lounge room. Laura was on the recliner next to the fire feeding a too-damned-spoiled wombat, and Trav was at one end of the three-seater. I threw myself beside him, leaned my back against his side, and pulled his arm around me. "Wondered where you went," I said.

Trav pulled the blanket on the back of the lounge over the both of us. "I'm all slept out."

"Morning, Laura," I said with a smile.

"Morning, Charlie," she replied.

By this time, Nugget had well and truly heard my voice and had obviously fussed until Laura put him down on the floor. "Righteo, righteo" she said. "There you go."

The little guy ran over to us and grunted and squeaked until I picked him up and put him on the sofa with us. Laura got up and handed Rumble Bear to me with a smile. "I'll go put the kettle back on."

Trav sighed and tightened his arm around me, and the three of us lay on the sofa looking out the window as a new day started over the desert. He kissed the side of my head and whispered something about perfect and forever.

Sounded about right to me.

WHERE THE AMERICAN GUY WALKS IN, ALL BLUE EYES AND DISARMING SMILES AND MY LIFE… WELL, IT DON'T GET ANY BETTER THAN THIS.

LIFE over the last five months had pretty much gone back to normal. Well, as normal as they were ever gonna get with Travis. Busy. That's what my life was. Busy as hell. And I'd never been happier.

Days off were rare, and days spent alone with Travis in the desert were rarer still, so we took the chopper and a picnic lunch to the lagoon, and we took our sweet time.

Summer had returned in all its blistering glory, and Trav and I spent the day alternatin' between swimming, makin' out, and snoozin' in the shade.

It was pretty damn close to perfect.

But we couldn't put off headin' home forever, and as the afternoon crept on, we packed up our things and walked back to the chopper.

I was used to him being here now. So used to him just fitting in, being a part of Sutton Station, and very used to him being with me. He'd been here a year today. Just one year. It felt like both a lifetime, and a blink of the eye. It was one year ago this very day that I first saw him in my kitchen.

As we walked back to the chopper, I guessed it was

time. Instead of walking around to my side—the pilot's side —I walked right next to him to the passenger side. Before he could ask me what I was doing, I pushed him against the chopper and kissed him. His surprise gave way to kissing me back and he pulled me against him.

When I slowed the kiss, he rested his forehead on mine and nudged my nose with his, his eyes half-closed. "What was that for?" he asked.

"Happy anniversary," I said, pecking his lips again.

He smiled widely. "You're such a sap."

"I can take your gift back if you don't want it," I teased.

"No! I want it. Actually I wanted it this morning, and you said I had to wait. Just how long have I gotta wait for?"

"'Til later," I said. "Anyway, you didn't half mind what I did give you this morning."

He grinned and groaned, rolling his hips into mine. "You can give that to me anytime."

I kissed him lightly. "I will if you want, but I was gonna say you can fly home."

I'd no sooner said the words than Travis was gone and I almost fell face-first against the helicopter. When I looked into the cabin, Travis was already in my seat with the headset on and a smile a mile wide.

"Hurry up," he said.

"So much for anniversary sex in the chopper," I said. He barked out a laugh as I climbed in and buckled myself in. "Do me a favour. Just breathe for a minute. If you're in too big a hurry, you'll forget something. Not much room for mistakes when you're twenty metres up."

His grin never faltered. Actually, I think it got wider. "Mistakes? Jeez, it's like you don't know me at all."

"If your smug-Yank attitude drops us out of the sky, I'll kick your ass."

Of course, that just made him laugh.

I pulled off my hat and slid on the headset he normally wore. Yes, he was all smug and smiles, but when it came time for me to actually give him instructions, he really was a very good student.

Travis had flown the chopper twice before. I'd shown him the dash instruments and gone through the checks and routines with him before, even when I was flying, I'd talk him through what I was doing. But he listened and nodded, paid attention like it was the first time we'd been through it.

He was a perfectionist, and he took learning new stuff pretty seriously. I knew he wouldn't be happy until he was the best he could possibly be, and I loved that about him.

"You ready?" I asked.

He nodded. "Yep."

"So take her up."

His eyebrows almost met in the middle of his forehead as he concentrated. But as soon as he had the skips off the ground and he took us up, he looked over at me and grinned.

And all in all, he did pretty good. Actually, he did real good. Even without the instruments, he had a good sense of direction and handled the weight of the chopper against the throttle perfectly.

We were about a twenty-minute flight from home, and I felt completely comfortable with him flying. It was kind of nice actually, being a passenger every now and then. It meant I could look out over the landscape instead. I got to appreciate the vast red dirt, the shrubs and trees. Looking over to the right, out Travis's side, there was a large mob of kangaroos in full flight over the dirt, obviously startled by the chopper.

I pointed to them, but Travis was too busy concentrating on the controls and what was out front. It made me smile, and when he risked a glance at me and found me looking at him, he was quick to ask, "What?"

"Nothin'," I said, shaking my head. "Just looking at you. Flyin' a chopper."

He smiled, but it was quick and he went back to focusing. I put my hand on his thigh and sighed. I still couldn't believe the fact he was still here. I still felt truly lucky that he'd not only dug his stubborn heels in and stayed the first time, but he'd gone home to the States and still came back to me. He was here for good, of that I had no doubt. And yet, a simple act of being out in the paddocks, working this farm and doing everyday things *with my boyfriend* was something I swore I'd never take for granted.

Each and every day with him was a gift.

I pointed out ahead and the homestead came into view. "Bring her down 'round the back of the house." All smiles were gone now, and he was back to concentrating. "How's your height?"

"Eighteen."

"Speed?"

"Twenty-five."

"Good. Start to slow her down." I pointed to the holding yard fence we were coming up to. "You'll want to be down to fifteen metres by the time we get over the fence, and down to about eight kilometres per hour. Bring her around to one-sixty-five degrees," I instructed, and he did it perfectly.

He pulled back on the throttle like he'd seen me do a hundred times and put the helicopter down on the ground with no more than a soft bump.

It shouldn't have surprised me that he did it so well, but I was impressed. "Perfect."

He cut the engine, pulled off his headset and gave me his biggest grin yet. "That was so fucking cool."

I rolled my eyes and pulled off my headset. "Right. Pilot's responsible for maintenance and log-book entries. I've got *stuff* to do inside," I said, getting out the chopper, swiftly ditching all after-flight checks.

I walked off toward the house and heard him call out. "That *stuff* better include my present!"

I snorted out a laugh and didn't even turn around. Truly, it wasn't anything too special. I bought us three days at Uluru at a five-star luxury accommodation and a box of those American chocolate biscuits his mom sent him once. It wasn't anything too extravagant, but he was gonna love it almost as much as me making him wait.

I was almost to the house when Billy came outside and leapt off the veranda. "Charlie," he called, running over to me. "George called from the hospital. Charlie, you better get in there."

The drive into the hospital was long and quiet. Travis drove and I got lost in my over-thinkin' mind. "She's been doing so well," I whispered. "It was just supposed to be a check-up."

Trav held out his hand and I took it without hesitation. "I'm sure she's okay."

Walking into the hospital, I was reminded of the time we first came here with Ma. The god-awful smell, the way staff looked at you like they weren't sure if they should offer congratulations or condolences. I hated them. Hospitals, not the staff. The nurse we accosted in corridor was helpful, pointing which way we should go.

We followed the signs and raced into the waiting room, and my heart just about stopped when I saw George. He was sitting there with his head in his hands like the first time we saw him with Ma, looking all sorts of helpless and lost. He stood up and took off his hat when he saw us.

"How is she?" I asked, my voice cracking.

"They won't tell me," he answered with a frown.

Oh, Jesus. "What kind of stupid policy is that?" I asked.

"Charlie," Travis said quietly, rubbing his hand on my back. "They'll tell us when they can."

I shook my head. "But we're family."

"Not technically," he answered.

I sighed—it was more like a growl—and threw myself into a waitin' room chair. But that wasn't any good, so I started to pace instead. And then two people in scrubs stood in the doorway, and our lives were changed forever.

It was Ma and Bacon; she was grinning, and he looked like he'd seen the light of God. "It's a girl" was all he said.

It's a girl.

Trudy and Bacon had a little baby girl.

I hugged 'em both, and then I hugged 'em both again. I was probably more excited than I should have been, and Lord knows Travis had told me I had to stop buying baby stuff. I couldn't help it. It was exciting and amazing, and Sutton Station was getting a new family member.

"Can we see her?" I asked.

We had to wait a little while, but when they finally let us in, Trudy was lying down with a wrapped-up bundle of pink blankets. I kissed Trudy on the top of the head and peeked in the blanket. There was a tiny, scrunched-up, wrinkled, pinkish, most beautiful sleepin' baby. "Look at what you did!" I said to Trudy, rubbing her arm. "You did so good."

She was exhausted and, truthfully, looked like she'd gone through hell, but she was just beaming. "She's perfect."

I nodded. "Of course she is."

"You came all this way?" she asked. "Just for us?"

"Of course we did," I told her.

Bacon came over and kissed Trudy and then he kissed her again. He picked up his daughter, looking like he just might burst, and he looked at me. "Wanna hold her?"

I shook my head. "Oh no," I said, shaking my head again. "She's too little." And she was. She was tiny. And breakable. And perfect, and did I mention that she was tiny? And breakable?

Bacon ignored me and shoved her into my arms. When I say shoved, I mean ever-so-gently put the most precious thing in the world in my arms. All I could do was look at this perfect little thing, and I was suddenly blinking back tears.

Trav put his hand on the back of my neck and kissed the side of my head.

"Hey," I whispered to the sleeping angel in my arms. "I'm your uncle Charlie." I swallowed thickly. "And this is your uncle Travis."

"I'm the funny, handsome one," Trav whispered, peering over the blankets. "He's the cranky one."

"Don't listen to him," I told her. "You stick with me. When your mummy and daddy want you to do boring stuff like chores and schoolwork, you come see me. We'll go horse riding and jumpin' in the river... well, maybe not the river because it's only got water in it when it floods, but there's a lagoon, we'll hang out there. And maybe Uncle Trav can find you your very own wombat—"

Bacon took her off me at that stage, and my arms felt suddenly very empty. I wiped my hands on my jeans. Trudy was lookin' at me like she was considerin' getting off the bed just to smack me in the mouth, so I told her, "Well,

I'd teach her to swim first, ya know, before I throw her in the lagoon. Actually, I wouldn't just *throw* her in..."

Trav put his arm around me. "Shut up, Charlie."

It was Grandpa George's turn for a hold, and he asked much more sensible questions like "What's her name?"

Trudy and Bacon both looked at each other and smiled. "Grace."

Grace. What a fitting, most-perfect name.

When little Gracie started to fuss, she promptly got handed back to her waiting mum, and we promptly got booted out. It was late anyway, and George and Ma were gonna stay in town overnight and bring the whole new family home when they were allowed.

Travis and I walked out of the hospital, and I think I pretty much talked non-stop from the elevator to the old ute in the car park about how amazing that little girl was and how Trudy and Bacon were gonna be great parents and how Sutton Station was gonna have the pitter-patter of little feet, then of course I wondered out loud if R.M. Williams made boots for toddlers. In pink.

Not quite ready to leave, I leaned against the door and sighed. "Did you see her little hands?" I asked him, which was stupid, because of course he had.

His smile kind of drained away the longer he stared at me.

"Trav, what's wrong?" I asked.

He stepped in close to me and lifted my chin so he could stare into my eyes. "Marry me."

I blinked. Like an idiot.

"What?"

"Marry me."

That's what I thought he'd said. And dear God, he was

serious. I swallowed hard, my mouth suddenly dry, and I tried to speak. And failed. Like an idiot. "Huh?"

He smiled, just a little, just one corner of his mouth. And then he did that thing.

The thing that fries my brain and steals my breath.

He nudged his nose to mine.

"Marry me."

"Trav."

He almost—almost—touched his lips to mine. He licked his bottom lip like he was gonna kiss me, but he did that nose-nudge thing again, and my knees went weak. "Marry me."

"You know," I whispered, all out of breath. "You know what that does to me."

He smiled his of-course-I-do smile, and spoke against my lips. "Then say yes."

Well, I probably would if I bloody could, but there was a serious synapses Travis-and-his-nose-nudging dysfunction in my brain.

So I nodded.

And he smiled.

It was his heart-stopping, eye-crinkling kind of smile, and he threw his arms around me.

And I was still blinking like an idiot.

I think I just got engaged.

To be married.

Travis pulled back from me with concern on his face. "You're not hugging me back."

"You used your wizard-spell-nose-nudgin' thing on me," I said. "I can't think straight when you do that."

He laughed, but at least he had the decency to try and look apologetic. "I'm sorry. If I asked you now, would your answer be the same?"

"Of course it would, but that's not the point."

He went back to grinning. "You really said yes."

"I can't believe you asked me," I said. I took his hand and shook my head. "Trav, this country doesn't recognise... We wouldn't technically be... you know, married." God, it felt weird even saying it.

"I don't care," he said simply. "We don't even have to actually get married, I guess. There doesn't need to be a ceremony or any fancy pieces of paper, Charlie. Just promise me, right now, swear your heart to me, and I'll consider it done."

"Travis—"

He shook his head quickly, his smile long gone. "I saw you in there holding that baby, Charlie, and you know what? It just all made sense. I don't even know how or why, but I just looked at you and thought, 'I wanna marry him.' How silly is that?"

"That's not sill—"

He cut me off. "Something in my head switched on. I know we've talked about our future and the word *forever*'s been thrown around a few times, and that's great, Charlie, it really is. But I want to make it real. And I want you to have kids."

Okay, he lost me on that one. "What?"

"Kids," he repeated. "You'd make such a great dad and just seeing you with Nugget and holding little Grace just now."

I shook my head. "No, no, no. Marriage I can kinda get my head around, but kids?" I shook my head again.

"Why not?"

"Because last time I checked, neither one of us has a uterus, Trav, that's why."

"There are options, Charlie," he said quickly.

I swallowed hard and lightly touched the side of his face. "Travis. I... I can't be a father... I'm sorry, but..."

"But what?" he said softly. He stared at me for the longest minute. "Charlie, don't tell me you don't deserve it."

I opened my mouth to argue, and for reasons I wasn't even aware of until he'd just said it, I'd had no clue I even thought I didn't deserve marriage and kids.

He shook his head slowly, and then he started to smile. "I've been here a year, yes?"

I nodded. "It's a year today since I walked into my kitchen and you stood up, all blue eyes and disarming smiles..."

He smiled at that. "And it's taken me a year to prove to you that you deserve happiness, a year to get you to realise that I'm not leaving you. That not everybody is gonna leave you."

I looked down at the ground. "Trav..."

He lifted my face in both his hands. "Then I don't care how long it takes me to get you to see that you can have marriage and kids, Charlie."

I shook my head in his hands. "I um..."

Shit.

"Do you want to get married, Charlie?" he asked me gently. "Do you want to have kids with me?"

Well, I didn't until you mentioned it just now...

He still had my face in his hands. "Charlie?"

I TRIED LOOKING AWAY, across the darkened car park, but I couldn't stop the tears. I nodded, because apparently I did want those things. I just didn't know that I did. Until now.

"Oh, Charlie," he said, pulling me against him. "I didn't

mean to upset you. I just saw you holding little Gracie and it looked *so* right. Please don't cry."

"I don't know why I'm crying," I said. "Stupid fucking tears."

Travis laughed and pulled back, letting me wipe my face. "I'll wait as long it takes for you to see you deserve it," he said again. "And I'll wait for you tell Ma before I tell my parents."

"Tell them what?"

"That we're engaged," he said with a grin. "You did say yes, yes?"

"Um..."

"There's no take-backs, Charlie."

"Take-backs?"

"No take-backs, no returns."

I smiled. "So it's a forever thing?"

He smiled his eye-crinklin' smile. "Charlie?"

"Yeah?"

"Fiancé."

My heart thumped in my chest. "Um..."

He laughed. "Too soon?"

I exhaled in a rush. "Jeez, Trav."

He laughed some more and kissed me. "Charlie?"

"Yeah."

"Take me home."

~ THE END

ABOUT THE AUTHOR

N.R. Walker is an Australian author, who loves her genre of gay romance. She loves writing and spends far too much time doing it, but wouldn't have it any other way.

She is many things: a mother, a wife, a sister, a writer. She has pretty, pretty boys who live in her head, who don't let her sleep at night unless she gives them life with words.

She likes it when they do dirty, dirty things... but likes it even more when they fall in love. She used to think having people in her head talking to her was weird, until one day she happened across other writers who told her it was normal.

She's been writing ever since...

nrwalker.net

ALSO BY N.R. WALKER

Blind Faith

Through These Eyes (Blind Faith #2)

Blindside: Mark's Story (Blind Faith #3)

Ten in the Bin

Gay Sex Club Stories 1

Gay Sex Club Stories 2

Point of No Return – Turning Point #1

Breaking Point – Turning Point #2

Starting Point – Turning Point #3

Element of Retrofit – Thomas Elkin Series #1

Clarity of Lines – Thomas Elkin Series #2

Sense of Place – Thomas Elkin Series #3

Taxes and TARDIS

Three's Company

Red Dirt Heart

Red Dirt Heart 2

Red Dirt Heart 3

Red Dirt Heart 4

Red Dirt Christmas

Cronin's Key

Cronin's Key II

Cronin's Key III

Cronin's Key IV - Kennard's Story

Exchange of Hearts

The Spencer Cohen Series, Book One

The Spencer Cohen Series, Book Two

The Spencer Cohen Series, Book Three

The Spencer Cohen Series, Yanni's Story

Blood & Milk

The Weight Of It All

A Very Henry Christmas (The Weight of It All 1.5)

Perfect Catch

Switched

Imago

Imagines

Imagoes

Red Dirt Heart Imago

On Davis Row

Finders Keepers

Evolved

Galaxies and Oceans

Private Charter

Nova Praetorian

A Soldier's Wish

Upside Down

The Hate You Drink

Sir

Tallowwood

Reindeer Games

The Dichotomy of Angels

Throwing Hearts

Pieces of You - Missing Pieces #1

Pieces of Me - Missing Pieces #2

Pieces of Us - Missing Pieces #3

Lacuna

Tic-Tac-Mistletoe

Bossy

Code Red

Dearest Milton James

Dearest Malachi Keogh

Christmas Wish List

Code Blue

Davo

The Kite

Learning Curve

Merry Christmas Cupid

To the Moon and Back

Second Chance at First Love

Outrun the Rain

Into the Tempest

Touch the Lightning

EWB - Enemies With Benefits

Holiday Heart Strings

Bloom

The Men from Echo Creek

Titles in Audio:

Cronin's Key

Cronin's Key II

Cronin's Key III

Red Dirt Heart

Red Dirt Heart 2

Red Dirt Heart 3

Red Dirt Heart 4

The Weight Of It All

Switched

Point of No Return

Breaking Point

Starting Point

Spencer Cohen Book One

Spencer Cohen Book Two

Spencer Cohen Book Three

Yanni's Story

On Davis Row

Evolved

Elements of Retrofit

Clarity of Lines

Sense of Place

Blind Faith

Through These Eyes

Blindside

Finders Keepers

Galaxies and Oceans

Nova Praetorian

Upside Down

Sir

Tallowwood

Imago

Throwing Hearts

Sixty Five Hours

Taxes and TARDIS

The Dichotomy of Angels

The Hate You Drink

Pieces of You

Pieces of Me

Pieces of Us

Tic-Tac-Mistletoe

Lacuna

Bossy

Code Red

Learning to Feel

Dearest Milton James

Dearest Malachi Keogh

Three's Company

Christmas Wish List

Code Blue

Davo

The Kite

Learning Curve

Merry Christmas Cupid

To the Moon and Back

Second Chance at First Love

Outrun the Rain

Into the Tempest

Touch the Lightning

EWB

Holiday Heart Strings

Bloom

Series Collections:

Red Dirt Heart Series

Turning Point Series

Thomas Elkin Series

Spencer Cohen Series

Imago Series

Blind Faith Series

Missing Pieces Series

The Storm Boys Series

Free Reads:

Sixty Five Hours

Learning to Feel

His Grandfather's Watch (And The Story of Billy and Hale)

The Twelfth of Never (Blind Faith 3.5)

Twelve Days of Christmas (Sixty Five Hours Christmas)

Best of Both Worlds

Translated Titles:

Italian

Fiducia Cieca (Blind Faith)

Attraverso Questi Occhi (Through These Eyes)

Preso alla Sprovvista (Blindside)

Il giorno del Mai (Blind Faith 3.5)

Cuore di Terra Rossa Serie (Red Dirt Heart Series)

Natale di terra rossa (Red dirt Christmas)

Intervento di Retrofit (Elements of Retrofit)

A Chiare Linee (Clarity of Lines)

Senso D'appartenenza (Sense of Place)

Spencer Cohen Serie (including Yanni's Story)

Punto di non Ritorno (Point of No Return)

Punto di Rottura (Breaking Point)

Punto di Partenza (Starting Point)

Imago (Imago)

Imagines

Il desiderio di un soldato (A Soldier's Wish)

Scambiato (Switched)

Tallowwood

The Hate You Drink

Ho trovato te (Finders Keepers)

Cuori d'argilla (Throwing Hearts)

Galassie e Oceani (Galaxies and Oceans)

Il peso di tut (The Weight of it All)

Pieces of You - Missing Pieces 1

French

Confiance Aveugle (Blind Faith)

A travers ces yeux: Confiance Aveugle 2 (Through These Eyes)

Aveugle: Confiance Aveugle 3 (Blindside)

À Jamais (Blind Faith 3.5)

Cronin's Key Series

Au Coeur de Sutton Station (Red Dirt Heart)

Partir ou rester (Red Dirt Heart 2)

Faire Face (Red Dirt Heart 3)

Trouver sa Place (Red Dirt Heart 4)

Le Poids de Sentiments (The Weight of It All)

Un Noël à la sauce Henry (A Very Henry Christmas)

Une vie à Refaire (Switched)

Evolution (Evolved)

Galaxies & Océans

Qui Trouve, Garde (Finders Keepers)

Sens Dessus Dessous (Upside Down)

La Haine au Fond du Verre (The hate You Drink)

Tallowwood

Spencer Cohen Series

Thai

Sixty Five Hours (Thai translation)

Finders Keepers (Thai translation)

Spanish

Sesenta y Cinco Horas (Sixty Five Hours)

Los Doce Días de Navidad

Código Rojo (Code Red)

Código Azul (Code Blue)

Queridísimo Milton James

Queridísimo Malachi Keogh

El Peso de Todo (The Weight of it All)

Tres Muérdagos en Raya: Serie Navidad en Hartbridge

Lista De Deseos Navideños: Serie Navidad en Hartbridge

Feliz Navidad Cupido: Serie Navidad en Hartbridge

Spencer Cohen Libro Uno

Spencer Cohen Libro Dos

Spencer Cohen Libro Tres

Davo

Hasta la Luna y de Vuelta

Venciendo A La Lluvia

En la Tempestad

El Toque del Rayo

Corazón De Tierra Roja

Corazón De Tierra Roja 2

Corazón De Tierra Roja 3

Corazón De Tierra Roja 4

ECB (Enemigos con Beneficios)

Floral

Chinese

Blind Faith

Japanese

Bossy

Portuguese

Sessenta e Cinco Horas

www.ingramcontent.com/pod-product-compliance
Lightning Source LLC
Chambersburg PA
CBHW032104180726
48284CB00002B/433